Presents

NIGHT TERRORS

An Anthology of Horror

EDITED BY THERESA DILLON

“You begin to sense - deep down inside you - that something has gone very wrong. Slowly, almost dimly, you regain enough consciousness to realize that you are suffocating, that some heavy weight is lying on your chest and crushing your lungs. Suddenly you realize your breathing has almost stopped, and you are dying for air. Terrified, you scream! At once, you seem to awaken. There is this thing hovering over you, crushing the very life out of your lungs. You shout at the thing, but it won't leave you alone.”

-James V. McConnell (1986) on Night Terrors

CONTENTS

From Under the Bed

David Bernstein

Kevin McCarthy was lying in bed, the comforter pulled up to his nose, when he heard the noise. It came from under his bed, a creaking sound, like something pushing against the wooden box spring. Kevin ignored the disturbance, chalking it up to the house's old age.

A few minutes later, floating into the sea of sleep, Kevin was startled awake by the sound of wood planks bending. He paused, hoping his mind would assure him that the creaking sound was still just the house settling.

The colonial, built in 1890, that housed his parents and his younger brother, Bobby, was built to last, but it wasn't without the occasional moans and groans, especially in the winter.

Just the house settling, he repeated in his mind. But when the noise returned again, Kevin could no longer pretend. It was definitely not the house.

He couldn't quite see around the room yet, as his eyes hadn't adjusted to the low level of light coming through the window. He lived on the outskirts of a small country town called Salisbury Mills, in upstate New York. The nearest house was two acres away and the only source of outside light came from the full moon.

Kevin remained calm and laid still, listening into the darkness. His vision finally adjusted to the point where he could now see across the room to his posters of bikini clad women, who posed seductively. The devious vixens began taking Kevin's mind away from the dark room to a more pleasurable place when the mysterious noise came again, followed by a thud that resonated up through the box spring, mattress and into Kevin's bones.

Something was definitely under his bed.

Kevin's mind envisioned him dashing to the door, flipping on the lights and running out into the hall, but fear kept him frozen in place. He knew monsters weren't real, but the fear of something grabbing him when he placed a foot down was present. Then a thought occurred to him and Kevin immediately began to smile.

Bobby! His little brother had to be hiding under the bed. Kevin was always scaring Bobby and the ten-year-old was undoubtedly trying to exact a little revenge.

Kevin exhaled, a wave of relief washing over him. He felt silly for letting his imagination get the better of him, but the fun he was going to have would make up for it.

Kevin sat up and began bouncing up and down on his rear hoping to panic his brother, make him yell for Kevin to stop, but Bobby remained silent. Kevin bounced harder, but still no pleas came from under the bed.

Kevin decided that if Bobby wasn't going to come out from under the bed, then he would go to him. It would be easy to turn the tables. He'd creep to the edge of the bed, then swoop down and scream. Bobby would be terrified.

Kevin jostled around slowly until he was facing the women on the wall. They stared at him with a mischievous look like what he was about to do was wrong. He should let his little brother have his scare and play along, but Kevin couldn't let him get away with it. After all, he'd managed to scare Kevin a little already and that was all he was going to get.

Kevin, still sitting cross-legged, inched up to the mattress's edge using his arms like a gorilla. He leaned over and looked down. The carpet was light blue, but it might as well have been black because there was nothing to see. Kevin braced his hands on the edge and leaned forward as far over as he could. Not a foot or elbow was showing from under the bed, Bobby had to be all the way under. Kevin decided to play into Bobby's plan.

"Who's there?" he said and waited for a giggle, but there was no response. "Anyone down there?"

Kevin was about to ask again when he heard and felt another thud. He jumped before quickly composing himself, listening, taking long deep breaths to calm his pulse. The little bugger was unparalleled as Kevin had nearly fallen off the bed. He smiled wickedly, determined to scare the crap out of Bobby and send him screaming out of his room.

Kevin slid his legs out from under his body and lowered himself into a push-up position. He inched forward until his upper body was hanging over the side like a diving board, arms trembling with excitement. Kevin went forward like a gymnast, landing on his hands. He took in a large gulp of air, preparing to let out a loud scream, but when he looked under the bed it wasn't his brother he saw.

Two bright red slits stared back at him. The sight caught him completely off guard. Kevin froze, unable to scream as his mind tried to make sense of what he was seeing.

A low growl came from the thing. Kevin tried getting back up onto the bed by pushing off the metal frame with his left hand while his right held his body from falling to the floor. The thing growled again, a foul, rotten, fish-like odor filled the air. Kevin wanted to gag, his left hand slipped off the frame causing him to fall further off of the bed, landing hard on both hands.

He tried getting up again, keeping his eyes on the thing when he saw it had a form. It was pitch black under the bed, but the thing was blacker than the darkness it waited in. It reached out with a clawed hand and grabbed Kevin's hair. He tried to scream, but couldn't. It yanked him to the ground. The room shook as his body collided with the floor. The creature was gurgling and trying to talk, but the words were barely comprehendible.

The creature began dragging Kevin under the bed, all his strength evaporated. He fought against the creature, trying to dig his hands into the carpet, trying to grab the steel frame, but unable to gather enough strength. He pulled in a big breath attempting to scream but all he could muster was a small groan. He was half way under the bed and felt a sharp pain begin to take hold over his shoulders when the door to his room suddenly flew open followed by bright white light.

The pain in his shoulders immediately ceased and whatever had been pulling him by the hair had let go. The smell of dead fish was gone along with the growling sounds the thing made.

"Kevin," his mother yelled, her pink nightgown shuffling about. "Are you all right?"

"Mom," he said. "Pull me out of here."

"What's going on in here?" Kevin heard his dad say.

Before Kevin's mom got to him, he'd wiggled his way out and sat on the floor, leaning against the bed.

"What were you doing under the bed?" his mother asked.

"You have a girl under there?" Kevin's father demanded, hands angrily on his hips awaiting an answer.

Kevin wanted to tell them what happened, but quickly decided against it. Only a week ago his Dad had caught him with a bottle of whiskey and had trust issues ever since. Kevin couldn't blame him. He would have to earn his father's trust back and raving about a monster wouldn't help. His dad would likely drive him down to the local hospital instead and commit him for drug abuse.

"I woke up under my bed and didn't know where I was," he lied.

Kevin's dad huffed, got down on his knees and looked under the bed. He got up as quickly as he'd gone down. "No girls," he said sounding satisfied. "It's cold. I'm going back to bed." He turned and left the room.

"Must have been a nightmare is all," Kevin's mom said. She hesitated then added, "Are you sure everything's all right?"

"Yeah," Kevin said as he wiped sweat from his brow.

"You can tell me if something's up. I know how your father can be lately, but I was a teenager once too."

"Everything's fine." Kevin wanted to tell her what happened, but he was too confused and knew he would have to deal with it on his own.

"Okay then," his mother said and rubbed his head. She stood up, said goodnight and left the room, closing the door behind her.

Kevin quickly jumped from where he was sitting, not wanting to be near the bed and stood against the opposite wall. Questions of what had attacked him and why the thing simply disappeared plagued his thoughts.

Perhaps the light being turned on had something to do with it, Kevin thought.

After awhile the adrenaline rush dissipated and Kevin grew weak and tired. He wanted no part of sleeping but knew he couldn't stay up all night. He checked under the bed again, a pair of white ankle socks lay lifeless like shriveled ghosts, then leaped onto the mattress, making sure his feet never came close to the bed's underneath.

The box springs screeched loudly, as if in pain, after which Kevin froze allowing the silence to take hold again. He sat in an awkward position listening for any strange noises, but none came. Kevin turned on the television and without realizing it, fell asleep.

He woke up Saturday morning around eleven thirty, thankful it wasn't a school day, and relieved he made it through the night without a second attack. He felt pretty sure that leaving the light on had something to do with it.

After returning from a badly needed bathroom visit, he sat at his desk and turned on the computer. He searched the internet for hours, looking for anything related to what had happened to him the night before.

The only information that pertained to what he experienced had to do with the famed boogeyman, but Kevin knew what he saw was no man. Most of the information was about how the boogeyman was created by parents to keep their kids from misbehaving. The origins of the boogeyman dated back to the sixteenth century in English literature, but some historians believed the legend was used as far back as when people lived in caves and huts to keep the children safe from predators.

Kevin had never really believed in the boogeyman, but after last night his feelings on the supernatural had changed. Almost every culture had its own boogeyman folklore and the stories were relatively the same: a man who hid in closets or under beds and scared little children. With so many accounts of boogeymen in so many different cultures Kevin was dismayed to find no information revealing how to kill a boogeyman, fictional or real.

After breakfast Kevin continued his researched and found a particularly interesting story. It was about a young girl who was savagely marred one night while asleep in bed. There was no break-in or DNA evidence to suggest that she was attacked by anything other than herself but she swore that a creature, its form black as tar, had attacked her. The creature grabbed her and pulled her under her bed but the teen claimed she couldn't scream and had become extremely weak. She was almost fully under the bed when her dog crashed through the door. The creature stopped attacking her and vanished. When asked by a reporter to give a description of the so-called creature, she only said that it was black as night and had two glowing red eyes.

Kevin was sure the girl, Rachael Bergnan, was attacked by the same creature that attacked him. He searched for more information about the girl—a phone number or address he could use to contact her. Unfortunately, the next article he found killed any hopes of speaking with Rachael. According to a local Topeka newspaper the young girl suffered a heart attack and was found dead under her bed. The article was dated a few days after her initial report of the creature. There was still no evidence for authorities to suspect the girl's claims were real. She suffered from panic attacks and died of a heart condition. Case closed.

Kevin swallowed hard. He felt positive that the creature he witnessed was the same thing that had attacked and ultimately killed Rachael. Kevin was brought out of his thoughts by his mother's voice.

"Kevin, your father and I are going to the market. Want to come?"

"Is Bobby going too?" Kevin didn't want to stay home alone, hoping his brother wouldn't go.

"Yes," she said.

He was about to say yes when an idea occurred to him and he would need to be in the house alone to do it. "No, I'll stay home, thanks."

After his parents and brother left the house, Kevin went up to the attic. The air was chilly, his breath showing in buffed bursts of harmless smoke. He moved silently, listening with every step.

The attic was lined with numerous cardboard boxes of various sizes. Kevin looked around for small boxes, gathering up as many as he could. He carried them down one, sometimes two at a time depending on the weight, to his room. He began shoving them under his bed, filling up the empty space. One box was filled with cutlery and the mere thought of knives under him while he slept was terrifying. He put that one back.

Soon the space under the bed was no more, filled with cardboard boxes. All his research into the boogeyman stated that beds and closets were doorways for the creature. Now the doorway under his bed was closed, so to speak. It was only a temporary fix, but it would do until he found a way to kill or at least get rid of the thing under his bed.

That night, Kevin went to bed around eleven o'clock. He tucked the covers deep into the mattress and slid in like a sardine. He turned on the television, but quickly turned it off. The silence was better, in a disquieting way.

Kevin saw the alarm clock's red numbers hit midnight. They reminded him of the thing's evil red eyes. He made a mental note to buy an alarm clock with different colored numbers—green would be nice.

His vision had long adjusted to the dark. The girls were in there normal seductive poses, but each one seemed to be smirking as if they knew something he didn't.

The underneath of his bed was tightly packed and although he felt safe, Kevin wanted desperately to stay awake. Unfortunately, he was too exhausted from not sleeping the night before. He tried a number of things to stop himself from falling asleep, thinking about Melody, a girl at school he liked, movies he wanted to see, books he had read, and even pinched himself a few times, but the dam of consciousness broke and Kevin drifted off to sleep.

He awoke to the sound of cardboard sliding on carpet, the tiredness leaving him as if his body had been dipped in ice-water. Kevin shot up, rubbing his eyes and clearing the dreariness from them. He looked down at the floor and saw five of the boxes he'd put under his bed. They were scattered across the carpet, each one pushed a different length from the bed.

Shock over took his body as fright traveled up his spine to his scalp where his thoughts seemed to vanish. A shushing sound, like sandpaper rubbing on wood, came from under his bed. The thing was pushing the boxes out of its way. Kevin didn't know how much time he had, but he got up and sprang from the bed. He sailed through the air as he had done so often the last two days, except this time his landing was obscured by an a cardboard box. The tip of his foot caught the edge of a box, the box gave under his weight, but tripped him up and he fell forward into the dresser.

Kevin crashed hard and loud, smashing his left cheek and forearm into the oak dresser. He toppled to the floor in a daze. A raspy hiss emanated from behind him and Kevin knew the creature was coming. Dazed and weak, he rolled over and got on a knee when something grabbed his ankle. It was cold, as if from some arctic hell. Kevin's strength weakened further, his will suddenly being stripped away. He could hear the creature's gurgled breaths.

Kevin turned and saw the thing. Its eyes glaring, its mouth open with teeth bared, but what scared Kevin the most was the creatures form. It had no defining features as if looking into a black void with red eyes and a mouth.

Kevin turned away reaching for something to hold onto. He grabbed onto the handle of the bottom drawer and pulled. The drawer withdrew with ease as Kevin was pulled toward the creature. The drawer slid all the way out, the lip caught on the inside of the drawer hole and prevented it from falling out. The creature tugged harder, Kevin tried to scream for his parents, but he didn't have any strength left in his voice.

Suddenly Kevin's other ankle grew cold and numb, the thing had both legs in its clutches. It was only a matter of time before it had him. He hoped his parents had heard the crash.

Kevin used his free hand and reached into one of the boxes near him. He searched with his fingers for anything he could use to fight off the monster. He found something metal and pole-like. He tried pulling it from the box, but the box folds were secure, each side of the folding lid tucked into the other. Getting his hand in was easy, but getting it out would require strength he wasn't sure he had left.

The numbness was spreading up Kevin's legs and to his knees. He had to act fast. He thought of his brother, sleeping in his bed, young and helpless and then thought of this thing going to his room. Kevin shook his hand violently, pulling at the box's closed top until in popped open. The metal object was an old flute of his mothers. He heard the dresser drawer begin to crack. Holding the flute at one end, he turned toward the creature and swung at it. The flute made a splatting sound as it connected, but the creature didn't flinch.

Kevin had one more option. He brought the flute to his lips and blew. The flute whistled, it was off and sounded terrible, but the sound was loud and true.

Kevin released his hold from the drawer, his fingers too weak. He slid across the carpet, knocking into boxes as he went, hoping his parents had heard the flute and would be coming in to check on him.

He looked down and saw the thing crawl under the bed and his legs along with it. He went all the way under up to his chest where he was able to reach up and use his arms to hold onto the bed.

His legs, lower region, and stomach were going numb. He felt himself being pulled and then the pain began in his foot where his toes were. He could hold no longer and was about to give into the creatures will when his mother began knocking at the door.

"Mom, mom," Kevin whispered, but it was too low for her to hear.

"Kevin, are you all right?" his mother said.

He couldn't hold on, his grip on the bed frame was slipping. He let go, his fingers brushing helplessly along the underside of the box spring. The creature pulled him under and Kevin felt his whole body go numb. He looked back and saw the boxes and thought how silly it was that they were the last thing he was going to see before he died.

The creature began making tearing noises then chomping sounds and Kevin guessed it was eating him alive. He only had pain in his foot so far and was glad for that. He was about to close his eyes when bright light filled the room. It filled the underneath of his bed and seared through the thing that was eating him like a razor though butter. It was gone in a matter of seconds. He heard his mother calling his name.

"Kevin, are you in here?" she said. "I don't think he's in here, Ed."

"Well, where the hell is he?" his father asked. "And what the hell are all these boxes doing in here?"

"I have no idea. He's a teenager, they do strange things."

"These are our boxes from the attic."

Kevin tried talking, but couldn't. He could see her feet beside one of the boxes and smiled.

"Leave everything where it is," his father said. "I've had it with his reckless behavior. He's getting grounded for the school year, so let him have his fun out with his friends tonight or wherever he snuck out to. I'm going to bed."

"Oh, hon, calm down. We were his age once too. We'll talk to him in the morning," his mother said and with that she turned the light off and shut the door.

Kevin closed his eyes and smiled, glad to have seen his mother's feet as the creature returned and began to eat.

Trepan

Bryan Oftedahl

Consciousness trickled into her mind like water over a long dried riverbed allowing her to slowly become aware of herself. She peeled her eyes open, waited a moment, then sealed them again realizing that open or shut made no difference since everything was darkness. Rising to a sitting position she lifted her hands as far as she could reach but felt nothing. Swinging her arms about only proved that if there were any barriers, they existed beyond her grasp.

She crawled into the dark with her hands sliding back and forth in search of openings, weaknesses in the flooring or any obstacles ahead. Eventually her hands felt something ahead, tough but yielding. Following it upward only proved that whatever it was, it rose higher than she could reach. Choosing another direction she slid her hands along the spongy surface of the newly discovered obstacle until she hit a corner. This continued for some time.

In her mind the dimensions of her surroundings came together to form the image of a floor and four padded walls. She was uncertain if anything was overhead but ignored this uncertainty by concentrating on specifying the dimensions. Walking heal to toe she found that each wall was the length of nearly forty-five of her feet. With the dimensions of the minute world haphazardly mapped she directed her attention to her self, her form.

Each foot ended in five stubby toes and each hand ended in five lengthy fingers. The nails of the fingers were longer than those of her toes. Her legs were longer than her arms and felt much more firm but her arms were smoother than her legs. Her hair, silky, ran from her scalp to her lower back. Her torso seemed full of activity as the upper half inflated and deflated with each breath while something near the center was beating against the fleshy walls.

She had no means of tracking the passage of time. She would sleep then rise and reaffirm her surroundings and herself. Sometimes she would forget to open her eyes while other times she wouldn't close them until they burned and itched.

As can be expected, change did eventually occur and with it came first fear then playful curiosity.

***

Champ rejoined the world in a strange state of peace, a first in so many weeks of waking up to the nightmare of finding the other half of the bed cold and empty before collapsing into tears under the weight of realization. He rolled out of bed and seemingly of its own accord his body began cleaning as if it understood the decision had been made before he did.

First, came the obvious need to wash and organize the insane mountain of rotting dishes, returning them clean and smelling of lemons to the cupboards. Second, came the scattered drifts of clothing, washed then dried with softener before being folded into the dresser or hung in the closet. Next, came the frustrating task of vacuuming with a piece of crap mini-vac that required its bag to be emptied after every three square feet or so. Then, Champ set to work scrubbing out the bathroom with heavy cleaners. The task left him tired and lightheaded but since the process had been started, it had to be finished. Finally, came the smaller things such as emptying the trash, wiping the windows, watering and grooming the plants and feeding the cat wherever he was. The last step of course was cleaning himself.

It was in the shower, the warm water running from his head down his slumped shoulders, that his mind began to wander the darkness behind his eyes. There was really only one thing he could think of and that thought chased away the unusual serenity he had woken with. The back of his throat began to ache despite his dedicated efforts of keeping the tears at bay. The concentration proved no match for the oncoming flood of emotions.

Champ recalled the shape of her face and proportions of her body with eerie detail as if she just stepped out of some dark cell and into the light. Her crooked left bicuspid, the tiny scar near her right eye, the thickness of her calves, these things he never paid much attention to before.

***

She felt warmth and knew without opening her eyes that her surroundings were not the same as when she had fallen asleep. She opened her eyes and gasped, curling into the corner. Now there was a distinct difference when her eyes were open from when they were closed.

What was it? Was it harmful?

After some time passed and nothing negative occurred she conjured courage enough to confront the change. High above her a ceiling rested on the tops of the walls. The ceiling looked much the same as the floor, sanitary white tiles, except for the thing hanging from it. It hung from the ceiling by two thin wires, one on either end while a black cable snaked from one side to a hole in the ceiling. Nestled inside it were two humming tubes producing the flood of fluorescent light.

A smile stretched her face. For the first time she saw her surroundings with her eyes, not her mind. The stuffed walls were colored a faded white. The floor consisted of several white tiles each only slightly longer than her foot.

Her skin was pale with a spackling of freckles across the shoulders and breasts. Her hair hung thick and black like the previous darkness.

As can be expected this change in her surroundings resulted with a change in her demeanor. The contentment she felt in the darkness was broken by the introduction of light. She danced the room spinning on her toes and loving this new sensation of sight, no longer blind to herself or her surroundings.

***

Once the tears started they couldn't be stopped. Champ reached between his legs and began tugging and pulling. Disgusted with himself he was still unable to stop. After the resulting mess flushed down the drain he fell to the shower floor sobbing and pathetic. It was then and there as he crawled from the shower that the decision was obvious, no room left to deny.

He brushed his teeth before shaving his face, cautiously preventing his eyes from meeting their reflection in the mirror. After shaving the scrag from his face he decided to do the same with his thinning patch of hair, feeling it only natural even if it meant sweeping the floor again.

Stepping out of the steam-clouded bathroom he moved to the closet for the one and only good suit; black pinstriped slacks, black silk vest, white button down dress shirt and black tie with silver diagonal stripes. The fact that it was the same suit he wore to her funeral felt comforting somehow.

In the bottom of a toolbox tucked away in the corner of the closet lay the kit and tool he had christened as his only hope for salvation. Its silver body and black handle he noticed kind of matched the suit. This fact was also strangely comforting. Resting on the nightstand next to the bed he once shared with her waited his guide, a textbook titled *The History of Medical Practice*.

The book easily fell open to the worn page, 317. Champ placed it on the back of the toilet for easy access, as if he hadn't memorized the chapter already. Plugging the ACRI-Cut perforator into the socket nearest the sink his eyes inadvertently fluttered to the mirror. There he froze, bloodshot eyes glaring at bloodshot eyes. Pulling the trigger started the machine vibrating in his hand, the vibrations caused the muscles up to his shoulder to tighten. The noise, a high-pitched whir, was much greater in his ordinarily quiet apartment than he had expected and for a moment he wondered if the neighbors might complain.

***

With the light, the ability to now see what lay around her also brought a want to see what may exist beyond the padded walls, tiled floor and high ceiling. There had to be something more, had to be. At first she tried to contain this resentment of her fate, this life in so small a world. Soon though the emotions overwhelmed her and she began throwing herself against the walls in hopes of breaking them down. She tossed her fists into the floor until the white tiles were splattered red. Everything she tried did nothing but fuel her frustration.

Most nights she fell asleep where the light fell onto the floor with her eyes streaming, her feet bruised and fists bleeding. She hungered for more change, could feel it so close yet refusing to come to her.

***

The justification for what he was about to do was all wrapped up in one beautifully simple formula. F=ma. Force equals mass times acceleration. To find the force required to bring a moving object to a standstill, or to take that still object and return it to its original motion you simply multiply its mass times its speed of acceleration. If an extreme occurrence brought his life to a standstill then an extreme occurrence, Champ speculated, was required to set it back in motion.

As if mechanical science had anything to do with life.

Without looking to the book he recounted its passages. '*It is perhaps the oldest form of surgery known to man with evidence of its practice found in remains dating back to the Neolithic period.*'

Reaching into the toolbox he removed an empty derma-syringe along with a vial of Epinephrine, to cause constriction in the blood vessels and a vial of Lidocaine, a local anesthetic. After injecting both drugs he reached back into the toolbox removing a vacuum-sealed scalpel which he aimed beyond the shaved receding hairline, a region known as the fontanel where three segments of the skull combine. He dug the blade into the skin and dragged it diagonally up then down to create a triangular opening exposing the bone beneath.

Again he recalled the passages in the book, '*Trepanning involves creating a hole in the skull exposing the dura mater resulting in a decrease of pressure and increase of the oxygen grade and brain-blood levels of the gray matter. Its practice has been used for a variety of purposes ranging from the curing of epileptic fits, migraines, mental disorders and even the release of demons.*'

Dampening his lips he grabbed the perforator and set it to top speed.

While leaning in toward the mirror, the perforator aimed at the exposed region of skull, that's when it happened. The dampness of the bathroom floor caused his right foot to slip and this loss of balance sent him crashing into the mirror. He watched as his reflection spider-webbed. The back of the perforator struck the wall behind the shattered glass forcing its 8mm/5mm bit inward.

There was a moment of darkness, barely a second, while the floor swung up to meet with the side of his head followed by the clanking of the drill on tile. The darkness cleared, he wrapped both hands around the handle and pulled with what strength he could muster, pulling the drill free and shoving it across the white tiled floor.

From some great depth the release of blood and inevitable mess aggravated him. He had just scrubbed those tiles not half an hour before.

***

Unexpectedly she was yanked from a deep sleep when her world was shaken by a violent blast. The fluorescent lights hanging from the ceiling swung back and forth tracing shadows across the room. An enormous hole appeared in the left padded wall providing a means of escape.

***

Rolling onto his back he felt the nausea clench his stomach. The shock caused the bone of his skull to feel chilled while his skin felt as if it were melting away. One arm crossed the belly that he was always so conscious of despite the refusal to do a few sit-ups each morning. His head shaved to the skin because he felt it was simply a piece of the ceremony, eyes bloodshot from tears he never could allow himself to cry willingly.

Shards of glass sprinkled across the floor reflecting the light from above. Splatters of red streaked across the tiles and up the wall toward what remained of the mirror. The bloodied silver and black drill, now silent, matching the color scheme of his stained suit, rested in the space behind the porcelain toilet.

Perhaps it was trauma induced hysterics but he could have sworn somebody was standing over him, bewildered and disgusted. With the last of his strength he forced a single word through his constricting throat, "Kaycie."

***

Champaign 'Champ' Delmont will lie there for a matter of weeks before the property manager begins receiving complaints about a smell. Notes will be slipped under the door but no replies will be received. Finally the manager will be forced to enter the apartment and deal with the problem directly. He'll stand in the bathroom doorway looking from the broken mirror to the book on the toilet to the congealed blood pooled around the body and for a moment he won't be able to move or think until his attention is drawn to the hungry cat scratching and mewing dismally outside the bedroom window.

For weeks following the discovery, Champ will be the spotlight of gossip for the entire complex. The kids will curse his apartment as haunted and make up tales about ghosts to explain the chill they feel while passing by. The adults will put in their two cents as to just why things turned out for him the way they did, theories and speculations. In the end he'll be forgotten just like he always feared.

He had rationalized it though. Once upon a time it was how the demons were evacuated, by creating a hole in the head. Trepanation it's called. One twitch of the index finger on the trigger and the demon would be gone.

It would all be gone.

Living Memory

Keith J. Scales

Twenty-five years. It was hard to believe that so much time could have passed since I last stood in this room. The sounds from outside were the same today as they had been back then. Crows in the yard, trucks on the roadway, a distant piano—though perhaps I'm imagining the piano. The wallpaper and carpeting had been replaced, of course. And looking around at the frilly covers, pretty curtains and porcelain knick-knacks, it's difficult to conceive, even for me, that murder had once been committed in this room.

The bed was still in the same place against the wall. And even after all these years I could still clearly remember seeing Christina, my beloved Christina, kneeling on that bed, looking up at me in surprise, hair rumpled, enchanting in the nightdress I thought she had bought for me but, as I now know, was intended to please *him.* I saw again her sleepy eyes grow wide with anger at my accusation, and her face drain white with fear when I threw the letter on the bed.

Music had never been an element in lovemaking, at least for Christina and me. According to that letter, it was different with Christina and him. *...the Rachmaninoff was so exciting, I loved it being so loud, I drowned in it when you touched me...* and further down the page, *...when I want to remember your skin I play our glorious Rachmaninoff...* and then the exquisitely detailed description of what they were going to do when she went away with him the next weekend, a fantasy written with such carefully chosen, suggestive words that I had not been able to prevent my own excitement when I first read the pages that I went on to read again and again and again...

Christina had stared at the envelope on the bed, the address plainly visible in her own flamboyant handwriting. And in that frozen moment, just before she reached cautiously for the letter, I suddenly realized that I was hearing music. Rachmaninoff. Very quiet, but distinct. Where was it coming from? And then I noticed the headphones dangling from her bedside tape player. So—when I opened the front door, moments before, she must have been lying on our bed, in that gossamer negligee, listening to melodies that reminded her of *him*.

She saw me notice the music. And suddenly it seemed as if she changed, somehow, as if from the inside out, into a person I had never met. Her eyes seemed to glitter with defiance and her lips twisted into a wicked smile of triumph, as though she had beaten me at some game I had no idea I was playing. In one graceful move she uncoiled her long slim legs, lay back against the pillows, put the letter to her lips with one hand and with the other yanked the headphones out of the tape player. The room was suddenly filled with a pounding piano concerto, gorgeous and swelling with passion. She shrugged at me, still smiling, and her nightgown slipped off one smooth creamy shoulder. And then, quite deliberately, she closed her eyes, as though transported by the music.

Time sped up again as the truth rushed in at me with the heavy chords of the concerto. My beloved was nothing of the kind. Everything I treasured was suddenly worthless, there was nothing to preserve, any more, no reason to go on. Arpeggios crashed in collision as I reached, almost without knowing it, for the knife in my jacket pocket. I said her name. She saw me slowly unfolding the blade and gasped. And as the crescendo mounted she laughed at me.

Standing in the same room now twenty-five years later, I cannot help but relive it all again. I had moved toward the bed and looked down at her. At that moment I had seen both Christinas. I saw the young girl I had pursued with such flair and who had given herself to me with such abandon, my wife for two and a half blissful years, in a marriage to which my every effort had been devoted. She had so many expressions, most of them playful or mischievous. But this new woman, this stranger, wore a look I had never seen on that face before, a look of hatred. Her hair hung loose over her shoulders, the way I loved to see it, her lips were parted and even as I stepped towards her with the knife in my hand I was hungry for her, I so desperately wanted everything to be as it had been, no letter, no Rachmaninoff, no next weekend with *him*—Christina loving *me*, wanting *me*, only me. Christina started shouting scornful, obscene phrases at me over that dreadful concerto, and I knew there could be no going back, there was nothing to go back to, no escape from this moment.

I don't believe I knew what I was going to do with the knife. Perhaps I thought to ruin her beauty. I had never been one to give into violence, but I had never experienced betrayal like that. And even as I reached for her it burst upon me that I did not know and probably would never know for how long I had been happily living in falsehood, the contented husband, foolishly unaware of her liaison with a man I had never liked.

I had thrown myself on top of her and she hammered at me with her small fists, snarling, startling me with her ferocity and profanity. I tried to cover her body with mine, to contain her. Her nightdress rose up her long, bare legs and I hungered for her sanctuary. But our limbs were meshed together in combat, not love, and her cries were not cries of ecstasy but rage. The music was thundering as we slipped to the floor, flailing and grunting, and our struggle became a terrible rolling, screaming, scratching, biting fight to the death. It took all my strength to force her head back down to the carpet. I straddled her body and started to babble questions, threats, but she laughed and screamed over the mercilessly pounding piano that I was stupid and when I raised myself up over her and lifted my arm to strike she cursed and lunged at my vulnerable parts with her knee, heaving with her pelvis, trying to throw me off. I don't know if she ever believed I might be serious. The amount of blood was horrifying.

Since that night, twenty-five cold years ago, I never think about the happy times we had, the confident years before I found that loathsomely salacious letter. Once in a while, of course, I may find myself in some part of town where something wonderful happened between us—a street corner where she kissed me impetuously, a doorway she pulled me into for caresses and then I cannot help but remember. But standing here again in this bedroom where so much had taken place, my mind is suddenly alive with memories of our early years, choosing wallpaper, breakfasting lazily in bed on Sunday mornings, pillow fighting, listening to the night rain patter against that very window. It is almost less painful to think through those last chaotic moments that brought an end to everything.

The shadows are growing longer inside the room. It's almost dark outside. I hear in my mind a sardonic fragment of distant, tinkling piano music and then, the bedroom door opens.

I turn, very slowly. Framed in the doorway is Christina, or so I thought. She stares at me. I stare back, bewildered by this woman who looks so much like the Christina I married, Christina in her twenties. We regard each other in shocking silence, and in that moment I understand that this lovely young lady with long dark hair to her shoulders is Christina's daughter, her eyes grow wide and she runs screaming from the room. From somewhere below in the house I hear a man's voice call out.

I should not have come back. And yet I know I will return again, in another twenty-five years perhaps, and maybe twenty-five years after that again, unable to stay away from this room, unable to forget, unable to find the peace and rest that belong to those who die an easy death. I hear steps on the stairs. It is time for me to leave before the man, whoever he might be, comes in and sees me standing here in my outdated clothes, drenched with blood, my throat slashed wide.

The Stripper

Stephanie Kincaid

The girl didn't belong in the Horny Toad. It was a filthy bar full of filthy people, most of whom were looking to do filthy things. Young attractive women didn't come here. And neither did men looking to hook up with young attractive women.

Randy hadn't come to the bar with any plans beyond drinking, except perhaps to drink some more. That changed when he saw the girl. The grime and gloom of the oppressive little bar didn't seem to touch her. She was immaculately groomed. Her rich brown hair fell in loose waves, not a strand out of place, as though she had just strolled out of a shampoo commercial. She was curvy, but only in the right places, and her lips were plump and moist.

Randy spent a full five minutes imagining things she could do with those lips; some sweet, some savory and some most definitely *un*savory. Randy's inner child existed in a permanent state of adolescence and it was one warped kid, particularly when Randy fed it liquor. He would have been content to sit there mentally violating the girl from every angle, but a tastier opportunity unexpectedly arose.

The bartender plunked a beer in front of Randy. "From the hottie over there. You lucky bastard. You know her?"

"Uh, no." Shocked out of his dirty daydreams, Randy didn't have the presence of mind to play it cool. It was clear from his reaction that he was as confused as the bartender as to why the girl would even look his way, much less buy him a drink.

"Go talk to her, stupid. You're not gonna get another chance like this. Ever."

Randy was many things—from eccentric to downright sick—but stupid was not one of them. He knew he had nothing to lose and he wasn't about to let the opportunity get away. He slid off his stool, snatched the beer from the bar, and walked as straight a line as he could manage over to the girl.

"Thanks," he said to her, raising the glass in a little salute.

"I saw you looking," she answered teasingly, her lilting voice floated on top of the music that twanged through the cramped room.

Randy started to stammer a denial, but she interrupted. "It's ok. I figured if I bought you a drink, it might loosen you up enough to come say hello."

"Hello," he said, careful not to grin too widely.

"What's your name?" she asked, waving at the stool beside her, on which Randy obediently sat.

"Walter," he lied easily.

"I'm Angelique."

"What do you do, Angelique?"

She cast her eyes down with calculated shyness. "Oh, you don't want to know that."

"Sure I do. Otherwise I wouldn't have asked."

"Promise you're not going to walk away as soon as I tell you?"

"Is it that bad?"

"A lot of men find it … disturbing."

God, he loved watching those lips make words. "Try me."

"I'm a stripper."

"Ok," Randy said nonchalantly. *Jackpot,* his brain screamed. He was willing to bet she could bend in ways even his twisted mind couldn't imagine.

Randy didn't even have to dream up an excuse to get her alone. After a couple more drinks, she asked him if he would escort her home. Her tone informed him that it was less a request than an expectation and he certainly wasn't about to let the lady down.

This is my lucky day! Randy thought, as Angelique led him straight to the bedroom. She put on some music that Randy was sure he'd heard before in a porno

"What do you want to do?" she asked playfully.

"Um … uh …could you show me some of your stripper moves?" *Damn.* His voice sounded clumsier out loud than it had in his head.

"Absolutely," she purred.

She walked toward him so smoothly that he never noticed the claws slowly extending from her fingertips. His smile remained, unfaltering, even as she flayed him. She performed her job with grace and efficiency. Before the pulsating song ended, every scrap of flesh had been stripped from his bones.

The Rest for the Wicked

Stephen Hill

Matthew Spencer woke with a start, his blocky face pressed up against the hard plastic shade of the airplane window. His sight was bleary and his hearing muffled, but the cramps that needled his legs and spiked his back confirmed the bad news. He was still onboard Flight 54 from L.A. to Chicago, and God only knew how much time was left.

A man of powerful build and intense focus, he shifted self-consciously, careful not to disturb the fastidiously pressed lines of his clothing. He was trapped within the cramped confines of the economy class seat, wishing he'd reserved earlier so he could have managed a business class ticket. He would still be petrified, but at least he would have been able to stretch out while he worked through the phobia.

Damn, he thought. He'd downed three Dramamine and four scotches before even stepping foot on the plane; so whatever had yanked him from slumber must have shoved him hard.

Squinting down at his Rolex, he tried briefly to calculate the time left onboard. As stressful as the previous day's meeting had been, Matthew wished he was back in the thick of it—selling those stubborn bastards on a campaign ad that would last well into the next year—rather than being on this or any other plane. He was good at selling and the victory gave him a rush. All that flying did was make him paranoid.

Slowly and uncertainly, he pulled his window shade up. The last time he'd looked they'd been taxiing down the runway at LAX, and sunlight was blasting across the hot tarmac. Now, there was nothing in sight but an endless chasm of black.

Prying his lower legs from beneath the seat in front of him, he sighed loudly and sucked in the regurgitated mash of rancid breath and broken wind from more than two hundred passengers. His tongue tasted like something left rotting on the lavatory floor.

Matthew's auburn eyes, so practiced at zoning in on a review board's vulnerability and exploiting it, peered over the seats in front of him. Relegated to coach, dozens of passengers' heads seemed to mock him, dark and immobile lumps that were tilted back in what Matthew imagined were lengthy and refreshing stretches of sleep.

While the main cabin bulbs were off, reading lights were visible above at least three of the plane's nocturnal travelers. Bitterness consumed him. He was positive that the few others awake were finally finding the time to read a novel, peruse a favorite magazine, or catch up on the day's events with a newspaper or two. God knew they weren't watching anything. There was no onboard movie during the four-hour flight.

Reaching into the seat pocket in front of him, he unearthed the present his daughter had given him before he left Chicago almost four days ago. "Thith will take your mind off the flight, Daddy!" she'd blurted, shoving the book into his carry-on bag.

He managed a smile, but groaned inwardly. His daughter understood his phobia at seven and to add insult to injury, she pointed it out with her damned lisp.

Edginess cut open the worry line between his brows. Matthew wished his wife, Andrea, would pay a little more attention to the kid's diction. It was embarrassing for him to know that he made his living with words, coaxing people into purchasing what they didn't even need, and his only child rarely got a sentence out without sounding like a drunk sputtering through a split lip.

He stared at the jacket of the book for a moment: *World's Stupidest Criminals*. Three mug shots and cartoon print zigzagging across the front cover promised tales of wacky shenanigans within; failed burglars getting caught with their pants down in ridiculous *what could they have been thinking?* circumstances. Matthew thought a better title of the book would have been *For World's Stupidest Readers*, but seeing his daughter was only seven, he figured perhaps he could cut her some slack.

Not much, but some.

He ran his hands distractedly through the dyed blonde highlights of his hair, then shoved the book back into the seat pocket. He began flipping through the flight's complimentary newspaper instead. He lost interest immediately and a moment later, his fingers were drumming the armrests.

The young stewardess who originally gave him the newspaper was the distraction he needed. One look at those voluptuous curves invited intense speculation on whether the swoop of the red mane that fell across her back matched the trim runway Matthew was sure she sported down below. He last saw her sashaying towards the rear of the plane carrying a magazine and wearing a smirk. The next time she passed, he planned on clarifying whether she favored a thong or a G-string.

He glanced at the empty seat next to him which had ended up as a curse only disguised as a blessing. Any number of beautiful women could have occupied it, thus providing added eye candy to the stressful flight but instead the seat remained vacant; taunting him. Too small to stretch out on, but just large enough to be a nagging reminder of what he didn't have.

Membership in the mile-high club was something his wife had suggested before one flight together several years ago. *What a joke*, Matthew thought. While the plane was up, there was no way he was getting it up. Not that Andrea had provided him with much reason to get it up on the ground these days either.

The plane lurched to one side, shuddering fitfully. "Calm down," Matthew muttered, closing his eyes. The sounds of the engine suddenly seemed distant, as his ears clogged with a steady and relentless hammering.

Is that my heart?

"Oh, God," Matthew gasped as he realized it was. Pain

stabbed out from the inside of his chest, as if tearing a scorching hole through his flesh. His eyes rolled to the back of his head and his teeth ground up against one another. The twinge he'd felt before he boarded the plane was now a thousand times more powerful and there was no sign of a Dramamine capsule or Scotch shot to douse the flames.

The pain consumed everything, blazing through his veins and boiling his blood. Hot sparks exploded across his closed eyelids and numbness sleeved his arms. He'd never known anything like this and now it was all that existed.

"Please stop," he whispered hoarsely through clamped lips. And then—as suddenly as it had arrived—the pain receded, leaving nothing but a cold sweat on his brow and a tremble in his limbs.

"Thank fucking God," he whispered.

As Matthew slowly opened his eyes, a young man of slight stature slipped into the seat beside him. "Sorry," the man said, glancing over timidly as he buckled up.

Although his new neighbor sounded sincere, Matthew's pain was forgotten, and his indignation flared like fireworks.

"The people sitting next to me down the aisle have a baby," the man continued, his face averted under a thick snarl of dark bangs. "I think they need the room more than I do." His narrow shoulders shrugged and he yanked nervously at the arms of his black sweater with spindly fingers.

The hull of the plane quaked as it slammed through a screaming wind. Matthew cast a menacing glare at the man and at his left elbow that rested on their shared armrest. Not only had space been lost, but—even worse—here was someone who could witness Matthew's fear firsthand, including the sweat springing from his forehead with each bump, or a possible scramble for the vomit bag.

To Matthew, it was all about self-respect. As long as someone was looking, it wasn't any more dignified to blow chunks at thirty-five thousand feet than it was at six.

Taking a napkin from his pocket, he dabbed at the moisture on his face and began to take inventory of his neighbor. The young man was good-looking in that sort of boyish, unthreatening way that Matthew figured got the ladies wet where it mattered. And, just like Matthew, it didn't appear he'd be sleeping anytime soon. His twenty-something face was set as if in white granite and his back was ruler-straight.

Matthew noted the young man's fine hands clenched over the fastened seatbelt in the lap of his black trousers. The only part of him that moved was one thumb, circling constantly across the cold surface of the buckle. In short, the man looked damn uncomfortable.

Matthew smiled inwardly and began looking around for a casual way to dispose of the napkin gripped in his clammy fist. He hated shoving it in his pants, yet tucking it back into the seat pocket in front of him seemed cloddish and weak. *Christ*, he thought. *Who am I trying to impress?* He pulled open the seat pocket and a shaky voice stopped his hand in mid air.

"Let me take that for you."

Before Matthew could answer, the stewardess plucked the napkin from his palm.

There you are, Matthew thought, and his eyes zoned in on her chest, noting the delicious weight that strained against the navy fabric of her uniform.

"Anything else?"

"Scotch for me," the stranger responded, "and…?" he turned to Matthew with a tired smile.

Taking in the grayish purple blotches under his eyes, Matthew realized his seat neighbor wasn't quite the pretty boy he initially appeared. "That's my drink," replied Matthew, and broke out in a grin that felt surprisingly natural. *Use it before you lose it*, he thought, and turned the smile on the stewardess. "Perhaps you'd like to join us with a third?" he asked, revealing perfectly white teeth.

Her green eyes were unreadable under thick blonde lashes. "Not while I'm working."

Before Matthew could answer, she was making her way back down the aisle. She looked back over her shoulder but there was no flirtation, just thinly veiled contempt.

Tease, Matthew thought to himself. *Or a dyke*. Turning to his neighbor, he offered what he hoped was a relatively dry hand. It was immediately held in a cool grip that was firm without being competitive. "Matthew Spencer," he heard himself say automatically.

"David," replied the young man softly. "You're not a good flier either, I take it?"

"Guilty," Matthew replied. His gut somersaulted slowly with the plane's next dip. "And, go figure, we're two of the only people actually awake in this hell."

David leaned back, "It makes you wonder just what we did to deserve this, doesn't it?"

The stewardess was at their side again, smeared in shadows from tiny light bulbs, and handing over two plastic cups half full of scotch and ice. David took his cup gingerly, as if handling a bomb that could detonate at any moment.

As Matthew reached for his, the stewardess's fingers released, and the cup plummeted. His hand grabbed and caught, but squeezed too hard. A splash of cold liquid sprung over the cup's lip and onto his lap, freezing his balls instantly.

"God-damn!" he gasped, staring up in astonishment. But the stewardess was already lost in shadows.

"You okay?" David asked.

"Peachy." He popped his seat tray free, tossing back the remaining gulp of scotch at the same time. He immediately surmised that the captain must have strained it through his boxers; not only was it the worst scotch he'd ever tasted, but the usual blossom of warmth in his stomach was replaced by several jagged stings.

A *ding* rang out in the darkness and with it the accompanying '*fasten seatbelts*' sign illuminated above every row in the plane. David sighed, checking his seatbelt for the tenth time in two minutes. "Why don't they just leave that on?"

A counterfeit smile pulled Matthew's mouth apart. "You don't think it's going to stop?"

David shook his head, staring at the glow of the seatbelt sign as if hypnotized by its simple, solid presence. His upper lip trembled noticeably. "For the rest of the way in, the forecast is awful."

There was a crackle of static and then the captain's voice came over the intercom. Abruptly Matthew forgot all about the scotch in his lap or the neighbor at his side.

"Ladies and gentlemen..."

God, Matthew thought, straining forward. *Was that a tremor in the captain's voice?*

"Ladies and gentlemen," the captain repeated. "Sorry if I've woken you, but we must ask that you *please* remain seated with your seatbelts fastened. We're going—"

As if on cue, wind shrieked across the jet's wings. Matthew's plastic cup jitterbugged to the edge of his tray and another burst of static cut the Captain off in mid-sentence.

Matthew swung a wild-eyed glance at David. "What the hell did that mean?"

"I think it means we're in for it."

Matthew's fingers tunneled into his armrests as he squinted into the inky darkness outside, then back at David, studying his face and gestures more closely—the skin drained almost completely of color; the fidgeting with his belt; the way his exhausted eyes couldn't make contact with Matthew's for more than a moment.

Yes sir, Matthew thought, *this guy's as terrified of flying as I am*. The revelation hammered home with a full-blown flash of delight. Reviled upon first glance, David had now become the most important person in Matthew's life. Still staring at him, Matthew managed a thin and weary grin. "May as well chat it up to keep our minds off this, what do you say?"

"I'd appreciate that."

Matthew pulled the plastic window shade back down. "I'll just be happy to get myself out of here and home to the wife and the kid." Even though he hated the weak sound of his voice, his openness brought with it a welcome feeling of release.

David considered Matthew with his fine, almost elfin features. "Kids?"

"A girl. She's seven."

David nodded as if he'd been expecting the answer. "It must be nice coming home to a family."

"You single?" Matthew asked.

David's bloodshot eyes grew wistful. "Yes."

"Well, you're a young guy," Matthew said. "I wouldn't start feeling too—"

Suddenly the bottom dropped out and the plane was plunging, choking off Matthew's words. As his guts were tossed to his chest, an elderly woman let out a squawk of surprise. Once again there was the familiar *ding* and the red headed stewardess ricocheted down the aisle. As she rebounded past rows of passengers, there were several cries for help, but she never stopped.

Matthew pressed his back against the seat as the plane slowly righted itself. David's hands remained gripping the armrests, but his eyes returned to Matthew's, latching onto them as if they were life preservers. "For one thing I'm not as young as I look," he continued as if nothing had ever happened. "And for another..." He paused, as if struggling for the right words. "From the very beginning I've wanted a family, and part of me is always jealous when I see just what people have." He nodded at Matthew. "It just looks like you've got it all."

Matthew marveled at the change in David's features over a few minutes. Perhaps airsickness was partly to blame, but his initial look of subdued cool had crumpled into complete despondence.

A man who has everything? Matthew grimaced. Something was gnawing at his insides that he hadn't felt in a long time. He opened his mouth to speak, and then thought better of it. *No*, he thought. *No, he couldn't da—*

BANG! The huge sound reverberated through the cabin, like nothing he had heard before, a savage metallic punch that shook the tray tables and chairs, and dumped his cup onto the floor. The plane pitched right, its turbines whining, and luggage crashed across the bins above.

Static hissed and again there was the sound of the captain's voice, buried beneath it. There was only one syllable this time, all authority lost amidst the uproar. "No!" And then with a final crackling sputter, the announcement was over before it had begun.

Say it! Matthew thought, panicked. *If I don't say it now, I might never get another chance.*

"I did it," he muttered under his breath, his stomach muscles clenched down like steel turrets. "I've been doing it for ages." He didn't even note the plane realigning itself, quaking stubbornly as it straightened across the night sky.

"What?" David's eyes stayed on Matthew, his brows knitting together in concentration.

"It's all bullshit," Matthew continued. "All of it. The marriage, the family, the wedding vows, everything." He leaned his head back, staring up at the empty eyes of the airplane vents. "What a joke."

"Look, you don't have to tell me anything you don't want to—"

"Screw it," Matthew said, louder now. The sound of the engines was rising to a wail. "We're going down anyway."

David stayed quiet. Whether it was due to patience or

terror, Matthew didn't know, and didn't care. It meant he could finally unload out loud and possibly come to terms with what he'd done. He took a deep breath and spat the next sentence out in a rush. "I've been cheating on my wife for years."

The plane was shaking hard, but David's eyes stayed riveted on Matthew. Light reflected off a forehead that was no longer damp. The pronounced tremble in his upper lip vanished. "And you're feeling penitent about what you've done."

Penitent? Where the hell did that come from? Matthew took fresh stock of his neighbor, noting that every sign of tension had disappeared. In harsh contrast, the plane was heaving worse than ever, riding a rickety roller coaster over impossibly steep hills that threatened to shake the flesh from his face.

Suddenly, Matthew felt deceived.

"No, not *penitent*," Matthew yelled, ears plugging up with cabin pressure. "Not penitent at all!" The acrid stench of fresh puke abruptly assaulted his nostrils from the row in front of him and it was all he could do to keep from being sick himself. Instead, he vomited up rage. "What I feel bad about is getting married in the first fucking place!"

"How so?" David asked calmly.

Matthew couldn't believe this; David's abrupt change in disposition was infuriating. This wasn't a man who was afraid of flying. Somehow, for some bizarre reason, it was all a charade. He was a liar. Betrayed, Matthew's rage peaked and he couldn't hold back even if he tried.

"How so? How *so*, you pompous asshole? How so means I wish I was able to tell my wife the truth about everything, just so I can stop sneaking around and finally *relax* when I'm fucking another woman in our bed!"

David's eyes were unblinking, his gaze and demeanor composed. "Are you done?"

The tone was judgmental and Mathew's temper was re-fuelled. "Are you looking for me to feel sorry about this?" he screamed.

The plane dipped and weaved sickeningly, and, even more sickeningly to Matthew, David's face remained unreadable.

"Come to think of it," Matthew continued, relishing his tirade, "I feel sorry for *myself* if anyone. If anything, my family has held *me* back!"

David was now looking at Matthew with something he recognized instantly — pity.

Your pity shouldn't be directed at me, Matthew thought indignantly. He was the one with the family and the money and the best that life had to offer. The only thing the two of them shared was a fear of flying and even that had turned out to be a false. Matthew strained against the seatbelt, everything forgotten but the pale, self-righteous face in front of him. His neck flushed crimson, the cords in his throat ready to burst. Bile rose to the back of his tongue and he tasted hot copper.

"You know you're the liar," Matthew blurted, stabbing the air with his forefinger. "At least I still have my self-respect." Dropping his finger, he remained leaning forward, as if waiting for the first excuse to pounce, to grasp, and to tear apart something with his bare hands. Yet David barely moved, and the judgment in his glance—if it had even been there in the first place—was gone.

And that wasn't all that had vanished. Only moments before, the plane had seemed stuck in a spin cycle. Now the engines were noiseless and neither the slightest bump nor tremble rattled the hull.

How long has it been like this? Matthew wondered. *How long have I been yelling and did everybody hear*? He was surprised nobody had said anything. Perhaps they were too scared? He did sound extremely aggressive.

Matthew slumped backwards, breaking eye contact with his adversary. He'd completely lost control, and—unbelievably—it was on account of one skinny man holding nothing more threatening than a seatbelt buckle. Even more humiliating; he'd lost control in public.

A moment passed. Then two. *Screw him*, thought Matthew with a passion he was shocked he still felt. *After today, I'm never going see him again.*

"Well, you're correct about that much anyway," David said quietly.

"Sorry?"

It was David's turn to lean forward and although there was nothing anxious in his manner, his gaze was uncompromising, insisting on attention without question.

"You heard what I said." The voice was spider's thread–soft but strong, ensnaring Matthew like an insect. "This will be the last time you ever see me."

Matthew answered automatically. "That's right."

"Now Matthew, I know you're a big proponent of first impressions. But isn't the last time you see someone also crucial to making a good impression?"

Matthew listened, incredulous as David continued. "I mean, if you—how would you say?—blow the exit, then you've really lost the whole interview, haven't you?"

Matthew shook his head brusquely. He was not going to be manipulated again.

David nodded as if he'd agreed aloud. "You'll understand I'm sure."

Matthew didn't, but David wasn't finished. "How you feel, and what you say when all is said and done in your life, and your soul is stripped bare—it's your last confession and it is extraordinarily important."

"What are you talking about?" Matthew struggled to find a voice that sounded natural.

The plane sliced through the air, sucked free of all sounds but their words. Nobody else coughed. Nobody else moved.

"I'm talking about your confession, Matthew. Your feelings about what's happened in your life up till now, or the lack thereof."

"What can you possibly tell me about…"

"Since you asked," David interrupted. "I can tell you about Andrea sitting up crying most nights worrying about you. I can tell you how she's tried to come to grips with what you've been up to, barely able to keep her mind on her daughter, let alone the house or the office."

Matthew's shock turned his voice to a whisper. "How do you know?"

"She's getting up later and later, and the later she gets up, the earlier she wants to go to bed." David looked away for moment, checking something ahead in the silent cabin. "Sadly, she's been thinking seriously about spilling her own blood on that lovely blue comforter you got from your sister last Christmas."

Panic crested in Matthew, tearing through the clenched knuckles frosted to his heart.

"But even if that did happen," David continued, "I'm wondering how long it would be before you had Wendy in that bed? Or Sheila. Or Linda. How long after Andrea's blood dried?"

Matthew fumbled with his seatbelt, clumsily pulling at the clasp that refused to give. "I don't have to listen to this."

"Give up, Matthew," David said coldly. "You're not going anywhere."

Matthew tried to ignore him, frantically reaching up and punching the stewardess button. No light came on. No bell went off. Matthew craned his neck over the seats. "Stewardess!" he yelled. "Stewardess!"

"Nobody can hear you, because nobody's here."

Matthew peered across the cabin, eyes wild. David was right. Of the myriad of gloomy shadows draped across the seats and aisles, none belonged to people. No darkened lumps poked over seats, no lights shone over books or magazines; it was as if everyone had leapt from the plane or had been vaporized by a bolt of lightning.

"It's just you and I," David said slowly. "Nobody has really been here for some time. Still, it was necessary to keep their images visible for the charade…and to confirm what I needed to know."

"But where are they?"

"Where they've always been—where you no longer are; the land of the living."

Matthew's eyes widened. "What did you say?"

"The pain in your chest you were experiencing a short time ago? The pain you'd never felt anything like before? That was when it happened. As of now, you've been dead exactly sixteen minutes."

"But... "

"Come on now, Matthew. Surely you must know who I am?" David's corneas blanched and whitened, swallowing the pupils in milk that quickly yellowed.

Matthew winced at David's transformation into something else. Something unhuman.

"And this isn't the end, it's actually a beginning." Cracks around the creature's eyes cut down across its cheeks, splitting them open and joining widening splinters around its mouth. The smell of rancid meat slopped out of decaying flesh, spiking the air with rot and decay.

Matthew felt a scream rising, then locking in the back of his throat.

"Everyone's hell is different," the Reaper intoned gravely. "Quite fitting that yours began on a plane, don't you think?" What little flesh was left on the creatures face melted away leaving behind a stained skull.

Panic was back, ferocious and unstoppable, speeding Matthew's dead heart up to a gallop, dumping fresh sweat down his face and torso. "No," he said aloud.

Outside, the sound of turbines rose to a high-pitched, stuttering squeal. The plane dipped, and Matthew's stomach cartwheeled. He snatched at his seatbelt but it cinched itself tight, cutting into his flesh and making him bleed.

"Your place is here," the Reaper croaked, now a talking corpse, slowly sweeping one skeletal arm in front of them. Its black sweater had become tattered rags that hung from emaciated shoulders and a sunken chest.

"Please," Matthew begged. The air was stale and rancid in his lungs.

"Here forever," the Reaper intoned. The remainders of its eyes collapsed, revealing the bony edges of empty sockets.

"I can't."

"But you are." The Reaper's wasted lips pulled up in a hideous grin. "And you may no longer recognize your fellow passengers."

The cabin lights flickered, the window shade flew up and a flash of lightening lanced across the wing, so close it blinded him. When his sight returned, the Reaper had vanished.

"Wait!" Matthew yelled, his eyes roaming the cabin as thunder broadsided the plane.

The Reaper may have left, but he wasn't alone. New shadows crawled and slithered, wailed and moaned. Several rows ahead, a high-pitched shriek climaxed in a sloshing gurgle of laughter. Muddy yellow eyes peered out between the seats in front of him. And in the aisle, a familiar mane of red hair now belonged to a slouching mass of gray flesh mottled with weeping sores.

Steel heaved mightily and a furious knocking beneath his feet sounded like the muffled pounding of huge fists, smashing their way in. Somewhere, bolts squealed in protest as they were ripped from their metal moorings.

No matter how loudly he screamed, Matthew could still hear it all.

Little Piggies

G. Winston Hyatt

Mr. Waynesbooth's cigar smoke formed a nimbus around the steer skull mounted high on the wall behind him. Unblinking as a snake, he steepled his fingers on his massive desk and asked, "Do you know why some folks call hogs 'horizontal men'?"

Merle shifted in his chair and tapped his foot. He figured he was in really big trouble when he got called up to the front office. Maybe even fired. Still, the supervisors, accompanied by two security guards, usually did that part of the job. He'd seen it when they let Gomez go.

Gomez had been one of the only co-workers Merle ever considered a friend. They use to hit up the Yellow Bull, a rundown tavern off Route 5, every payday. Though it stood miles away from the United Meat Packing plant, the syrupy reek of slaughter somehow persisted there. Looming over the prairie like a vigilant giant, the plant's observation tower could be seen from the Yellow Bull's front lot. Merle hadn't been to the bar since his drinking buddy disappeared. It just wouldn't have been the same.

"Horizontal men. Nossir," Merle said. "Don't reckon I ever heard that."

Mr. Waynesbooth nodded and pursed his lips. With a hairy knuckle, he stroked his chin. The boss said nothing, leaving Merle to stew in his own confusion.

He was sure he hadn't done anything that deserved firing. Now and again he'd cut some corners, sure, little things when they were busy. The damn knife sterilization rule was a bitch. There was no way they could expect him to keep up on a busy shift and sterilize after every goddamn pig. He'd never been written up, he'd never missed a shift, and he'd sure never done something bat-shit crazy. He'd never snapped.

Merle had no idea what'd made Gomez start cutting off hogs' snouts and gouging out their eyes with a boning knife—before they were even stunned. He'd screamed some sort of nonsense as he hacked away, but his words drowned in the mutilated animals' squealing. Gomez always seemed like a regular guy until then. He hollered and ranted on as the security guards dragged him away. No one had seen hide or hair of him since.

Mr. Waynesbooth cleared his throat before saying, "The hog's organs have a one-to-one correlation with our own. In the same places, you understand, on four legs instead of two. Heart, liver, lungs, all of it. Strange, isn't it?" He brushed some dust from a ruby-colored lapel, and then adjusted his bolo tie. "Tell me, Merle—can I call you Merle?"

"'Course you can. You're the boss."

"Tell me, Merle," Mr. Waynebooth said, his drawl dripping slow as black molasses. "How you feel about pigs?"

"Honestly, sir? I don't care much for 'em," Merle replied. "If they get a mind they ain't gonna go somewheres, they'll try to run. They'll kick and scream if the stunning tongs don't get 'em right on the first time. Pigs do all kind of fussing and carrying on. Not like sheeps and cows. I can handle the hogs, though."

"I understand where you're coming from." Mr. Waynesbooth laughed heartily, and Merle smiled, relaxing a bit. "Pig's got a mind of its own, Merle. That aside, how do you feel about United Meat Packing? Now, I know it's hard work. I worked as a pig-sticker myself for my daddy as a youngin."

"I love it," Merle replied. What was strange was that he meant it. The words came out automatically. "I worked at Triton Meatworks for ten years and hated every goddamn minute of it, but that all changed when y'all took it over. I actually like my work now. Maybe it's the music that's always playing. And them new bells for the shift changes. Get a real feeling of, y'know, a real feeling of *accomplishment*."

Mr. Waynesbooth leaned forward with his elbows on the desktop. He smiled and nodded.

"That means a lot to me. Especially from a real working man, not some bullshit pencil-pusher. You see, Merle, United Meat Packing is my family. It's in my blood. I like to think of everyone who works here as part of that. You do good work."

"Thank you, sir."

"You have a Certified Drivers License, correct?"

"Well, I did. Never renewed it, since I ain't done no truck driving in so long."

"But you can drive a truck."

"Sure. Like riding a bike."

"Good, good. You see, Merle, we're pulling a bit of a move against our competitors. Going to do a massive buy-up of all the livestock in the region. Need drivers for the trucks. Now, this is just for one day. We'll pay you well. You know the county roads, right?"

"Like the back of my hand."

"Good. I'll need you punched in for work at five in the AM tomorrow. You'll get your route maps and instructions then. You with me on this, Merle?"

"You bet, Mr. Waynesbooth, sir."

The shift-change bell rang, its humming tone radiating across the room and filling the smoky air. Merle smiled as the warmth washed across his body.

"Good." The boss nodded. "Merle, I want you to go home and go to sleep. We'll need you rested for the pick-up and delivery work tomorrow. We'll see you bright and early, right?"

"Yessir."

Merle showered, drove home, and promptly went to sleep. The ceaseless ringing of his phone pulled him out of empty dreams that night. It started clanging at two in the morning and rang straight through until three. He finally groggily sat up in his bed, a mattress thrown in the corner of his doublewide and stumbled across the narrow dark space of his living room to answer.

"Merle," rasped a voice through the receiver.

"Who the hell is this? I gotta be at work in a couple hours. Big day."

"Merle, it's Gomez. Listen to me and listen closely. It's a temple."

"What? Gomez, man, it's good to hear from you and everything, but I don't got time for this kinda crazy—"

"Listen!" Gomez sounded panicked and angry. "They tried to kill me, but I got away. I know what U.M.P. is all about bro, but I couldn't put it together till now. All the sanitation guys know too, I bet, but you never hear from them. Think about it. Bobby, Dave, Sanchez, all the guys transferred to clean up the blood. The ones working under the drains, you ever hear from them?"

Merle thought about it. "No, I ain't heard nothin'."

"Either they're dead, or they never leave. Ever. Listen, Merle. I don't know for what, but it's a temple, a church or something. Like the observation tower, what's the story there? Ever notice they built an observation tower with no windows? And what does a meat packing plant need a tower for?"

Merle didn't say anything.

"Think!" Gomez pleaded. "The music. The bells. And worst of all, what's under the drains. They're feeding something under the plant. This is real, I swear to Christ. There's nobody to help. United Meat Packing runs half the state. They're all in on it. I got to go. They're lookin' for me, Merle, and I've spent too long here trying to get a hold of you. You were the only one I ever really talked to there. Stay away from the plant."

The line went dead. Merle shook his head and laughed. He glanced over at the clock, crimson numbers glowing on the wall beyond the kitchen doorway, as he hung up the receiver. He could get another half-hour of sleep before work.

He arrived just before dawn. The United Meat Packing plant was a concrete fortress silhouetted against the pale sky. Merle parked his truck in the gravel lot outside before joining the numbers silently marching to the gates. Music rang out from an unseen source; a triumphant tune, synchronizing his heart with his steps. Workers gathered in the outer yard in perfect regiments. There was no carousing, no chatter. The tower, like a black monument to some unknown thing, loomed overhead.

They waited in unmoving lines before Mr. Waynesbooth, who stood wearing a red suit and cowboy hat with his hands on his hips. Two blank-faced men in blue U.M.P. coveralls walked up and down the ranks, handing out folders to the men. Merle took his and tucked it under his arm. The music stopped and the tolling of a bell filled him with its resonance.

"Today's a big day for United Meat Packing. We can't have any mistakes," Mr. Waynesbooth exhorted. "Your routes are marked on the maps. The dots are your stops. Open the doors at the dots and allow the livestock to enter. The doors will lock when the pick-ups are complete. Bring the product here and then we'll get down to business. Simple stuff. Your vehicles are primed and ready. Be proud!"

The bell tolled once more. The men cheered as a fanfare blasted from the speakers, introducing a brisk battle-hymn. Merle marched with the men to the stockyard gates, whistling along to a song he'd never heard but somehow knew. Massive rust-stained doors of solid steel creaked open, the squealing of their hinges barely audible over the blaring melody.

The stockyard had been cleared to make room for the livestock transports. Row after row they stood with engines idling, their exhaust pipes retching out clouds of blue diesel fumes. One by one they drove from the gates to gather their product. Merle thought something seemed strange as he waited behind the wheel to head out, but he couldn't place what. He recalled Gomez saying something about a temple. Something under the drains. Feeding.

He hesitated, but the music playing through the vehicle's speakers calmed him. The bell hummed in his ears.

Merle shrugged, released the brake, and put the vehicle into gear. He whistled softly, incessantly, as he joined the long line of yellow school buses rolling out of the slaughterhouse gates.

The Hole in the Fence

Craig Saunders

It was thirteen minutes past twelve by Sam Jefferson's watch. The glow faded and the numerals slid into darkness.

He pulled on his cigar, relishing the smoke as he drew it into his lungs. He wasn't supposed to be smoking. An early stroke had seen to most of his pleasures. No more fry-ups on a weekend. No more beer. No more cigarettes. Not that he'd had much of an opportunity to smoke these last three years. He couldn't even smoke in his own home nowdays. His new wife had all but taken over the house. Pink settee, foot stools, lurid throws that clashed with his duck picture that hung over the fireplace under sufferance of his beloved.

It wasn't that he regretted giving up on some of his freedoms. She only had his best interests at heart. Especially since the stroke. She looked out for him. She did.

The tip of his illicit cigar glowed in the still midnight air. It was chilly, but he didn't dare wear his bathrobe over his pajamas. The smoke stink would linger. As it was he was reduced to sitting in the dark, like some fugitive from justice.

He puffed luxuriant smoke, trying to make a smoke circle. It didn't work. He hit the light button on his watch. Twelve twenty precisely. The witching hour plus twenty.

He stood on his awol leg and dragged himself into the shadowy underbrush of the laburnum tree. Perfect night for a surreptitious piss in garden. If he was caught smoking he'd be for the high jump, might as well go the whole hog.

He pulled himself out of the slit in his pajama bottoms and let a stream of steaming piss flow into the too-long grass. He sighed with relief and not a little pleasure.

"Hey!"

He turned, dribbling on his leg as he hastily tried to stuff himself back in his trousers.

"Who's that?"

"Over here."

He looked around, but there was nobody there. His heart was beating too fast in his chest.

"Here, by the fence. See me?"

The fence was too dark. The hole in fence was covered.

He thought about getting a knife from the kitchen. Someone was prowling next door. He looked around slowly, seeing if he could find the owner of the mysterious voice.

He walked toward the voice, blood thundering.

"Hi," said the voice as he neared the six foot high wooden fence.

Now that he was closer he could just make out an eye peaking at him through a hole in the fence that split his property from the neighbor's back garden.

"Evening," said the disembodied eye. "Fine night for a piss in the garden."

"You saw that?"

"I don't mind."

"Who are you?"

"I'm your next door neighbor. Jeff. I'd shake your hand, but I can't reach over this fence. Pretty big fence. You put this up?"

"Yeah. Didn't know anyone had moved in next door. Pleased to meet you. I'm Sam."

"I'm glad we've got the introductions out of the way. I've already seen your penis. Seems only polite."

Sam laughed. "Interesting introduction. You'll forgive me if I don't ask you to reciprocate."

"Perhaps when we get to know each other better."

Sam ignored this in the spirit it was intended. “How are you settling in?” he asked instead.

“Fine, just fine. You know how it is, though…moving and everything. It’s never as easy as they make out in the movies.”

“Do it yourself?” Sam asked.

“Yeah, just me and a van. Haven’t got a wife. She passed away this last year.”

“Oh, I’m sorry to hear that. Must be tough.”

‘Nah, she was a bitch,” Jeff replied. “Never got to enjoy myself. Wouldn’t let me smoke in the house. Wouldn’t let me drink. Not that I’m a big drinker. But I enjoy sinking a few watching football with my feet up, you know?’

“All too well,” Sam said, nodding conspiratorially at the hole and the eye. “It’s pretty much the same for me here. I don’t get to smoke in my own home. I’m reduced to sneaking a few puffs in when the missus has gone to bed.”

“I bet you miss the old days.”

Sam didn’t know why, but he felt himself warming to the eye. “You know, Jeff. You know. Sometimes I wish…”

“I know, Sam. Sometimes you wish. Sometimes it’s best not to voice those wishes though. Especially not in the midnight hour. You never know who might be listening.”

“I wouldn’t mind if it was one of those magic genies,” Sam smiled.

“No such thing as genies, Sam.”

Suddenly the conversation had turned and Sam found himself wondering why he was discussing his inner most thoughts with a complete stranger through the fence.

“Well, I’d better be getting back inside. She’ll give me hell if I wait up too long.”

“Funny, isn’t it, how we forgo our freedoms for a sure thing…”

Sam just nodded. “Good night. It was nice to meet you.”

He paused for a moment, feeling something more was expected of him. The eye was still peering at him from the safety and anonymity of its hideaway on the other side of the fence. He didn't know why, but he felt he should ask it…him…over for dinner.

"You'll have to come over for dinner one night. When you've settled in, of course."

"I'd love to. Be nice to meet your wife, too. Well, I'd best get on with the unpacking."

The eye disappeared. Sam went to bed, mulling over the strange meeting with the disembodied eye and comfortable voice.

***

It was twelve fifty by Sam's watch. The glow on its face faded and he rose with his ever-present limp and carried his reluctant legs toward the border at the bottom of the garden to bury the evidence of his smoke.

"Hi," said a voice behind the fence.

Sam smiled. It seemed his neighbor was nocturnal too. "Hi," Sam said. "Don't suppose you're an early sleeper, then."

"No, since my wife died I've little reason to go to bed early."

"I suppose not. How's the unpacking going?"

"Slowly," said the eye. "It's surprising how much crap you accumulate over the years. I should throw some of my wife's things away, but I just can't bring myself to do it."

Sam nodded in what he hoped was a commiserating manner. He didn't really know what it was like.

"It must be hard on you."

"Not so much. There are benefits to being single. I can smoke in the house now. I can leave the toilet seat up. Sometimes," he whispered, "I even drink in the mornings."

Sam sighed at the thought. "Even on a weekday?"

"Anytime I want. It's my house again. I don't know if you'll understand, but I feel like a man again…"

"I can understand that."

"It's surprising. Most people forget that feeling. That perfect freedom…"

Sam was silent for a moment. Imagining it.

"Anyway," the voice said softly. "I'm off."

Sam fantasized for a time, sitting on his deck chair on the decking. Then he rose and went in to his wife.

***

The weeks passed and Sam still hadn't *seen* his neighbor. Yet he talked to him every night as he smoked his midnight cigar. He even took to sneaking a few whiskeys as he smoked. He began brushing his teeth twice before getting into bed, rolling away from his wife and thinking about what Jeff told him about his life as a bachelor through the hole in the fence.

He began to wish he could have his neighbor's life. All day, doing whatever he wanted. Watching sports on the television, eating microwave meals with no nutritional value. He could eat hotdogs and drink beer for lunch. Hell, he could even piss in the sink if he wanted to.

Not that he really wanted to. But, still, it was the principle of the thing. He was like a prisoner in his own life. His wants, his needs, had all been put on hold while his wife tried to keep him in check. Sure, she said it was for his own good, but was it? Really?

Or did she just want to take his fun away. Telling him what to do all the time. Hovering when he wanted to watch the TV. She knew he couldn't work, not with a bum leg. What else did he have to do during the day?

Why, it would be so simple, so easy to do it…he could just get a divorce…but that wasn't what the eye that belonged to the hole in the fence thought.

There would be money to lose. His house would be split in two. He'd end up living in some dank one bedroom flat in the middle of town. It was a good street he lived on.

No, there was a better way. Jeff never came right out and said it, but he certainly hinted at it.

***

"Have you thought any more about what we talked about?"

"Tonight," Sam answered, voice cracking slightly.

"You don't sound too sure."

"I am…it's just…" Sam trailed off.

"That's not the sound of a man who's got his thoughts straight. A man's got to get his mind right," said the ever-present voice. "It took me all day to pluck up the courage when I did it. Take the day. Reason it out. I think you'll see it's the right thing to do…but don't rush it. It's not every man who's brave enough to take that final step. You think on it."

Sam puffed some air into the chill night.

"I will."

The eye behind the hole went away, for a time. The orange light of the street filled the opening.

Sam watched the hole for a while. Thinking, but not really thinking. Drifting, was more like it. Drifting into the hole, through the wood and out into the artificial light of the suburban garden.

He sat on his deckchair until his watch showed two. Then he went to bed.

***

A day passed and come midnight Sam stood before the hole in the fence again, his shoulders shaking.

"Where are you? Jeff?!"

His voice cracked. In his hand he held a Philips screwdriver. In the dim light of a half moon his hand seemed black. His other was still pale in the silver light.

"I'm here, Sam. I'm always here. I see you did it."

Sam hated the eye and the voice. He hated the hole in the fence.

All this started with the hole in the fence. The hole in the fence had made him do it.

He saw the eye through his fence. It seemed to be laughing at him. There was humor in that eye, sometimes blinking, sometimes just staring at him.

"You lied to me."

"Don't give me that, Sam. You wanted it. You wanted to be free."

"It wasn't supposed to be like this!"

"Shut up, Sam. Don't be such a baby. Be a man. You're a man now. This is the way it's supposed to be. Freedom, Sam. Can you taste it?"

Sam looked away from the eye, down at his hand. He could taste it. He could smell it. Acrid and foul, dripping from his hands.

"Fuck you."

He drove the screwdriver into the eye and at last the hole in the fence fell silent.

***

Sam Jefferson lay in his pajamas in the long grass of his garden, a screwdriver driven firmly into his own brain.

The police stood on the back lawn, shaking their collective heads and staring down at the body.

"ID'd him yet?"

"He's the owner. Sam Jefferson. Positive ID from his Driver's Licence. Same with his wife upstairs."

"Neighbor's hear anything?"

"Next door's empty," said the officer. "The woman two doors down heard him talking to someone late last night, shouting, like he was having a fight." She shrugged. "We're canvassing the neighborhood."

"Probably talking to himself," replied the detective.

He lit a cigarette and waited for forensics to arrive. Open and shut case, he figured. The *why* of it might have interested some people, but not the department.

If you stab yourself in the eye with a screwdriver, motive is irrelevant. Crazy is all it is.

He flipped his notebook shut and flicked his stub into the border along with the cigars that rested there.

Holy Is as Holy Does

Pete Mesling

He awoke knowing he was a different man than he had been the night before, that his life prior to this morning had been preamble. Today was a new beginning for Daniel Collier and he breathed it in deep.

The early morning light streamed in through his window and he threw the threadbare curtains wide. He stood naked before the rising sun, which warmed his flesh through the glass.

There would be time enough for reverie at the top of the hill, so he quickly donned his rustic attire, fetched a light breakfast from the kitchen and was out the door. He hitched up the team and as he rode off on his buckboard, the house felt large behind him. Too much house for one man. But he vowed he would not be its only inhabitant for long. There was a wife in his future and children. If one of those children turned out to be a boy, he would inherit an army of followers, because Daniel Collier intended to lead the pioneering people of America into a bright age of prosperity and greatness.

It would all begin on the hilltop.

Dandelions carpeted the crest of the hill and he was tempted to lie down in their luxuriance, divest himself of his clothing and roll in them like an antediluvian god. Maybe later. He wasn't at the very top yet. A voice had been calling him there in his dreams, but it had taken him until now to work up the courage to make the climb. Now he was so convinced good news awaited him that he couldn't imagine why he'd put it off.

From the rocky summit he could see all corners of the prairie terrain. To the northeast, ranchland flourished. Cattle followed paths from one grazing pasture to another. In the west, fields of young wheat rolled like a wavering green blanket in the morning breeze. In the blink of an eye it would be autumn and the healthy greens he saw before him would turn to brittle gold for the harvester's scythe.

The sky cracked open and Daniel fell to his knees in spontaneous prayer. He trained his gaze on a bright figure that floated down from the rent in the heavens. His dreams had not lied. Here came the bringer of truth, angel of light. Tears poured out of his eyes and his hands shook as he held them in ready acceptance of his Savior's word.

The winged-being halted in the air several yards above him, batting its wings to stay aloft. Its form was female perfection, naked yet chaste. The smile it wore showered grace down upon him. He knew that a lifetime of waiting was about to be recompensed as the angel opened its beautiful mouth and sang him his destiny.

***

"The path to righteousness is not a gilded path!" he shouted to the dozen or so members in attendance at the prayer meeting. "Nor is it lined with fine-smelling flowers. That path exists, if you haven't the stomach for the one true calling. Take, if you want, the beautiful and easy path that leads to an ocean of flames. I'll take the uneven, bramble-strewn way that leads me unto the glory of God!"

As the barn filled up with the exuberant praise of its worshippers, Daniel wondered what it would feel like to get a similar reaction from a crowd of fifty or more.

"We will meet with resistance along the path that has been laid for us. Some will find our ways and customs odd. But there is no room for doubt that we are meant to rise to prominence among the competing denominations in this New World. Let those who oppose our subservience to the will of God tremble at the wisdom of His justice. Let them answer to Him for taking a stand against our piety.

"The good Lord has more in store for you and me than parrying the blows of the ignorant. He will watch over and protect us from the repercussions of men. We need only concern ourselves with the expansion of our church and our adherence to the will of the Almighty!"

He dabbed at his forehead and neck with a handkerchief. All of the cheering congregants were men. That would have to change. Already he grew tired of the wind-battered faces of these farmers. Where were the bankers and the bankers' daughters? He had certain ministerial claims over the women of this region, but he was the only one aware of the fact yet.

He paused dramatically after the cheers of support died out.

"Go out into the world now and sing the new gospel. Enjoy your families in the coming nights. The church elders will have a mission for you soon. Great wealth wants to come into our church, but it is dependent on the absolute commitment of everyone present here today and as many more as we can bring into the fold in a month's time."

The church elders consisted of exactly two members: Daniel and his faithful friend Theodore, who was seated in the barn with the other men, savoring every word that spilled from the minister's mouth. These were humble beginnings, but Daniel was convinced that an undertaking was only small if it was handled small. This new church of his would have to grow to meet his expectations and ambitions. *It* would rise to meet *him*. He wasn't about to shrink his ideals.

***

Back at Daniel's house, he and Theodore sat across from each other near a thriving fire, sipping at glasses of deep red wine. Daniel had been considering banning wine, for purposes other than libation, but the timing wasn't right. With gold in the church coffers he would introduce an additional list of thou-shalt-nots, but for now he was happy to share in a bottle with his friend.

"The letters pour in, Theodore. Even the newspapers are

against us. So much resistance to the idea that a modern prophet could be handed an amendment to established scripture."

"They're the ones who will pay the price for their folly, in the end," Theodore said in his serene but firm manner of speaking.

"In the end, yes, of course. If only I had more like you. Such confidence in the future!" Daniel said this with a histrionic clenching of his fist. "But we have yet to carve that future, Theodore. We must bend it to our will. A party of settlers will be passing through our county next week. I understand they'll be carrying gold. A lot of gold."

"Uh-huh," Theodore said.

"Paiute country, too. Sure would be a shame if those nice folks met up with a bunch of bloodthirsty savages."

"That *would* be a shame. And all for a little gold."

"For the good of the church, Theodore."

"Won't the survivors say it was us who massacred everyone? Or won't there be any survivors?"

"Come with me," Daniel said, exchanging his wine for a candle. He led Theodore to the back of the house where a closed door stood at the end of a corridor. Daniel chose a key from a ring and unlocked the door.

The two men entered a small, windowless room. Everything in range of the candlelight was covered with white sheets. Furniture, crates … Daniel couldn't even remember everything that was still waiting here to be unpacked since his arrival out west. He crossed directly to the tallest item in the room and smiled at Theodore.

"What do you suppose this is?" he asked.

"I'm sure I have no idea."

"Remove the sheet."

Theodore reached hesitantly for the sheet, as if pulling it away might reveal a caged animal. But once it was fully removed he exhaled loudly in relief. "Why, it's a wardrobe."

"Precisely. A wardrobe. But not just any wardrobe. This

wardrobe is special."

"What do you mean, special?"

"Look inside." He knew Theodore would go to the ends of the earth for him, but it was good to reinforce the man's allegiance from time to time.

With a glance at Daniel, Theodore stepped to the wardrobe and threw open its doors. Daniel purposely kept the light of his candle from revealing the contents of the tall wooden closet, but the dense odor of aged leather wafted out immediately. Finally he tilted his candlestick so that it illuminated the interior.

Theodore took a step back and looked at Daniel. "I don't understand. This is Indian dress, is it not?"

Daniel smiled and nodded. "Easier to make our own Indians than convince the real ones to join our cause, yes?"

"Where did you get these?"

"I've … been collecting them. You aren't going cold on me, are you?"

"No, it's just—"

"Good, I wouldn't want to have to make public certain indiscretions from your past."

"There'll be no need for that. I'll organize the ambush straightaway."

"I knew I could count on you, Theodore. I am blessed to have you at my side."

Theodore gave a perfunctory smile as Daniel shut the wardrobe.

"Our wine has had sufficient time to breathe, I should think," Daniel commented as he led his underling into the corridor and locked up the room before returning to the fire.

***

Standing atop a bluff overlooking the site that was about to go down in history—the good Lord willing—Daniel Collier had doubts. Not about the nature of his plan or the justification for it, but doubts about whether or not his men could be relied on to carry out their orders. They all seemed to be behind him in this, but he knew that when the wagon train was stopped and women and children began spilling onto the road to see what was going on, the men would have second thoughts.

He ducked behind a nearby cottonwood and sat down with his back against the knotty trunk. The smell of prairie grass, slightly sharp, was strong and he found himself twirling errant blades of the stuff around his index fingers.

A small group of men was huddled nearby and Daniel could see how ridiculous the disguises looked. It was one thing to have the appropriate attire and quite another to know how to fit it properly. They would fool some of the settlers, but others would see right through them. He had thought it would be a good idea to leave some survivors behind, to spread the word of what happened. He knew the incident would grow in scope with each retelling, which might keep outsiders from moving into the area in droves. But maybe they *would* have to kill them all, as Theodore had suggested. His church wasn't yet strong enough to shoulder the blame for something of this magnitude.

The rattling grind of wagon wheels on dry earth came with shocking suddenness. At the first sound of the settlers' approach he was up like a shot, crouching as he went from man to man and issued the command to take up battle positions. He knew it would be no battle. It would be a slaughter, a decimation. But it could do his men's fighting spirit no harm to have them think this wagon train was a threat to their personal safety. That's how he'd sold it and that's how they'd bought it. Stolen gold it was in those wagons, according to his story. And each and every member of the Blackert party was as cold blooded as they came. Only he and Theodore knew that the Blackerts and their associates had come upon their gold through the sale of prime land farther east. They'd simply pooled their income, joined forces, and pulled up stakes in search of warmer climes.

Daniel and his men set themselves up along the edge of

trees that gave way to a steep drop leading down into the meadow the Blackert party would soon be passing through. Theodore and his contingent manned a ridge opposite, armed with bows and tomahawks for the sake of realism. Some of the men on the bluff side also carried Indian weapons, but everyone had a rifle slung at their side for good measure.

The settlers came snaking into the meadow presently, trailing great plumes of dust. It was a holy vision, almost as holy as the angel who had visited Daniel on the hilltop all those months ago. He yearned for the means to preserve the next hour for eternity. The Bible itself contained no scene more memorable than what was about to unfold on the plains of the Utah Territory before his very eyes.

He let out a holler, which passed among the men until it reached Adam Jacoby, Lance Hatford and Jules Warren, the party assigned to stopping the train. Daniel watched with wide, hopeful eyes as the men thundered down the hillside on horseback, whooping in their best imitation of a Paiute war cry and swinging tomahawks above their heads. Daniel let out a second holler, this one signaling the remaining men to descend upon the rest of the stalled wagon train. Their descent was a visual signal to the men on Theodore's side to do likewise.

It was at a leisurely pace that Daniel navigated the slope down to the meadow. He had no interest in partaking of the violence, but he wanted to bear witness. His horror mounted, however, as he neared the scene on foot. There was no beauty here. The screams of women and children being dragged from the backs of wagons by their hair filled his ears. The men folk were quickly dispatched with rifles, but women were cruelly slain in front of their children. Young girls were stripped naked and beaten to death. Boys were forced to take it all in before meeting with similar fates.

Daniel circled the mayhem in disbelief, as if he were Dante being led through a ditch of hell by an unseen Virgil. What kind of monster had he created? It wasn't supposed to feel this way. Here was Lance, tearing chunks out of a woman's neck with a hunting knife. There was Jules, tying a boy no more than twelve to a wagon wheel by the neck and striking the flank of the horse at the front of the wagon. The horse whickered and fled, and the boy's throat took the full weight of the wagon at each rotation of the wheel. Daniel clearly heard the boy's broken screams, but he probably only imagined the *blump, blump* of his head smacking the uneven earth as the wagon charted an erratic course across the meadow.

He spotted Theodore in the madness and went to him.

"Theodore, what goes on? They carry this thing too far," he said, laying a trembling hand on his friend's shoulder.

Theodore's eyes were dead coals. "Do not ever speak to me of this day," he said. To Daniel's dismay, the man returned to the fray and began clubbing children to death with the blunt end of his tomahawk.

"Theodore!" he screamed, but his friend was lost in a hurricane of bloodlust. Disgust rose up in Daniel and he turned away from the bloodshed he'd called for. His great religious moment felt more like a badge of shame as he wound his way back into the hills toward home, terrified and alone.

***

Theodore would come to him. Sooner or later his trustworthy companion would deliver a report of the afternoon's proceedings. *Someone* would come to him. They couldn't just leave him to suffer his burden and puzzle out the next steps by himself.

But it grew dark all around him and still no one came to put his mind at rest. Did they not understand how keenly he felt the impact of the day's events? Did they not appreciate the responsibility he shouldered?

"Come to me!" He flung his empty whiskey glass into the fireplace and fell into his chair.

A knock at the back door. A single knock. Odd.

"Well, it's about time."

He dragged himself out of the chair and stumbled his way to the back of the house. "Been a long time since you've been good and drunk, Daniel," he slurred to himself and laughed. "Can't hold your liquor."

He released the latch of the back door, but the door wouldn't budge. Looking up he remembered bolting it. He'd be bolting his doors from now on, he had a feeling.

"That you, Theodore?" He fumbled with the wooden bolt. "Good idea, coming to the back door. Can't be too careful."

Another solitary knock, followed by silence.

Finally the bolt slipped out of its notch and Daniel was able to open the door. At first all he saw was the boughs of a couple of old oak trees in the distance, cradling the crescent moon as a cool evening breeze blew through them. But when he looked down, his eyes met the stolid faces of two small children, a boy and a girl.

"This is one of my faces," the boy said, "but I have another one."

"Wha—"

Whatever Daniel meant to say was cut short by horrified disbelief as he watched the boy reach up to his own forehead with both hands and peel the skin of his face downward until it hung from his chin in a loose, gory flap.

"You did this to me." The boy's voice was wetter now. He turned his head toward the girl, as if giving her a cue.

"Do you want to see what you did to me?" she asked, too sweetly.

Daniel shook his head but no words would come.

The girl looked over at the boy. "He doesn't want to see." She gave an exaggerated pout and looked back up at Daniel. "But he's going to." Something dark had come into her voice, and she set about undoing the middle buttons of her dress, which he noticed were bloodstained. A bullet had ripped through the center of her little body, leaving behind the hideous wound she now flaunted at him.

"You have changed us," the children said in unison. "Now it's our turn."

He tried to slam the door on them, but they were too quick. They shot around him and ran upstairs, giggling all the way. Daniel teetered for a moment as fear squeezed out the dregs of his whiskey drunk. When he finally managed to shut the door—and refasten the bolt—it was on sober but wobbly legs that he gazed at the foot of the stairs.

"I'll teach you to cut my face off with your Indian axe!" The boy's voice could have been coming from any of the upstairs rooms.

"Shoot *me* in the tummy, will you?" the girl's voice charged. "We'll just see about that."

"You've got the wrong man," Daniel said, mounting the stairs. "I swear I didn't touch either of you. I harmed no one."

The children giggled some more.

Don't go up there, a voice in the back of his mind cautioned. But he knew he had to. What else could he do? Run? Flee from his own house? Never. If only his guiding angel would come to him now, tell him what to do, the way she had told him of his destiny. How later, in his dreams, she had wiped away his doubts and showed him the wisdom of murdering the Blackert party.

But wait, that hadn't turned out to be so wise. He was confused. Why had the angel misled him?

The last step groaned under his weight and brought him out of his thoughts, back to his predicament.

"Okay, children. Where are you?" He tried to sound calm but didn't. "Come on out, and let's talk this through." He contemplated going back for the candle, but he decided it wouldn't be of any real use. The feeble moonlight would suffice. That and the flickering firelight from below.

"You're a bad, bad man." It was both voices together again, but he still couldn't tell which room they were in.

Two rows of doors ran parallel to the staircase. He had hoped at least one of these rooms would be home to a child one day. How had he lost sight of that simple wish?

He turned back to the first door on the left side of the stairs. It popped free of its latch with ease and he steeled himself for a lunge into the dark room.

But something caught his attention at the far end of the hall. Where moonlight stole in through a grimy window, he could make out the dead-still outlines of the two children. His blood seemed to drain away at the sight of them, so smug in their accusatory stance, their fearless communion with the dark. He envied them and he hated them for seeing more than he saw. For knowing more than he knew.

"Wretched spawn!" he shrieked.

As he ran full speed down the length of the hall he could see the shapes of their heads turn to look at each other and again they giggled. Their laughter crescendoed and echoed in his brain, but he would soon put a stop to that!

He leaped into the air, wanting to pounce on the little brats, but in midair he realized they had vanished beneath him and he had overshot his jump. The window shattered in a spray of broken glass as he sailed through the casement. For an elongated instant he caught the leer of the moon, obsequious yet damning. Then, just before he fell to the ground, it was the face of an angel. His guiding angel.

Twinkle, Twinkle

Jessy Marie Roberts

Megan shifted beneath the thick, thermal sleeping bag and rested her head on Jacob's shoulder. "Cold?" he murmured, dropping a quick kiss on the crown of her blond head.

"No," she said with a contented sigh. "This is amazing, Jacob. I've never seen such brilliant stars. And I didn't know it could be this dark at night."

"That's why they call it big sky country," he teased, finding her hand under the covers and entwining his fingers through hers. "The best view in the whole world for stargazing. I've been coming to the top of this hill for as long as I can remember to look at the sky. I used to have a telescope up here, but dad got rid of it years ago."

Megan propped herself up on her elbow and smiled at her fiancé. "I'm glad you brought me to Montana to meet your family. We've been together for so long and I never met anyone, I started to think you were ashamed..."

Jacob pressed his index finger against her lips. "Stop right there, Meg. I've never been ashamed of you. It's just, well, they're not open to a lot of things. I didn't think they would understand our relationship."

Megan sighed and dropped back beside him, her eyes staring up at the clear night sky. "What part? That I'm a single mother, or that I'm fifteen years older than you?"

"Both," Jacob admitted with a small shrug. "They're pretty traditional. But now that they've met you, I know they'll grow to love you as much as I do."

"Well," Meg teased, rubbing tickling fingers up the length of his body, "at least they can't say I'm marrying you for your money. I might be a scandalous cougar, but I'm not a gold-digger."

"Maybe I'm the gold-digger and I only want you for your money," he growled, flipping Megan onto her back and pressing wet, open-mouthed kisses down the length of her slender, iridescent neck.

Meg giggled and tossed her head back, allowing Jacob easier access to her sensitive neckline. She gasped as he nipped at her collarbone. "You like that?" he asked, his voice deep and husky with desire.

"Jacob, look at the sky," she gasped, pushing against his shoulders. "It's incredible!"

"Forget the sky," he whispered, licking his way up her neck to bite at her earlobe.

"Stop it, I mean it," she cried. "This is a once in a lifetime sight!"

With a frustrated moan, Jacob fell to the ground beside his fiancée. "They're just st..." his voice trailed off as he stared at the glistening sky, mesmerized by the twinkling stars streaking down through the heavens to dance in the air just inches from their faces.

"Is this real?" he asked, incredulous, outstretching his arm and wiggling his fingers in the luminescent spheres circling their bodies.

"My God," Megan said, breathless. She lifted her hand into the smattering of brilliant light. "It's so warm. I feel so alive."

They slowly rose to their feet, their bodies encapsulated by the startling, gleaming balls of glowing warmth. They lifted their arms toward the sky, tilted their heads back in ecstatic surrender, as the stars swirled around them in a twisting, sparkling light. Faster and faster the stars spiraled around their bodies until suddenly, as fast as they had arrived, they disappeared, streaking toward the small town nestled at the base of the hill.

Jacob and Megan stared at each in awkward silence until Megan forced a fake laugh and squatted to roll up her sleeping bag. "I think I've had enough stargazing. Think we can head back to our motel room now?"

Jacob nodded. "What just happened?"

Tears streamed down her face. "I don't know. I feel so empty, so lost."

He wrapped his arms around her waist and pulled her tight against him. "Me, too," he admitted, his voice cracking with anguish. "I never wanted it to end."

They held each other and wept until their throats were raw and their cheeks were caked with salt. Finally, their tears spent, they collected their blankets and pillows and made their way to his old Chevy pickup truck and buckled themselves in for the twenty minute drive down the weaving fire access dirt road into the small town where Jacob had grown up.

***

"Why can't we go straight to the motel?" Megan whined, pressing her face against the chilly glass of the Chevy's passenger side window. "I just want to go to sleep."

Jacob shifted the truck into park outside the beat-up farmhouse where he had been raised and his parents still lived. The old one-story place needed some serious sprucing up. The paint was chipping away and the front porch was beginning to sag. He made a mental promise to return home before the wedding, without Megan, so he could help his dad with the chores.

He felt inexplicably guilty for leaving home for college, for applying to and being accepted into law school. For spending his summer vacation naked and sweaty and falling in love with his sexy pre-law professor, Dr. Megan Remerick, instead of coming back to Montana and checking in on his parents.

"I'm a terrible son," Jacob whispered, then said louder. "I don't know what is wrong with me. My stomach hurts and my chest aches. I just want to crawl inside that house and have my mom make me a cup of her special hot chocolate."

"Well, I just want to be left alone!" Megan sniffled and trailed the back of her hand across her dripping nose.

The porch light flicked on and the weathered storm door creaked open. Jacob's mother's blue-haired head peeked out from the lighted crack, a welcoming smile stretching over her frail, withered face. "Jakey? Is that you, my son?" she called.

"I miss my mother," Megan wailed, dry sobs wracking her athletic frame.

"You live next door to her," Jacob said, plastering a wobbly smile on his face and waving at his mother. "You'll see her as soon as we get back to Palo Alto. Are you going to come inside or stay out here by yourself? I really don't care."

Megan's eyes tightened at the corners as she shot him a pouting glare. "Fine. We'll have one cup of cocoa and then we go to the hotel. I need to put this whole experience behind me. I've never been so miserable in my life."

"Fine," he agreed, his tone sharp and nasty.

He shut off the truck and stepped out, racing up the front steps to embrace his mother. "Jakey, you're squeezing me too tight!" the elderly woman laughed, her blue eyes bright with pleasure. "Now let me go. I'm making a batch of cookies. Nothing like a midnight snack!"

"Sorry, mom," he said, choking back sobs. He fell to his knees, burying his face in the folds of her pink, flowered house jacket.

"What is it, dear?" she cooed, brushing his hair off his forehead. "Why are you so sad?"

"I don't know," he screamed, the words coming out in halted, tortured syllables.

"Well, I know just the thing. Come inside and I'll make you some hot chocolate to sip on while we wait for the cookies to come out of the oven. How does that sound?"

Wiping his red-rimmed eyes with the hem of her worn nightgown, he stood up on shaky legs. "Yes. Please."

Ignoring Megan, Jacob followed his mother inside the house and let the screen door slam on his fiancée's face, leaving her in the frigid, black night. With a disgruntled harrumph, Megan opened the door and trailed after him into the kitchen.

***

Jacob sat at the small oak table in the kitchen, his mother humming as she mixed the cocoa mix and marshmallows into a chipped coffee mug. "It's lovely to have you home, son," she said, her face the picture of contentment.

"I'm sorry I don't come home more often," he whimpered, his shoulders heaving as another round of inconsolable weeping overtook his usually even-tempered countenance.

His mother set the coffee cup in front of him, the hot, sweet steam inciting his nostrils to twitch and his mouth to salivate with nostalgic longing. "There now, son. I don't remember you blubbering quite so much as a child."

"I can't stop," he croaked as he brought the hot liquid to his quivering lips. He looked to the corner of the kitchen, where crumpled in a distraught heap between the old, green refrigerator and the portable dishwasher, sat Megan. Both he and his mother had begged her to sit at the table to enjoy a cup of chocolate with them, but she insisted on remaining curled up in the corner, an occasional grieving hiccup escaping her lungs.

Jacob's dad soared into the room, one hand tucked against his flabby belly, the other outstretched to his left, his butt tucked tight, his hips twisting, his feet striking out in flaring kicks. "Dance with me," he beamed as he strutted around the small kitchen in an imaginary tango.

"Dad," Jacob cried, "be careful! Your arthritis!"

His dad laughed, his eyes brilliant with cheer. "I haven't felt this good since I was in the army! I always wanted to be a dancer, you know. Your grandmother taught me to dance when I was a small boy, happiest time of my life. If I hadn't enlisted to fight the Germans, I would have been a professional!"

The old man ratted off a Latin beat with his tongue, prancing about in hold, leading his imaginary partner around the table and then dipping her with agile grace. "Please, Marge," he begged, skidding up behind his wife and wrapping his arms around her, swaying with the rhythm of his hummed beat.

She swatted him away. "Stop it, George!" she shrieked. "I'm baking snickerdoodles. And making sure Jacob has plenty of hot chocolate! You dance and I'll cook and we'll both be happy as larks!" she exclaimed with a giggle as she checked the oven's temperature a second time and slipped the first cookie sheet of cinnamon and sugar coated dough into the heat.

Humming louder, George tangoed to where Megan sulked in the corner. Leaning over, he pulled her to her feet and wrapped one strong arm around her waist, drawing her opposite hand into his and pointing their clasped hands toward Jacob. "Pick up those feet. Put back your shoulders. Crane your neck," George coached Megan. She crumpled against the old man, her feet dragging across the floor as he propelled her through the motions of the dance.

"Let me go," Megan pleaded, trying desperately to withdraw her hand from her partner's pervasive grasp. "I can't go on. I just want it all to end," she shouted.

"Me, too, darling," Jacob screamed, then took another scalding swig from the constantly refreshed mug. Blisters formed on the insides of his lips, the tip of his tongue, and the roof of his mouth as he guzzled the piping hot liquid. Every time he would swallow some of the cocoa, Marge would top off the coffee mug with more boiling refreshment from the open kettle on the gas stove.

The oven timer dinged and Marge reached in and pulled out the cookie sheet, forgetting to use a pot holder. The burning tray singed her skin, the cloyingly sweet smell of the cookies overpowered by the sharp, putrid scent of burning flesh.

"Mom, your hands," Jacob cried, gooey blobs of marshmallow sliding down his chin to plop on the scarred table. "It's my fault!" he exclaimed, "I should have grabbed the damned cookies for you! Forgive me, mother!"

He slid off the chair to his knees, covering his tear-stained face with his hands.

"Oh, it's nothing, dear," Marge said, rolling more dough with her swollen, angry red hands, and then dipping it in cinnamon sugar. "More snickerdoodles coming up. Go ahead and dig in!"

Jacob slouched over, falling into a desperate heap of unmitigated despondency. George marched by, clacking out the Latin tune at the top of his lungs, Megan dangling in his arms, her head cocked at an unnatural angle.

"Meg?" Jacob called, catching her limp arm as she and his dad shuffled by. "Are you okay?"

Marge spun away from the stove, flinging hot cookies at Jacob with her spatula. "She's dead, Jacob! Can't you see she's gone?"

"Dead?" Jacob repeated, his mouth agape. "But, how?" he sputtered.

"She was struggling with her posture," George said with a chuckle. "I adjusted her neck for her."

"Adjusted?" Jacob shrieked, jumping to his feet. "You broke her neck? Oh my God! The love of my life is dead! And we never even shared a honeymoon!" He clenched his fists and pushed his elbows straight, then shook his head from side to side, screaming in pain and anger.

"There, there, dear," Marge consoled her son, patting him on the back with cookie-coated fingers. "Why don't you sit down and I'll make you some more hot chocolate."

Jacob stopped howling and sat down as commanded. The table was covered with coffee mugs, each filled to the brim with hot cocoa. He picked up the first cup and slammed the liquid, then picked up the second cup and polished it off in one breath. "More," he cried, alternating his frantic drinking with huge, ravenous bites of fresh baked snickerdoodles.

"*Pa –pa- pa, ba-dum-dum,*" George yammered as he swooshed by the table, his dead partner cradled in his stiff arms. Without warning, Megan fell to the linoleum amidst a mound of cookies. Seconds later, George fell atop her, clutching his heart.

"Dad?" Jacob stuttered. "Mom, I think Dad is dead."

Marge glanced away from the third batch of cookies she was setting on wire racks to cool. "Why, it appears so, dear. Why don't you have another cookie?" She set a heaping plate of cookies in front of him, pushing aside coffee mugs for room.

Stuffing a cookie into his mouth, Jacob grabbed his mom's hand. "Mom?" he asked around the mouthful of dessert.

"Yes, dear?" she asked, looking him in the eye.

"You have stars in your eyes."

"So did your father, dear. My God, those cookies smell delicious!" she exclaimed with a glorious, beaming smile. Opening the oven door, she stuck her head in to sniff the cookies.

She never pulled her head out.

Sitting in the kitchen, eating cookies and drinking hot cocoa, Jacob watched his father's corpse crush his fiancée's dead body while he inhaled the pungent stench of his mother's head baking in the oven.

When his snack and drink were finished, Jacob grabbed a plastic grocery bag from the pantry, pulled it over his head, and duct taped it around his neck, effectively cutting off his air supply.

His last thought before he fell unconscious was how warm the swarm of stars had been.

***

That night, beginning in a small town in Montana and spreading across the North American continent, people were possessed with the ecstasy of the stars or overcome with despair at having been touched by the light and then left, forgotten.

By morning, everyone was dead.

Good Samaritan

Murphy Edwards

Stacey slid another quarter into the coin slot and clicked the dryer on. She flopped back down on the cheap padded bench, dreading the sticky feeling of the dirty vinyl cushion on the backs of her legs. His eyes were probing her. She could feel it. She pushed her hair back and wiped her face, trying not to look up.

He had appeared on the corner outside the Laundromat while Stacy was cramming a load of jeans and tops into a washer. That was over an hour ago and he had been there ever since. Still staring. Still pacing. Still mumbling obscenities to a newspaper box and kicking in its metal sides.

She pulled the clinging T-shirt away from her sweaty skin and watched her clothes do a spinning dance in the dryer. The lilac smell of fabric softener made her wish she was home. She thought of her mother and missed the days when she could fling open the closet door to find her clothes freshly washed and hanging in a tight little row.

Stacey always waited till nine o'clock to do her wash. No crowds—less noise, plenty of washers and dryers—open till midnight. She even had time to study between the wash and dry cycles. It was usually ideal, but tonight she wasn't so sure.

"Cut it off...Shoulda' done it sooner...Put an end to it..." The drunk continued to ramble in broken sentences, stopping only to stare in the window and kick the newspaper box. "Had it comin'...All of'm did..."

She tried not to notice and eased over to the dryer to check her clothes. Still wet. *Why do things take so long to dry? Damn manager must keep the temperature cranked down to make more money.* Stacey pictured the laundry manager's house, plastic buckets full of quarters stacked from floor to ceiling. She closed the dryer door and fed it another quarter.

"I'm Creepy Willy!…Don't wanna' mess with me!"

Stacey inched her way back to the bench and picked up a coffee stained copy of National Geographic, trying to ignore Creepy Willy's words. She heard keys jingle at the back entrance and squirmed nervously behind her magazine. Her legs made a slippery squeak on the vinyl seat.

A tall, clean shaven man walked in, his arms full of wet clothes, keys dangling from the waistband of his shorts. His T-shirt hugged his body, showing off a set of muscular arms and well toned abs. He nodded politely and began fishing quarters out of a plastic sandwich bag.

The racket outside started up again. "Never got caught...Too smart for it...Careful Willy...always careful..."

The box took another kick sending newspaper pages flying down the sidewalk. Stacey peered over the magazine, hoping the man at the dryer would notice the disturbance.

"Takes all kinds huh?" he said without turning.

"Excuse me?"

"Takes all kinds. That guy out front there, ya' know? Takes all kinds."

Stacey lowered her magazine. "Yeah, I guess it does." She closed the magazine and began to fan herself with it. Pearls of sweat hung from her upper lip.

"You come here a lot?"

Stacey wiped her forehead with the back of her hand and stopped fanning. "Why?"

"Oh, just making conversation is all. My name's Erik by the way."

"Stacey." She glanced outside in time to see another newspaper fluttering down the sidewalk. "Don't remember seeing you here before."

"Probably not. My dryer's on the fritz. Stuff always seems to break at the worst possible time."

"That's the truth."

The newspaper box let out a loud metallic crack. "Bastards...shoulda' kept quiet...used rope instead...Creepy Willy loves the rope!"

"So what's this guy's story?"

Stacey wiped a sweaty tear off her cheek. "I don't know. He just showed up on the corner about an hour ago and he's been pacing like a cat ever since." She eyeballed Erik as he bent to pluck a wet sock off the floor.

"He try anything yet?"

"No, but I have to admit, he's beginning to freak me out." She admired Erik's biceps as he tossed his clothes into the dryer across from hers.

"Shoulda' killed her...waited till dark…cut her up real bad...no witnesses…Creepy Willy strikes again!" The ranting was growing louder.

"Looks like Ol' Willy has a few screws loose!"

Stacey turned to agree and caught Erik checking out her breasts through her thin cotton shirt. *Maybe I should have worn a bra. It was too hot out though*. "Maybe he's just a drunk."

"He does seem a little out of it."

"You know what really bothers me though?" She didn't wait for an answer. "The stuff he keeps mumbling. They never caught that Eastside Killer the reporters are talking about and..."

"Eastside killer?" Erik interrupted. "What's that?"

"You haven't heard?"

"Well, I'm a new student. I just started this semester."

"It's been all over the news. Somebody is picking people up at random and killing them. Always keeps a souvenir from the victims."

"Souvenir? You mean like jewelry or panties? Stuff like that?"

"No, I mean like toes, or fingers, or ears. Stuff like that."

Erik fed another quarter into the dryers and eased up next to Stacey. "You're kidding right? I mean, this sounds like one of those college ghost stories."

"Actually, I'm not. The worst part of it is, they have no idea who's doing it. No leads, no motives, no real evidence. Nothing."

"Except for the missing body parts, right?"

"Right."

"I don't know. Sounds like an urban legend to me. I don't really believe all that serial killer stuff the media puts out. It's so easy to hype that stuff up just to scare the hell out of people and cause a panic."

Stacey leaned in closer to Erik, bringing her voice to a whisper. "Normally, I would agree, but last week they found a girl from my dorm dumped behind Eddie's Pub on Marcum Street."

"That's only a block from the east wing dorms."

"Yeah. And both of her pinkies were missing."

"Jesus! I'm sorry. I mean... I had no idea".

Stacey's bottom lip began to tremble. "The worst part is, she was last seen with some local guy. Not a student, just a townie. Some painter. Tattoos, oily black hair, ragged jeans. Kinda' like that guy," Stacey said, jerking her head towards the street.

"Shit! Maybe we should call the police!"

Stacey felt her thigh rub against Erik's, their sweat blending together. "He really hasn't done anything yet, except molest a newspaper box and freak me out a little." She pulled a rubber band from her pocket and started to pull her hair back in a ponytail. "It's so damn hot in here!"

"Here, let me."

"Thanks."

"Any time."

Stacey loved the feel of Erik's fingers running through her hair. She pictured them alone together in a steaming shower, shampoo foaming in her hair and running down her body. "You think that guy out there really *could* be the killer?"

Before Erik could answer, the pacing outside became more frantic. The tattooed man pulled a switchblade from his pocket, flicked it open and began stabbing it into a telephone pole. Splinters of wood flew over his shoulder and littered the sidewalk. Blood began to ooze from between his fingers as he continued to stab. "Don't wanna' make Creepy Willy mad…not in this lifetime…Willy will find you…set things straight!"

Stacey stopped the dryer and started shoving damp clothes into her basket. "To hell with this! I gotta' get outa' here! I can't take it anymore."

"Listen," Erik said. "I've got an idea. I know you don't know me that well, but why don't we leave together? My laundry's about dry and I don't think he'll try anything if someone's with you".

"I'm not sure I should," she said, looking at his chiseled body.

"My car's right outside. We can go out the back. I'll take you right to your dorm. We'll be out of here before he has time to do anything."

She watched his cool blue eyes staring at her intently and tried not to blush. "Maybe I shouldn't."

"But you live on the east side right? I wouldn't feel right having you walk home and there's no way I'm leaving you alone here with this nut outside."

Stacey twirled her ponytail around her dainty index finger and thought it through. "Well...OK, I guess you're right."

Erik nodded. "Of course I am."

Once in the car, Stacey began to relax. They had pulled out of the parking lot before Creepy Willy realized they were leaving. She watched him disappear in the side mirror as they headed for the east side. "I really appreciate this. I don't know what I'd have done if you hadn't showed up."

"No problem." Erik grinned and nudged her shoulder. "Us college kids gotta' stick together. Right?"

Stacey nodded in agreement just as they passed the entrance to the east dorms. "Hey, we missed the turn!"

"I know, but with all the excitement I thought maybe you might need to cool down and get a drink." He switched on the air conditioner, adjusting the setting to high.

"I really should get back." She caught a glimpse of Erik's powerful arms bulging under his T-shirt and let out a sigh as the cool air from the vents began to wash over her sweaty thighs.

"Come on. What could it hurt? It's not that late. Besides, I'm a newbie. You need to fill me in on all the campus gossip."

"Well, maybe just a quick one. It might help me forget about that creep at the Laundromat and get a good night's sleep."

Erik shot her a quick smile, revealing his perfect white teeth. "That's the ticket!" He eased the car into Augie's Quick-Stop Liquors and cut the ignition. "What'll it be?"

"Beer's fine with me."

"Beer it is. I'll be back in a flash. Don't go anywhere."

Stacey scrunched up her nose and began to blush. "Alrighty."

Erik returned with an ice cold six pack and a bottle of bourbon. "Where to?"

"Oh, I don't know. Let's just cruise around a little."

"Sounds good to me." He unscrewed the cap on the bourbon and passed it to Stacey.

"Oooh, no thanks. That stuff makes me crazy!"

"You sure?" he asked.

"Believe me," she smiled. "You don't wanna' know. I'll stick to beer."

Erik pulled a frosty can off the plastic ring and handed it to her. "Bottoms up!" He tilted his own can and took a long swallow.

"Yep," Stacey giggled, popping the tab on the beer and sipping the froth. She watched Erik, cool and lean behind the wheel as they cruised out of town and onto the open highway. By her third beer, she had filled Erik in on all the campus news. The weird professors, the geeks, dorks and preps. She left out the jocks, since she was sure he fell into that category. No use ruining what was turning into a good evening.

"So tell me more about this Eastside Killer"

Stacey held the icy can to her cheek, then took another sip. "It's strange. The only thing they know for sure is someone is out there killing college students."

Erik uncapped the bourbon and took a long pull. "How many students has this nut-job killed?"

"Eighteen so far."

"That's insane!"

Stacey watched Erik stare at her petite fingers wrapped around the sweating beer can. "I'll say. But that's just the ones they know about for sure." Her shoulders shook violently, trying to shrug off the goose bumps. "Look...could we talk about something else? I don't like thinking about it."

"Sure. Just one more thing though. Why do you think the killer cuts body parts off and keeps them?"

Stacey's polished pink nails clicked nervously on the pull tab of her beer. "Look, I said..."

"OK, OK I'll stop. I'm just trying to figure out why a person would do shit like that."

She took another gulp of the cool suds. "Who knows why people do shit? It's a messed up world ya' know?" She slid closer and put her hand on his leg. "I don't want to think about it."

"You're right. Let's talk about something else."

Stacey finished her beer and tossed the can to the floor. As the Chrysler rolled down the deserted two-lane, she began to hum along to the tune playing on the radio. Her hand drifted behind Erik's back and finger-walked around his waist. "I'm glad you were there for me tonight Erik." She felt the tip of his nose graze her earlobe.

"Hey, no problem. I was glad I could help. Besides, if I hadn't been there I wouldn't have met you."

Stacey nodded and leaned her head against Erik's shoulder. "I hate to think what might have happened if you hadn't showed up."

"All kinds of weird-o's out there, that's for sure." He nibbled her tiny ear.

Stacey's earlobe tingled under the pressure of Erik's teeth. "Yep. You never know who you might run into these days." She tightened her grip around his waist. "This world isn't as safe as it use to be."

"That's for sure," Erik muttered, as he eased the car off the pavement and stopped at the end of a deserted gravel lane. "This OK?"

"Perfect," Stacey cooed.

Erik never felt the syringe inserting between his ribs, sending a lethal dose rocketing through his veins. His head crashed against the steering wheel just as Stacey clamped the garden pruners around his index finger and pushed the handles together. Her eyes began to sparkle as she wiped the bloody pruners on his shirt, shoved him out the driver's door, and took his place behind the wheel. She had to hurry. There was just enough time to wipe down Erik's car and return it to the Laundromat. She'd swing by Augie's Quick-Stop on the way and pick up Creepy Willy's usual fee—a pint of the cheap red stuff. It was a small price to pay, and after all, he earned it.

Ten Seconds

Michael Hughes

Raymond's typing came to an abrupt halt and he froze, gaping out the window at the sight of an interloper climbing over his backyard fence. "Oh, God," he uttered to the empty room as the unwelcomed guest landed in his yard, crushing half a dozen purple flowers.

Ray figured that he had about ten seconds. Ten seconds to run downstairs and lock the back door before *it* got inside.

He pushed back from the table so fast that he knocked over the glass of scotch that had been sitting next to his laptop. The glass shattered on the floor as he leapt from the chair.

Ray's foot landed in the puddle of brown liquor that was now pooling across the dark hardwood floor. His stomach dropped as his feet went out from underneath him and he crashed to the ground. Ray scrambled back to his feet in a panic and bolted toward the staircase.

Ray's fans had waited two long years for the final book of his trilogy. Earlier that day he had finally found his groove after a torturously long dry spell. Energy flowed through him that afternoon, igniting his imagination. His fingers had furiously pounded the keys of his laptop, guided by a mind that seemed to roar. Until he saw *it.*

As he sprang toward the staircase Ray cursed himself for neglecting to shut the back door earlier that afternoon after sitting on the porch and scratching edits all over his manuscript. The buzz he had put on might explain the lapse in judgment.

Nine seconds.

He could hardly breathe when he reached the top of the stairs and his heart palpitated at an accelerated rate. The famous sixty-year-old fiction author had a heart condition, happened to be a bit wobbly from intoxication, and suddenly had to rely on his less than world-class speed to save his life.

Today had started like any other day for Raymond Michael Loftus—otherwise known to his readers and most of the world as Raymond M. Lovejoy. Raymond, semi-retired and recently bachelorized due to the unfortunate passing of his wife, arose around noon, a routine occurrence in his second life, and wandered into the kitchen like a mummy in a semi-depressive trance.

He felt like the feeble Mr. Loftus upon waking and not the genius Lovejoy, although after about three cups of coffee and some liquor, he came to life.

Ray pushed his thick black reading glasses up the bridge of his nose while perusing the newspaper and eating a bowl of Crispix—well, half a bowl at least, signaling that it was near time to visit the local Shop 'N Buy.

Within minutes after breakfast Raymond opened the liquor cabinet. Although he had been a beer drinker for most of his life, hops and barley just didn't cut it anymore—it failed to produce the desired effect—and if he was honest with himself he would have to admit that it was more of a required effect for daily functioning.

Thus, he had recently transitioned to vodka on a full-time basis and mixed it with whatever accompanying beverage was at hand. Today he would use cranberry juice—an efficient companion to the alcohol because as he destroyed his liver, the juice addressed his bladder, an organ that had been deteriorating for the last few years in as unremitting a fashion as his heart.

Snapping back to reality Ray felt his chest tightening and his heart racing while the world around him seemed to be doing the exact opposite – transitioning into slow motion. He was unsure if his palpitations were from fear or his heart condition.

Eight seconds.

After he had knocked off three cranberry and vodkas that morning (or, more aptly, vodka with a splash of cranberry)—it was time to write now that the inner muse had been satiated.

His friends and wife, who all wanted him to quit drinking, had often scoffed at the notion that Ray's best ideas came when he was inebriated. To which Ray argued that book one of his bestselling *Urchin* trilogy was written during a six month drunken haze. Not to mention that without his favorite creative lubricant there never would have even been an "Urchin"—a fact that Ray had tried to explain to both his friends and his wife to no avail. The Urchin books were brilliant; they garnered rave reviews and were even characterized by one famous critic as a contemporized version of The Omen.

Ray had modernized the story with the main character, a young victim of demonic possession who grew up to be a serial killer, outfitted in a gray-hooded sweatshirt to resemble one of the most popular young rap stars of the day. Raymond was such a gifted writer that readers could actually empathize with the evil character. Plus he had cleverly concocted Urchin to have very dark nondescript features, which left the specifics of what the malevolent young man looked like up to the reader's imagination—a feat in which Raymond took great pride.

Raymond tried hurdling two steps at a time, kicking his legs wildly as cold fear shot through his veins. Then his eyes surreally became fixed on, of all things, the wallpaper. He zoomed in on the tiny yellow and beige triangles and boxes with dark double-lined borders that were speckled with little brownish dots. And then he came to a stark moment of clarity and halted. With his eyes burning into the wall he said, "This wallpaper really is atrocious."

Seven seconds.

Ray remembered the frigid Saturday in late fall ten years ago when he had stormed out of the house after he and his wife Karen argued violently, for what seemed like an hour, about his endless procrastination. It had been the third week in a row he postponed going with her to get wallpaper. In his meek sober moments he was all about getting new wallpaper, and all about upgrading the love seat and couch, and all about planting flowers in the backyard, and all about taking a pottery class, and all about playing cribbage with the Hickersons, and all about…

But she just didn't understand. She never understood how precious a writer's time was to him. Nor did she understand that it was college football season to boot, not to mention that on that particular day, the day of the great wallpaper incident, the Michigan – Ohio state game was airing. Ray remembered thinking to himself at the time '*of all days to pull this shit.*'

Six seconds.

Raymond calculated that after reaching the bottom of the stairs he would have to cover about sixty feet through the dining room and kitchen before getting to the door. He also had to account for the second or two it would take to lock the damn thing. Worst of all, Ray had to account for the fact that in order to accomplish his mission, it was paramount that he avoid a heart attack. And the way his heart was thumping, that was a legitimate concern.

His thoughts soon returned to the wallpaper incident. He remembered storming out of the house by himself and later returning with the vile wallpaper. This only started another argument because, of course, she not only despised the wallpaper design but the colors nearly made her physically ill. At one point he raised his hand as if to backhand her but stopped. And the shock in her face had been etched in his mind for years.

Her blond hair was pulled back in a pony tail that day, her lips glossy with a subtle shade of red lipstick, and she wore a bare hint of dark purplish eyeshade. The former prom queen still wore a light sexy tan too, and although nearing forty, she was still the object of many a man's desire in the Dayton, Ohio suburb. An average looking mutt ten years her senior, Ray admitted the obvious—he was lucky to have her. Thank God she loved the James Joyce quirky writer-type—although he always wondered if she really understood what she was getting into.

He never hit her that day or on any day for that matter, which is why he found the accusations disgusting that he had anything to do with his lovely wife's death. But his abrasive tongue had done worse damage than any fistful. He knew she represented the only truly pure thing in his life. He loved her but had never shown it. Perhaps if he even tried she might not have taken her own life.

Five seconds.

Ray could remember the torturously palpable silence that enshrouded the room as they went about papering the walls. He'd done a horrible job because it was tough operating and producing anything of quality after consuming a 12-pack of Old Style. Karen ended up redoing half of it. He recalled watching her work so hard to put up the wallpaper that she hated with a passion. And Raymond Lovejoy, once again, had sucked the life out of his beloved. But what she had said to him on that and many subsequent occasions was short, sweet and piercing: "You're such a taker Raymond."

Those five simple words were a dagger in his side. They always left a mortal wound that he may not have felt at that moment or even on that day, but inevitably he suffered for his selfish acts. He learned later in life that his misdeeds do come home to roost.

Four seconds.

He finally neared the bottom of the staircase and swung his head towards the front door. He emitted a sigh of relief when he noticed that at least the front door was locked. However, relief turned to panic because, as if writing his own sad award-winning ending, Raymond tripped on the last step, and everything seemed to transfer back into fast forward mode.

At full speed Raymond drove his shoulder into the hardwood floor and omitted a scream that echoed throughout the empty house. But the raw fear and adrenaline coursing through his body quickly overcame any pain he felt and he sprung back to his feet.

Three seconds.

For the first time since he was a child he began to pray. He prayed out loud while pumping his legs. Ray swore he would not take this experience for granted, would change his ways and quit the drink to make it up to Karen.

Two Seconds.

The mental oath triggered an inexplicable phenomenon, because Raymond swore he could actually feel Karen's presence in the room. He even thought he heard her voice, which gave him momentary warmth. The warmth however was quickly replaced by a chill as he realized it *was* her voice and it sounded unnatural and raspy. He sensed anger in the voice. He nearly stopped running when he finally comprehended what she had been hissing the entire time: "Murderer."

One Second.

Raymond had no time to absorb the accusing voice, because he had to act—now. He screamed as he left the ground and threw all of his weight into the door, slamming it shut. He spastically locked the door in record time as the mental stopwatch in his head clicked to zero.

Ray felt a triumphant joy course through him. He crawled to the kitchen counter and pulled himself up, breathing heavily. He began laughing hysterically despite the pain in his shoulder. The pain didn't matter now, he felt reborn, like he had been gifted with another chance at life.

Ray's elation was shattered as the bolt and the entire section around the doorknob exploded. Debris shot across the kitchen. Ray dropped back to the floor and threw his arms up to cover his head. His body shook with fear as the door swung open and banged against the wall. A sharp, hot pain gripped his chest and prevented any air from filling his lungs.

A figure filled the doorway wearing a gray-hooded sweatshirt that cloaked his face. It swaggered into the kitchen and stopped within a few feet of Raymond. The hooded entity slowly leaned forward, causing Ray to lean back. Ray tried to force his body to turn and run, but couldn't move—he was paralyzed. Then, from under the darkness of the hood came a voice: "You're such a taker Raymond."

It was not his wife's voice. It was raspy and deep like Urchin's—or at least what Ray always imagined Urchin's voice would sound like.

As Urchin laughed deliriously he grabbed the top of his gray hood and pulled it backwards, completely exposing his head and face. It was what Ray always thought evil would look like. Urchin's lumpy albino-colored cranium was covered with grotesquely jagged blood-red scars.

But as Ray studied the beast's features more closely, it told a different story. Urchin's lips curled into a sickening smile and the thing let out another high-pitched snort, revealing dark, rotting teeth. Ray further analyzed the abomination's eyebrows, then his nose, and then his chin. And his draw dropped.

As the picture came together and recognition set in, Ray thought he was going to be sick. Sick because he was looking directly into the face of one Raymond M. Lovejoy.

The Face in the Sand

Lawrence Conquest

The older Charlotte got, the more the incident preyed upon her mind. At times she felt sure that it was all a fabrication, just a childhood fantasy and nothing more. But still she worried at it as though it was a rotting tooth, uncomfortable at the reaction it provoked within her and yet seemingly unable to resist returning to prod the aching wound time and again. Now, after all these years, how could she truly tell what was real and what was a lie? What was memory anyway, but the past retold as a convenient fiction?

She had replayed the incident over and over in her mind like a favorite film, until the actions of the cast became meaningless movements and the dividing line between reality and fantasy had become hopelessly blurred. Was everything she remembered real, or did the story merely contain a grain of truth that had grown like a lustrous pearl with the embellishments of over two decade's worth of retelling? She smiled grimly at the apposite image of a grain of sand lodged within an oyster's shell, an irritant that worried at the maddened creature until it was forced into action. Always it came back to the beach.

Finally, on a clear summer morning some twenty-seven years after she may have killed a man, Charlotte decided it was time to face her demons. After all, she thought, they do say that criminals always returned to the scene of their crimes.

Feeling the years fall away from her, Charlotte Straw picked up the telephone and prepared to book a train ticket to Poole.

***

Their family had been on holiday for almost a week now and Charlotte could sense that their time in Poole was nearing an end with talk turning time and again to the return trip to Bristol and the even more dreaded return to school.

"The only reason you even need an imaginary friend is because you don't have any real ones."

"That's not true!" replied Charlotte, though the response had come to her lips automatically and no sooner had she uttered it than she began to sense the uncomfortable ring of truth that underlaid her sister's accusation.

Charlotte knew that Kate was annoyed at having been tasked with looking after her nine-year-old sister, and the shopping trip to nearby Lilliput had in truth been little more than a thinly veiled excuse for their parents to spend some time together alone. Charlotte didn't mind her sister—most of the time, but recently she could sense the resentment radiating from her in hot waves like a repelling force.

"What sort of stupid name is Muffy, anyway?" asked Kate.

It's a good name, for a cat, thought Charlotte, but swiftly decided against revealing the fact that her best friend was not only imaginary but also non-human. She may be young, but she wasn't entirely stupid, and she wasn't going to give Kate any more ammunition to belittle her. Charlotte paused for a while, watching her sister flick idly through the teen magazines on the supermarket shelves and gave herself time to think up a suitable witty reply. "You smell."

The force of the blow from Kate's rolled up magazine wasn't enough to hurt, but the shock was sufficient to make Charlotte burst into tears. Like an overstuffed fly she ducked out of her sister's swatting reach and fled down the supermarket aisle, dodged past an old lady apparently dancing with a frozen chicken the size of a small poodle and burst into the high street.

Lilliput was thronged with mid-day shoppers and Charlotte had little difficultly losing herself among their anonymous ranks. It was obvious to her that Kate didn't want to be seen with her younger sister in tow, didn't want this embarrassing reminder of her own youthful lack of independence.

Well fine, Charlotte thought, *she could always amuse herself. And if not, well, there was always Muffy*. Charlotte tried to will the cat into being there, but it slunk shyly away into the shadows, embarrassed at having had its fictional nature spoken aloud.

Somewhere in the distance she thought she heard Kate calling for her, but if so it was a pretty half-hearted effort. No doubt Kate would fully enjoy getting her little sister into trouble and once deprived of her company maybe she'd have more success with the gangs of teenage boys that accumulated like litter on the street corners. Boys. Charlotte didn't know what her sister saw in them, and besides, everyone knew you weren't supposed to talk to strangers.

Alone in the crowd, Charlotte angled herself away from the center of town and headed towards the beach.

***

Charlotte lay on her back, a mound of sand serving as a readymade bed, and watched the sun as it slowly set over Sandbanks.

Charlotte knew she should have left for the hotel hours ago, and her parents would be worried sick about her by now, but the sound of the waves as they lapped gently at the shoreline was hypnotic, lulling her into a state of drowsy tranquility. She had wandered along the beach in a deliberate quest for solitude and as the light had faded so had her fellow tourists' numbers thinned, leaving Charlotte now the sole inhabitant of her section of beachfront. The beach was divided into thin strips of golden sand, bordered by the lapping sea to one side and the busy lights and lavish homes of Sandbanks Road along another. Each strip was separated by a narrow walkway that terminated in a jetty overhanging a man-made collection of rocks. Water sprayed in foamy flumes about the barnacle-encrusted stones, the violence of the sea transformed into a soothing susurration that seemed to whisper half-heard secrets in Charlotte's ear.

Charlotte shifted uncomfortably, feeling her neck crick from having laid so long upon her sandy bed. Fully aware that she was merely delaying her inevitable departure, she turned and ran her hand over the dune, sculpting the sand to provide a more comfortable headrest. As her fingers worked at the gritty sand she became aware of a compacted hardness beneath the surface, as though a rock or shell lay buried only inches away. She dug a little deeper, determined to pry the offending object loose, and found her fingers scraping against a soft, pliable surface. Pulling upwards, she removed a small plug of compacted sand, then froze in surprise at the sight of what she had uncovered.

Staring back at Charlotte through the freshly uncovered hole in the beach was the incongruous shape of an open eye. It lay there, glossy and bloodshot, looking like a poached egg that had been left on the sand by some forgetful diner.

Feeling as though she was in a dream, Charlotte gingerly stretched out a hand and began to smooth away the sand from around the unblinking eye. She tried to tell herself that it was just a washed up fish, or some other unfortunate sea-dwelling creature that had found itself out of its natural habitat, but with every sweep of her hand the truth became harder to deny. Rising from the golden crust, its contours gradually emerging from the granular depths like an island from the sea, was the unmistakable shape of a human face.

The features were still encrusted with a patina of sand, but the profile was unquestionably male, its leathery skin scored deeply with sedimentary grit. The back of the man's head still remained buried beneath the beach, but Charlotte had brushed the sand away from mouth to forehead, and the exposed countenance now appeared to lie upon the sand like a discarded mask.

Feeling an equal mixture of curiosity and terror, Charlotte edged a little closer, leaning over the profile as if doubting the evidence that lay before her. She could see herself reflected in the glazed eyes as they stared blindly up at the sky, a slightly chubby girl with long brown pigtails, a puzzled frown skewing her normally pleasant features. Abruptly the stereo mirror images flexed and danced beneath her as the man's pupils dilated, the face shuddering as it pulled in a whooping breath through a suddenly open mouth.

Charlotte yelped involuntarily and backed away from the face so fast that her legs tangled beneath her, making her fall to the ground. Dragging herself clumsily to her feet, she turned to face the road, and began to run. She was halfway towards the bright lights of Sandbanks Road when a voice from behind brought her up short.

"Stop! Wait!"

Her legs felt like dead weights as she turned to face the beach. A guttural coughing drifted across the bay, a barely human counterpoint to the lonely gull cries that peppered the early evening air.

"Please, Miss? You must help me!"

The voice sounded sepulchral, almost as though air was being forced out unnaturally through long-dead lungs. But how could the man be alive? How could he have remained so still beneath the sand—how could he breathe? She felt a yawning sickness in her stomach as she realized that she had been resting only inches above him, her comfortable bed built upon the roof of another man's tomb. Had he felt the awful weight of her pushing down upon him in the dark? Had she awoken him from some unfathomably deep sleep, or from a state of existence deeper still?

"Please come back, I promise I won't hurt you!"

The man sounded desperate now, and Charlotte felt a terrible sympathy for his plight. She knew that she should fetch an adult to help, but casting her gaze along the beach revealed the sand to be otherwise deserted. If anyone could help this man, it would have to be her. On legs shaky with nerves, she retraced her footsteps back down the beach.

“Thank God, you’ve come back!” the face wheezed in a tone as dusty as the grave. “Please, you have got to help me!”

“How did you get in there?” asked Charlotte.

“I…I can’t quite remember. It’s all a bit of a blur. I was lying on the beach, and Robert and Joseph were playing. Yes, that’s right, they were playing, building sandcastles. Then, then they wanted to bury me in sand, and – I think I must have fallen asleep. I don’t remember anymore. But where are they anyway? Robert? Joseph?”

“There’s no-one else here Mister. Can’t you dig yourself out?”

“I don’t think so, I can’t seem to move my hands. The weight of all this sand, pushing down on me, I can barely breathe as it is. You’ll have to help me.”

Charlotte knew that he wanted her to dig him out of the sand. But something about his story didn’t seem right. Something about the man made her feel uneasy and she wasn’t sure if she wanted to get involved. Surely if she went away someone else would come along and solve this problem? She was only nine-years-old, she shouldn’t have to deal with this.

“How do I know you’re real, Mister?”

“What? Of course I’m real. Why haven’t you started digging?”

“My sister says I have an overactive imagination. Maybe I fell asleep on the beach, and you’re just a bad dream? Maybe you fell asleep too Mister, like you said, so perhaps you’re dreaming too. Maybe if you go back to sleep eventually you’ll wake up and everything will go back to normal. Besides, the tide’s coming in.”

This last comment made the man explode into panic, his speech degenerating into a string of shouted gibberish whilst he fought, with no avail, to free himself. Charlotte was sad to see the man so afraid, but she knew best how to calm him.

"Everything has its place, that's what my mum says. I've found lots of strange things on the beach here Mister, though I'll admit that you're probably the strangest creature yet. Sometimes these things don't look so well, a bit like you don't look so well right now. Anyway, I always want to help, and I'll fish them out and show my mum, but then she always tells me to put them right back where I found them. They're happier where they are, apparently."

Charlotte began to scoop up handfuls of sand, pounding them into clods which she began to smooth over the face of the thing on the beach.

"And besides," she said under her breath, "I'm not supposed to speak to strangers."

The man continued to struggle for a while, but as the plugs of sand and grit stopped up his mouth his terrible cries gradually lessened.

Within a few short minutes the entire face was hidden from view and Charlotte smoothed the sand over until all trace of the man was gone. Gingerly, the young girl leaned over the mound and pressed an ear flat against the sand. She fancied she could still hear what sounded like a thin, wheezing breath, somewhere down in the dark, but after a time the noise was gradually drowned out by the roaring voice of the incoming tide.

Charlotte retreated to the road and watched a while, waiting until the sea hid sand from view, than began to walk back to the hotel.

***

Of course, it was madness to think that she would find any physical evidence now, some twenty-seven years later, of the face in the sand.

Nevertheless, as the miles between Bristol and Poole lessened, Charlotte could feel an uneasiness growing within her, as though some malignant force was drawing her towards an inexorable doom. Her fellow passengers lolled in their cushioned seats like lifeless mannequins, their bodies given merely the semblance of life by the gentle rocking motions of the train. She felt claustrophobic, hemmed in by the silent creatures, unable to move without making unwanted physical contact. The fat man next to her seemed to encroach upon her territory with a series of infinitesimal motions, the stale stink of his tobacco breath an expeditionary force presaging his covert moves.

Finally the train disgorged its remaining passengers at the terminal, the milling crowd spilling across the dull steel and concrete structure like multi-coloured flecks of vomit. Charlotte stumbled away from the station, grateful for the space to stretch her stifled limbs, and sucked the tangy sea air deep into her aching lungs.

A short taxi ride later and Charlotte stood once more on Sandbanks Road, facing the sea. She carried no baggage with her. She didn't expect to stay long. There was absolutely nothing here for her, nothing except the past.

She planned her arrival carefully. The day was hot, and the beach was thronged with the comforting sight of numerous sun-seekers, their bronzed bodies scattered across the shoreline like pieces of washed up driftwood. The beach was safe and there was absolutely nothing here for her to fear. So why did she hesitate?

Charlotte chided herself mentally and forced herself to step off of the tarmac road and onto the soft pliable surface of the beach.

There, that wasn't so hard was it? No terrors from beneath the sand had risen up to claim her, no vengeful cries had welled up from its unknowable depths. Forcing a hollow smile upon her face, Charlotte wandered slowly down the beach.

Of course, she couldn't remember exactly where the incident had taken place, but she walked a good distance along the shore, until she felt certain that she must be somewhere within the vicinity. Still, she made sure not to wander too far from the lolling sunbathers, taking a small comfort in the knowledge that others besides herself inhabited this boundary between land and sea.

She noticed a pair of young boys had been busy excavating a crater in the sand, the scooped out well reaching as high as the pair's chests. Seeing Charlotte approach, the boys levered themselves from the hole, their emaciated bodies dappled with flecks of sand, and ran off laughing along the beach. Charlotte smiled after them, thinking of the childish games she had played with her sister in happier times, and perched herself upon the lip of the well.

She closed her eyes, idly kicking her legs against the damp sand walls of the pit as she concentrated. This was it, if she was going to get any benefit from this trip, then she needed to face her fears now, in the bright light of day. Either the incident had happened as she remembered it, or it had not. If it had, well, she was only a child at the time, and if she had acted wrongly then she had not done so out of malice. But how could the man on the beach have ended up so deeply buried, and where had the two children that he mentioned disappeared to?

Charlotte dimly heard the giggling laughter of the two young boys as they ambled further down the beach, and felt a chill touch of coldness creep up her spine. What if the man *had* been playing with his children, exactly as he had said? What if they had been burying him in the sand and some kind of tragic accident had occurred, an accident that caused a sudden collapse of sand to bury all three together? What if the man's sons had never left him at all, but had laid alongside him all the while, their small bodies pressed tightly against his own by the fierce hug of the beach? Did he finally notice the cold touch of their tiny limbs as Charlotte began to entomb them all? Was it this realization of his children's fate that caused him to scream at the end, or merely the knowledge of his own impending doom?

Charlotte punched her hand into the sand besides her, frustrated and angry at herself. This was getting her nowhere—she had to stop speculating and separate the fact from fiction within her mind. She opened her eyes, letting her thoughts glide for a while with the gulls above, their wings outstretched as the wind seemingly held them aloft with invisible fingers. She breathed deeply and attempted to calm her nerves. The sun-warmed sand felt curiously comforting as it held her hand in its delicate grip and she pushed her arm a little deeper into the granular substance.

With a sudden wrench, Charlotte pulled her hand free of the sand and staggered to her feet. A desperate scream began to force its way through her lips and she began to run towards the reclining sunbathers, frantic to outrace whatever was behind her. Roused from their slumbers, they turned their faces as one towards the screaming woman, but something about their outlines seemed wrong. The bathers were encrusted with clots of golden sand, their outlines rendered indistinct, and Charlotte couldn't tell where the people ended and the beach began. The beach itself seemed a living thing, the swell of each curve, the turn of a hip, the crest of each dune, an upthrust head. Yawning mouths seemed to crack open beneath her feet as she ran, the hungry maws gulping and sucking at her footsteps, causing her to lose her balance and pitch forward.

Winded, Charlotte tried to tell herself that what her fingers had just brushed against in the depths of the beach was merely the wet skin of some burrowing sandworm and not the loathsome touch of cold dead fingers, reaching up from the grave to clutch back at her own.

Sprawled upon the baking sand, Charlotte risked a quick glance over her shoulder.

Outracing the tide, her past rushed hungrily up the beach to meet her.

***

By evening, the water's calming touch had swept the surface smooth again, and not a single trace remained of what now lay buried beneath the sand.

Scent

Joshua Scribner

"I know where Freddie Claypack is."

Sheriff Arn Cowan jolted. His hand slipped to his pistol, wondering who had snuck up on him.

It was a boy, short, but adolescent by the razor-burn-stubble mixture on his face. His hair was brown and bushy. He wore a jean jacket and blue jeans. His hands dangled safely at his sides.

Arn lifted his hand from the gun. "Who let you back here?"

"No one. I walked right in."

"That's impossible. The dispatcher and the clerk both know better than to let someone enter my office unannounced."

The kid smirked. "I waited outside until I knew they were both away, one to the bathroom, one to get a cup of coffee, then I walked through the front door and back to your office."

Arn studied this odd character. He'd seen him around town, but couldn't associate him with mischief. "You can't see into the station from outside. How would you have known when they were away from their desks?"

The arrival sucked a deep breath into his nose. He then gave a slight smile. "Irish Spring Body Wash, Pert Shampoo, Edge Gel, and Degree Cool Rush Deodorant, which, by the way, you could use a new application of."

Arn reflexively looked at the damp area under his left arm, and then, in his mind, recounted his morning grooming ritual.

"You're batting a thousand, kid."

"Always do. Shall we talk about your lunch and the peppermint candy you had afterward, or are you convinced enough with my ability that we can get to the issue of Freddie Claypack?"

Arn recalled the deep breath the kid had taken. "You can smell things others can't."

"How perceptive of you, and how open-minded." The kid seemed truly impressed.

Arn nodded. "I was a detective in L.A., before I moved out here. I've worked with a lot of frauds, but I've also worked with a few of genuine ability. You seem to be in the latter group, so let's talk about Freddie Claypack."

The kid stared at him for a few seconds, his face incredibly still. "Freddie didn't run away, like everyone thinks. I'll lead you to him, but I have my requirements."

Arn shrugged. "Most do. What do you need?"

"I need for only you to know what I can do. I want a normal life until I'm older, and the less people who know about my ability, the more likely I can have that."

"Fair enough."

The kid looked away, took in another sniff. Arn suspected he was checking for people nearby. "I can't tell you where he is. It's too complicated. I have to lead you to him."

Arn stood. "Fine by me. Can you tell me if he's alive, though?"

The boy didn't respond.

"I just like to know what I'm coming into."

The boy nodded. "He's dead."

***

The kid said his name was Brody, informed Arn they'd meet near the woods and then snuck out the same way he came in.

"How far?" asked Arn when they met up.

"Couple of miles."

Brody sniffed the air periodically and adjusted his route accordingly. They traveled for about ten minutes before coming to a creek. Brody jumped from rock to rock. He then waited on the other side, as Arn took much longer.

"Not as nimble as I used to be."

Brody chuckled. "I doubt you were ever a rabbit or a cat."

Arn wanted elaboration on the comment, but he didn't ask for it. He just continued to follow Brody deeper into the woods, until, after another ten minutes, Brody elaborated on his own.

"We all have past lives, Sheriff. Our spirits harbor many different things. For most, the path of lives is varied and their soul becomes muddled and confused. For others, the path is not so varied. Each life similar to the one before it and the soul becomes cohesive and consistent."

That was a lot to think about and enough to keep Arn in his head as they trekked. A few times, he thought he heard something, the slight sound of footsteps or a tiny branch breaking. Placing a hand on his pistol pushed the fear away, allowing him to return to his higher thoughts. He didn't know how long he was considering Brody's comments, before Brody stopped walking.

"I dream every night. Sometimes, it's in woods like these. Sometimes it's on an arctic plain. I even dream of the desert. Wherever the place, what I am and what I'm doing is always the same." Brody was silent for a few seconds, and as still as a dead man. Finally, he said, "Freddie Claypack is on the other side of these trees."

Brody moved to the side, and Arn moved forward. He stepped around a few branches, into a clearing, were a mangled skeleton lay.

"I'd say he's been gone over," Arn said.

As Arn knelt for closer inspection, he felt his pistol lift from its holster.

Arn shot up and turned around. Brody had the Colt pointed at him.

"Don't do anything foolish kid."

"And you, Sheriff, don't go for the gun on your ankle. I know it's there. I can smell it."

There was rustling in the surrounding woods.

Brody's face grew into a satisfied smile. "My dreams tell me what I've been. I've been a wolf. I've been a coyote. I've been a jackal, and many others. Several lives in a row, I've even been a wild dog, and it's left a mark on me." Brody sniffed the air very audibly.

The commotion in the trees grew. Arn knew he'd soon have to chance a move at his gun.

Brody's expression was still, like a predator locked in on its prey. "Freddie Claypack used to hunt in these woods. He shot one of them. Just like you shot one of them near the Resnick place, after a few sheep disappeared. You hung its corpse on the fence so the others would see what they were up against."

A growl reverberated. Arn looked to see a grey wolf creeping into the clearing. "I'm going to have to protect myself, Brody."

Brody laughed, this time loudly. "Make your move, Sheriff, but remember, we run in packs."

Arn went for his gun, but before he could get a hand on it, ripping pain shot through his back. He didn't even seen the first attacker. Another wolf got his leg. A third came from the side to get his throat. They dragged him to the ground. He caught a glimpse of Brody walking away, sniffing the air.

Tomorrow's Headline

Adrian Ludens

Michelle Watkins thought her day couldn't get any worse. She was wrong.

She'd just dropped off the dry cleaning when the telltale swirling orbs of white light assailed her vision. Michelle knew a migraine was rapidly approaching. She groaned inwardly and gripped the wheel. From the back seat Casey, his voice dripping with the sweet purity of youth, sang: "Robot pa-rade, robot pa-rade..."

"Casey, honey," Michelle had to raise her voice to be heard. "Mommy is getting a headache. Can you please stop singing?"

Casey caught her eye in the rearview mirror and stopped singing. He started kicking the back of her seat instead.

Michelle sighed and yanked the Impala's shifter into reverse. On the street behind her, the driver of a late model Chevy pickup leaned on his horn. Michelle winced as the sound grated her ears. "Go ahead then," she said aloud as if the pickup's driver could actually hear her, "Save yourself ten seconds."

The pickup roared up the street and Michelle looked out the rear window before cautiously backing up again. She would detour to the drug store before heading home, she decided. It was only four blocks from the dry cleaners and then eight or nine blocks back home. She could turn on cartoons for Casey and then hide from the pain in the familiar confines of her darkened bedroom.

At the stoplight Casey started kicking her seat again.

"Casey, quit!" Michelle admonished. This triggered the song again. Michelle rubbed her eyes in a fruitless attempt at clearing her vision which swirled in a bluish haze. Nausea would be setting in soon, then the crippling pain.

The light turned green and Michelle was eager to push down on the gas but a chubby kid lugging what appeared to be a trombone case hadn't made it across the street yet. She ground her teeth with frustration until the kid reached the curb then pressed down on the accelerator.

Michelle sped the two remaining blocks and eased the Impala into the first empty parking spot she found. She closed her eyes and massaged the back of her neck in a fruitless attempt at relieving her discomfort. Michelle inhaled deeply, held it, then exhaled slowly. She repeated this exercise four more times. Then she opened her eyes and was chagrined to discover her migraine had advanced to the next stage. In the center of her gaze floated the dark spot of nothingness that usually preceded the nausea. She held her hand up in front of her face but saw only her fingertips. The palm appeared to be curiously nonexistent.

"Robot pa-rade," Casey sang tunelessly from the back seat. Michelle glanced into the rearview mirror but found that she could not see him. There was only a dark circular void where her son should have been.

Sighing, Michelle pressed the release button on her safety belt and opened her door. Then she opened the back door and leaned in to unbuckle Casey.

"I don't wanna go in!" the boy complained.

Michelle paused, considering. She could be in and out in five minutes. Then she shook her head slightly and withdrew her protesting son from his car seat. Casey kicked and tried to wriggle away.

"I wanna stay here!" he cried angrily.

"You have to come in with Mommy," Michelle told him. "I can't leave you in the car or some strange man might try to steal you."

Casey abruptly stopped his fussing and gaped. "What strange man?"

"I don't know," Michelle replied, as she walked with him toward the drug store's entrance. "Maybe someone hiding somewhere," she finished vaguely.

The automatic doors slid open and Michelle and Casey stepped into the drug store's fluorescent interior. The dowdy cashier looked up briefly, nodded a hello and continued scanning items for a bored looking bearded man in a Red Sox T-shirt.

Michelle glanced at the local newspaper rack. The headline read: "State Homeless Numbers Up". Other headlines above the fold included a fatal car crash out on the Interstate and the search for a lost hiker in the nearby national forest. Michelle shook her head. Seemed like nothing but bad news. She was almost afraid of what tomorrow's headline might be. Michelle took Casey's hand and led him into the drug store.

Her vision had cleared but now the pain was starting to creep in from the base of her skull. Tendrils of burning discomfort would soon shoot through her brain. Every second counted. The pharmacy was tucked into the corner on the opposite end of the store and Michelle took Casey's hand and headed in that direction.

The pair had to stop at the intersection of aisles for the tallest woman Michelle had seen in years. The woman looked as if she stood about six foot three. She had wiry gray hair and a stern expression. Her cart was filled to capacity with cartons of diet soda. The woman plodded past and Michelle caught sight of her companion; another elderly woman barely over five feet tall, her hair dyed a garish orange hue. A small package of facial tissue made up the entire contents of the cart she was pushing. Stifling a giggle, despite the increasing discomfort of her migraine, Michelle continued down the aisle.

"Mom, can I go look at the toys?" Casey asked, wresting his hand from hers. Michelle looked at him.

"Will you be good and stay right here until I come back?"

"Yes."

"And you promise not to talk to strangers?"

"Yes."

Michelle sighed. Her temples were starting to throb with pain. "Okay, I'll be in the next row."

"Okay," Casey replied absently, already gazing at the colorful diecast cars in their little blue packages.

Michelle rounded the corner and jostled against a man who was apparently browsing in the next aisle. He was a man of average build, short cropped brown hair and unremarkable features. The only memorable feature the man could boast were his light green eyes which held Michelle's gaze for a moment before a wave of dizziness swept over her. Michelle staggered and everything went black. She fumbled out a hand to steady herself, sending several plastic bottles of vitamins clattering to the tile floor.

Michelle kept her eyes closed and waited for the dizzy spell to pass. She opened her eyes to see the pharmacist staring at her from behind his counter. The man she had bumped into was nowhere in sight.

She gave the pharmacist what she hoped was a reassuring smile. "I'm all right," Michelle croaked in a hoarse voice that she hardly recognized. Embarrassed, she stooped to pick up the bottles.

"It's okay, I'll get them," the pharmacist said, coming around the counter.

Michelle nodded and moved self-consciously down the aisle to the headache medicine. There was one brand that worked rather well on her migraines and Michelle scanned the shelf for it. She stopped short, amazed.

Michelle no longer felt the tendrils of pain encroaching on her temples or the base of her neck. Her vision was fine and she didn't feel any nausea either. Her migraine had miraculously disappeared. Michelle realized that after bumping into the man with the striking green eyes, her migraine symptoms left her. Smiling to herself, she strode back to the toy aisle.

"Casey..." she rasped. Michelle started to clear the frog from her throat but stopped short. Casey was not there. A tidal wave of panic rose and washed away her irritation at seeing that he'd wandered away. She immediately turned and looked in all four directions. A little red-haired girl followed her mother down one aisle. The others antagonized her by being empty.

As she turned the corner at the end of the aisle, Michelle reflected that bad things happened to people—even children—all the time. She silently prayed that nothing bad had happened to Casey. Michelle moved toward the cash registers, looking carefully down each aisle as she passed. She saw the tall and short elderly women still caravanning together down one aisle and a stock boy opening boxes halfway down another. A man and a woman, obviously a couple, browsed the magazine rack. No Casey.

Then Michelle realized something that made her feel like she had been kicked in the stomach: she hadn't seen the green-eyed man she had bumped into either. Had he heard her telling Casey to wait? She had practically announced to anyone listening that the boy would be unattended. Michelle mentally cursed herself and broke into a panicky jog, heading to where the register lanes and the entrance were located.

There! Michelle saw the back of Casey's head. He was walking toward the exit.

"Casey!" Michelle shouted. Her voice again sounded strange in her own ears. Her son turned and stared with surprise in her direction. His mouth hung open and his eyes were wide with fright.

"Casey, you stay right there!" Michelle rasped. "I'm coming to get you."

Terror twisted her son's face and he spun around and ran. He was gone out the front door before she could circumvent the customers crowded with their carts at the checkout lines.

Frustration overwhelmed Michelle and she screamed, "Stop running!"

She jostled through the crowd, furious that no one seemed to care about her situation. In fact, several customers were eyeing her suspiciously. Some even gave her dirty looks as she pushed past them.

Michelle could see out the sliding glass doors and into the parking lot now. Casey was being carried toward a dark windowless van by a woman wearing the same outfit Michelle had on.

"STOP!" she shrieked as she reached the doors. The door slid open but before Michelle could pass through, something large and hard drove into her hip and sent her flying. Michelle crashed into the local newspaper rack and then fell awkwardly to the tile floor. Pain shot through her right elbow and her left hip throbbed sharply. Stunned, she looked up to see the tall gray-haired woman towering above, glowering down at her. The diminutive orange haired woman pursed her lips disapprovingly.

"You got him good, Agatha," she commended.

"Probably some pree-vert," the tall woman said, her eyes never leaving Michelle.

A man with a bad comb-over and a green vest hurried up. "I've phoned the police," he announced.

"Get out there and stop that van!" Michelle cried, motioning frantically with one hand as she struggled to her feet. A group of grim-faced customers barred her path to the exit.

"I don't think so buddy," the man who had been in the magazine aisle with his wife replied.

"Get out of the way!" Michelle growled. She wondered again at the strangeness of her voice.

The manager stepped closer. "Just stay calm and we'll get this all sorted out. We don't need any trouble."

"That woman has my son!" Michelle appealed.

The cashier who had nodded hello shook her head. "No sir, that little boy came in with his mamma and he left with his mamma."

Michelle began to tremble. This was insane. It couldn't be happening. Then Michelle thought about her voice again. A vague idea formed.

"May I walk down your cosmetics aisle while we wait for the police to arrive?" she asked the manager. Michelle tried very hard to appear calm, but the sound of her voice made her want to scream.

The store manager looked at Michelle closely, then nodded. The crowd parted and Michelle strode carefully through the aisle until she found the rack of lipstick testers. Above the testers was a small mirror for customers use when trying out colors.

Michelle took a deep breath and looked in the mirror. A stranger stared back at her. Short cropped brown hair framed an unremarkable male face. Bright green eyes held Michelle's gaze for a moment before a wave of lightheadedness swept over her. Michelle staggered back and began to scream. She screamed until her vocal cords simply refused to work any longer.

It took eight people just to hold her down until the police came.

***

Michelle awoke in a hospital bed. A policeman sat in a chair in the corner of the tiny room. Michelle guessed that he was there to guard her but was staring raptly at the television on the opposite wall instead. She glanced at the screen and saw that the local news was on.

"Looks like we owe you an apology buddy." The policeman sounded awestruck. "How in the hell did you know she was gonna kill her kid?"

Michelle looked up and saw herself on the television screen. She wore an orange jumpsuit and manacles on her hands and feet. She struggled as police wrestled her into the back of a police cruiser. Michelle's heart seemed to jump in her chest as the woman on the screen turned and shrieked directly at the camera. "I'm the arresting officer!" she cried. "She switched bodies with me!" The door of the police cruiser slammed and the woman's cries became inaudible.

"That woman is crazier than an outhouse rat!" the policeman remarked.

The news anchor was speaking again. "A closed-casket memorial service will be held for Casey Watkins this Friday at..."

Michelle stopped listening. Every fiber of her being felt scorched and desolate. Only the formality of the actual act of dying remained. She beckoned to the policeman who stood up and moved toward her, his eyebrows raised quizzically. Michelle's eyes darted to the enticing black steel handle of the Beretta holstered to his hip and watched as it moved closer... closer...

Are You the Fairest?

Piper Morgan

I couldn't take it anymore. I screamed but no one heard me. Some stopped to glance at themselves, but most just bustled about. People stopped to judge... but they didn't always judge themselves. Maybe they should. Why do you have to stare at yourself five times over the course of an hour? So much beauty, love, passion, jealousy, hate, and ugliness. Is the ugliness why you look so much?

Who am I to judge? you ask.

I'm the mirror you look into as you go in and out the front door of the fancy restaurant.

I wasn't always like this. I was born a beautiful creation. You people have made me this way.

Ages ago, a brilliant craftsman thought of me as a wonderful gift for his daughter. I'll leave out all of the boring technical details, but for the frame he used smooth brass, forming several small swirls, each with the gentlest of curves. Once my frame was ready, he placed me—the rectangular mirror—in the center. He looked at the final project, satisfied with his handiwork.

The craftsman went to his daughter and turned me around to face her. "Michelle, I made this for you."

She took me in her arms and started to cry.

"Don't you like it?" her father asked.

Wiping tears away, she whispered. "Yes, father, thank you." She walked down the hall to her bedroom and leaned me against her bed. Michelle took a small round mirror off the wall and set it beside me.

Hello, I said to it.

I'm glad to finally be out of here, was his reply.

Before I could find out what he was talking about, Michelle grabbed me and hung me on the nail. She plopped down in a chair and stared at me. Tears rolled down her cheeks. "I hate you. You're so ugly," she snarled. "You're hideous."

I gasped. *Why are you so mean?* I asked. *We've just met, and so much love and hard work was put into me!*

"You're poor. You're so pathetic and repulsive, your own mother left you behind. She took your sister, but you weren't good enough for her. I hate you!" she screamed and ran to her bed, burying her face in pillows.

Every day, Michelle sat in front of me, saying the same terrible insults. Every day, I felt more miserable and pathetic. *Why?* was all I could ask.

After months of hearing the same awful things over and over again, Michelle grabbed her father's straight razor and sat in front of me.

What are you doing? Michelle, what's going on? I asked frantically.

"I hate you. You deserve to die." She ran the razor along the veins of her left forearm. Dark red fluid dripped from her arm.

No! I screamed. *Someone help her! Michelle, you have to stop!*

Crying, she put the blade in her left hand, and with forced effort, she cut her right arm. She looked at me then fell to the floor with a thump.

Michelle?! Father, where are you? Michelle needs help! No one heard me.

Hours later, I heard shuffling outside the door.

Hey, in here! We need help!

A knock. "Michelle?" A pause then another quick rap. "Michelle, are you in here?"

Yes, in here!

The door slowly opened. "Hey Michelle? Dinner is..." Father stopped when he saw his daughter laying on the floor, surrounded by the crimson puddle. He ran and knelt beside her. "Michelle? No Michelle!" He wailed. "What have I done?" He held his long gone daughter in his arms and cried.

I cried with him, but no one noticed.

When Father finally stopped crying, he looked at Michelle. "I am so sorry." He left the room and came back a few minutes later with something in his hand. He looked at me.

Father, what are you doing?

Crying again, he turned his back and knelt beside Michelle again.

There was suddenly a loud boom and something warm and wet splashed across me.

I screamed but no one heard.

For a long time, I hung on that wall and waited. Anger and bitterness surged through me. *Why?* was all I could ask.

After someone eventually found Michelle and Father, I was taken out of the room and put in various boxes and dark rooms. No one even cleaned me.

For months, I sat in a musty warehouse... waiting, seething, hating.

Finally someone walked by. "Justin, look at this." She knelt beside me. "I think this would look great in the restaurant."

"Yuck. It's a mess."

She picked me up. "We'll just clean it up, and it'll be good as new."

I scoffed. *Ha! That will never happen again.*

So here I hang, watching as you pass me by. Hating you; wondering why.

Summer Heat

Lawrence Salani

The sticky, heat had reached an oppressive height today. A lethargic, sickly feeling crept over Jason, the room was stifling and still the temperature continued to rise. He detested the hot weather because the heat always brought *them.*

Belinda, his girlfriend, had come to visit, but regrettably Jason had to ask her to leave because he hadn't been feeling well all afternoon.

"I'll call back again tomorrow and see if you feel better," she said as she walked towards the door, her short, colorful dress swaying to the movement of her hips.

He had known Belinda for a long time and had trusted her enough to give her a key to the house. Asking her to leave had been difficult, but the hot weather always affected him badly, and the pain he knew all too well was beginning again.

She turned and gave him one of her sexy smiles as she opened the door. "Get well soon and drink plenty of water," she laughed as she stepped into the dazzling sunlight outside, leaving him alone.

It must be at least 100 degrees out there, Jason thought to himself, as he looked out the window at the brightly lit gardens.

Drinking iced water had only resulted in making him feel bloated and now he simply wanted to lie down and sleep. The throbbing in his head was relentless and the small pain that formed in the space between his eyes was getting worse.

I have to lie down.

Making his way to the bedroom, Jason lay on the bed near an open window and looked up at the clear, blue sky. The blue was so deep, so bright; the sky had never been so cloudless and beautiful.

Occasionally, a sweetly scented zephyr, from the open window, would briefly caress his body. The fleeting coolness, perfumed by the flowers from the garden outside, left him longing for more.

"This damned heat," he whispered, looking at the swirling waves of steam rising from the green foliage outside. "When will it end?"

His skin felt sticky and uncomfortable, as he drifted in and out of sleep. He desperately needed to sleep, but the insidious headache and muggy atmosphere was keeping him awake.

As Jason looked into the bright, cerulean sky, his mind finally began to drift. It felt relaxing allowing his mind to float into the cool, deep blue. The blue slowly faded to grey then turned to darkness and he felt himself falling into the swirling, dark void. Floating in the empty space away from the burning heat felt amazing, and as he fell, memories drifted around him, like a gigantic, ravenous piranha circling about him ready to devour him and lead him into another nightmare. The intense heat had always led him into frightening dreams and he always woke up screaming.

He saw it in the distant darkness; at first it was intangible, but then it started to take shape. It *was* the darkness, but it had form. The form was not wholesome as normal things should be. It crawled on four legs, which resembled human arms and legs, but the sinewy, hairless body seemed more canine than human as it hid in the shadows. It was a travesty that should not exist.

Ripples of fear surged through Jason's body as he stared at its shadowed form, for he knew that it was aware of his presence, and as he looked, a long slit in its distorted, egg shaped head began to open exposing a row of pointed, razor sharp teeth. It moved out of the shadows toward him, allowing him to see the full horror of its shape. He fled screaming.

The brightness of the blue sky dazzled him when he awoke. Looking around the room, he realized that he had been dreaming again and he could feel sweat trickling down the sides of his body as he began to relax. The dreams were always the same; the thing would be waiting for him in the shadows and the sweltering heat only made the image seem more real, more potent.

Luckily, night was approaching and its arrival would bring slightly cooler temperatures. At least he hoped. The dreams were never as bad when the temperature dropped.

The re-occurring dreams had always been frightening, but the most disturbing had been when he encountered a group of four of the things beneath a twisted and blackened tree. The creatures had defiled a grave. The tombstone was lying on its side surrounded by mounds of dug up earth. Inside the dream, Jason kept hidden in the shadows to avoid detection from the monstrosities. Finally, curiosity got the better of him and he decided to edge closer to the group so that he could see better. What he saw made him recoil back into the shadows with terror. They were feeding upon the human corpse.

Jason watched as one of the creatures gnawed on a femur while the others stripped the flesh from the body. He felt safe hiding huddled amongst the shadows until one in the group sensed his presence and scurried towards him.

It came so close that he could smell its vile, carrion breath upon his face. He wanted to run, but could only fall to his hands and knees, as his stomach constricted. Vomit burned his esophagus.

The thing with the distorted, egg shaped head, its slit now closed, beckoned him to follow as it turned around and walked back to the group on its four legs; it had thought him to be of its kind.

His body shook as he neared the nightmare beings, but he needed to continue the pretence, he assumed failure would surely result in being eaten alive. So crawling on his hands and knees, Jason reluctantly joined the group.

The stench was gut wrenching while he sat amongst the creatures and watched them rip flesh from the torso and eat the putrid meat. Fear felt like a burning stone in his stomach, but the greatest horror came when the thing that had beckoned him to follow threw an arm that had been torn from the body towards him and waited for him to partake of the unholy feast.

In a mindless daze, he looked at the repulsive appendage that lay on the ground in front of him. Refusal meant death; nevertheless, he still procrastinated. What they were asking was inhuman and against everything he believed, but raising his eyes towards the thing that had led him there, he could see the slit in the faceless deformity slowly begin to open revealing a gaping hole surrounded by razor sharp teeth.

He silently prayed to his God for forgiveness as he looked down at the rotted arm. He reached for the limb trying to block out the sickening sounds of breaking bone and the tearing of flesh coming from the others. The dead flesh was cold to his touch and the revulsion was more than he could withstand, but he could wait no longer. He was being watched.

Lifting the cold, bluing arm, he closed his eyes as he bit into the flesh and tore a fragment of meat away. To keep himself from spitting out he tore at the flesh again, this time exposing the bone. Surprisingly, the flesh tasted sweet. He continued to masticate the human remains knowing it was the only way could he hope to escape, to live again.

The wild, unearthly feast had continued until the corpse before him was reduced to a broken skeleton. Afterwards they left him in his despair and disbelief, cringing in the darkness. The warm night breeze blowing through the silk curtains had finally startled him awake that night. The dream had been so vivid that night that it had remained in his consciousness even today. Mostly, he remembered the taste, the sweet taste.

Trying to dismiss the thought, Jason looked back out the window. The sun had finally set and the heat was not as intense as it had been during the day. Hopefully, he would be able to sleep soundly tonight. Usually they didn't come when the weather was more temperate.

The cool night passed peacefully and Jason was undisturbed by his nightmare visitors but the following morning, the radio announced news of a prolonged heat wave over the coming week. Looking at the morning sky, he could see the sun in the distance; a blazing, yellow ball on the horizon. Although it was still cool now, he knew that the midday sun would be intense and he needed to prepare himself for the oncoming heat.

As the morning progressed, he closed all the windows and blinds in an effort to keep the house cool, but as the sun slowly drifted across the sky, his precautions did little. The heat consistently rose inside the house and he suddenly sensed *their* presence within the darkened corners. They were hungry and in need of flesh. He could hear their scurrying movements throughout the house and he knew that soon the heat would become insufferable.

The midday heat proved to be more than he could endure; the pain had returned and he needed to lie down. When he returned to his bed, Jason felt slightly better inside the shadowy room, but for some reason could only think of the taste of human flesh. It was then that the thought became a craving.

The nightmare creatures crawled within the darkened corners of the room; their deformed faceless heads and muscular, hairless bodies moved in and out of the shadows as they waited for him to drift into the darkness once again.

They were hungry; he sensed their yearning, for their pain was now his. He needed to satisfy his hunger; to experience the sweet taste of flesh again.

A loud knock on the door echoed in an unearthly silence as he lay in the darkened room; his mind floating in the blackness.

After a short time the knock was repeated, startling him into wakefulness. He could hear movement then the rattle of keys before the door opened and someone entered the house.

The shadows moved eerily within his room.

"Hello." The voice was soft and feminine and suddenly realization dawned upon him as he lay within the dimly lit room.

As the door closed, the cry was repeated.

"Hello, Jason, where are you?"

They yearned for the soft flesh, for the yearning was now a searing pain in his stomach that only human meat could suppress.

He could now hear footsteps, as Belinda moved around the house searching for him until, finally, the footsteps stopped behind his bedroom door.

The knock on the door seemed to reverberate throughout the room and caused the creatures to move in anticipation within the shadows.

The pain grew intense and he could smell the warm flesh. The handle began to turn and then the first ray of light shone through the opening gap of the door. Her silhouette stood in the doorway, as she adjusted her eyes to look inside the dimly lit room.

"Are you alright?" she asked as she stepped into the room and cautiously made her way towards the bed where he was lying.

"Yes. I'm fine now," Jason said, sitting up on the bed and looking over her shoulder at something, crouched on four legs, that was moving towards the door.

A strange, scraping sound behind her caused Belinda to stop before she reached the bed where her boyfriend was seated. It was when she turned to see why the door was closing that the screaming started.

Tattered Notes Found in a Cheap Motel Room

Lee Clark Zumpe

THIS MORNING

Speeding north as the first traces of dawn bled into the horizon, Graham nervously glanced into his rearview mirror half-expecting to see something pursuing him.

He picked up a little piece of paper on the car seat.

The jumble of letters and symbols seemed completely unintelligible to him, now; he could not see their meaning—he could not imagine that they had ever been comprehensible.

LAST NIGHT

Graham slipped off the interstate just after dark, rolling down the slick exit ramp toward a blinking traffic light. The rain kept coming, cascading down from the solemn gray canopy that had blanketed the region all day—only night had obscured the grim swirling veil. Now, a heavy black shroud unfolded overhead, sending raindrops down to shimmer in street lamps and headlights.

He stopped first at a gas station. He stood beneath the awning covering the pumps as he filled his tank and watched his breath spill across the cold wind in diminutive gray wisps. Inside, he paid for the gas and picked up a bag of chips and a sandwich smothered in shrink-wrap.

"Where's the closest place to get a room for the night?"

The attendant swiveled on his stool, sipping coffee. The kid—young enough to still be in high school, with dirt beneath his fingernails and grease smeared across his jeans—seemed thoroughly shocked by the question.

"Well, I guess," he finally said, after struggling some

moments to form words. "You could go back under the overpass there and down about a mile—on the left is a motel that used to be one of them Vacation Inns 'til they went out of business."

"Is it open?" Graham leaned against the counter, hoping to glean a little more information. He noticed a number of men's magazines scattered across the floor behind the attendant.

"Yeah, somebody here local bought it and renamed it the Hillside Lodge."

"Great," Graham could not help but eye the covers of the magazines as he continued to talk. "I've been driving since four this morning and I think I've reached my limit for the day..." Trying not to be too obvious about it, Graham stared at the faceless women sheathed in leather or latex gracing the publications. He saw figures in black facemasks using strange and unfamiliar implements of torture—or pleasure. "Does this motel—the, er, Hillside Lodge—does it have pretty good service..." Among the magazines, he identified several disturbing names: *Bound and Beautiful, Pain Bliss,* and *Wicked Worship.* "I mean, you know, is it clean?"

"Clean as any little roadside motel I guess." The attendant lurched forward, gently setting his coffee down on the counter. His gaze pushed Graham backwards a few steps. "Anything else I can do for you, sir?"

The tone of his voice—the tint of his green eyes rattled Graham.

"No, no thanks. I'll go check the place out...thanks again."

Graham joined a dozen other cars parked in front of the Hillside Inn. The clerk welcomed him with a mild snarl.

"Need a room?"

"Yeah..."

"How many people?"

"Just one for one night..."

"Just one?"

"Yeah, just me," Graham said, somewhat agitatedly, "I'm

traveling alone…"

"Alright, sir, cash or…"

"Cash."

By the time he had settled into his room the rain had started coming down even harder. Graham could hear it washing through gutters outside, pouring into growing puddles in the parking lot. If it continued like this all night, he worried that the road might be flooded by morning.

For twenty dollars he had not expected luxury. A small, cramped room, sparsely furnished, reeking of cigarette smoke—though cheap and seedy, he found nothing so foul that it would keep him from sleeping.

He had been in worse places.

He sat on the edge of his bed nibbling at the sandwich and munching chips. He had nothing but water to drink—the vending machine at the motel stole a dollar in change before he noticed the "Do Not Use" sign resting on the damp floor.

The television offered only three channels—all local. Two of them promised to preach to him twenty-four hours a day and urged him to call for a prayer. The other station played nothing but fishing and hunting programs.

As he prepared for bed, he accidentally brushed his room key off of the nightstand and onto the floor. As he crouched down to retrieve it, something beneath the bed caught his eye. Graham got down on his knees and peered into the shadows beneath the mattress. It had been a while since anyone had taken the time to clean.

Among cobwebs and condom wrappers, Graham found several tattered sheets of notepaper covered with writing. At first, he thought it might have been a child's handy work: the scratches and scribbles seemed random and meaningless. Even where strings of words seemed to appear, he found only gibberish.

Oddly, the more he examined them, the more sense they made.

He began to find some kind of dark logic behind every squiggle line, significance in each eccentric character.

Sitting there on the floor in his room, the words suddenly began to lift off the aged paper:

"...what day it is...I have been here so long I am not sure anymore...they keep me here, chained to the wall, their prisoner and slave..."

Graham felt himself shudder involuntarily.

"...no light—how they do it I can't guess, keep me drugged during the day maybe; and rain all the time—they're always wet when they come here, and I can hear it pouring outside the boarded window..."

Graham absently shook his head, frowning. *Nothing*, he thought, *but a twisted practical joke. Nothing but a bad gag.*

Graham placed the notes on the nightstand and pulled himself off of the floor. He rubbed his eyes as he staggered across the room toward the television. As he reached for the power button, he noticed for the first time that the television was chained to the wall. Of course, motels commonly secured their property against their untrustworthy guests; Graham had seen it dozens of times.

It proved nothing.

"...tonight was the worst it has been so far—if they do it again, I don't think I can survive—I'm not sure I can make it even now...so much blood..."

Graham noticed a pair of headlights sweep across his drawn curtains.

"...doesn't matter what happens, they've taken everything away from me; I don't want to go on—not after all this, I can't face living with these memories; I don't even know who they are, even if I escaped, I could never identify them, I couldn't be sure they wouldn't come after me again—God, they're coming now, I hear them; 2:00 a.m., just like last night...they'll be wearing their black suits, they'll have their razors and their pinchers, and they'll tie me up until I can't move, can't breath, but they won't let me go back to sleep—they'll prick me and cut me and keep me awake with drugs until they're done with me, I wish they…"

Graham thought he heard a voice outside the door. Instinctively, he turned off the lights in the room. He crammed the notes into his pocket, and gathered his belongings. He dressed quickly, watching for shifting shadows outside the window—watching the door, waiting.

The clock winked at him from across the room.

2:00 a.m.

A key slipped into the lock, the doorknob wobbled.

Graham found his fingers winding around the face of the telephone.

"Hello?" Graham recognized the voice immediately. A flickering light outside in the hallway revealed the glaring green eyes of the gas station attendant.

Graham rushed at him, wrenching the telephone out of the wall. He caught him on the forehead with a crushing blow. The man virtually crumbled into a trembling mass and blood surged out of his skull and onto the carpet. Graham struck him three or four more times, until he stopped shaking, stopped breathing, stopped coughing. Only his fingers moved, wiggling like worms trying to dig down into the floor.

Graham dragged the man into the room, horrified but exultant. He had done only what he had to do to keep from suffering the same torture as the room's former lodger; he had saved himself—and perhaps others—from the depravities practiced by this lecherous degenerate.

Society would praise him as a hero.

Still—fearful of the investigation that would surely ensue— Graham abruptly decided to get back on the road. He did not need the attention, he shunned the spotlight; becoming a hero would only cause him grief. He would remain anonymous—just a faceless vigilante who registered under an assumed name at a roadside motel.

Graham left all but one page of the notes in the room; one he kept with him—a keepsake from his heroic deed.

THIS MORNING

Try as he might, Graham could not make any sense out of the marks scrawled across the face of the paper. Swerving in and out of traffic on the interstate, he tried desperately to reassure himself he had done the right thing—tried to find the haunting narrative that had convinced him to act as he had—but the voice that had spoken to him so clearly and zealously a few hours earlier had completely abandoned him now.

As more light fell across the tattered page, the scratches seemed less and less like words, and more like inarticulate stains and smudges…

…more like random spatters of blood.

Lunatic Mile

Barry Napier

A wail of pain swept so suddenly through the house that Rosetta nearly dropped the plate of roast beef that she was carrying to the table. She cut her eyes to the right, towards the hallway where the cry had come from. Frowning, she set the plate on the table next to the potatoes and carrots.

Her two grandchildren eyed the meal with mixed reactions.

Gabrielle, the youngest, wouldn't eat much of it but Rosetta kept hoping that the girl's appetite would eventually change. Gabrielle had a taste for flesh, but not of roast, steak or burger. On occasion, she would eat chicken, but it had to be freshly killed and raw. When her hunger pains grew too extreme, Gabrielle would gnaw at her own body. Several months ago, she had started with the pinky of her left hand. That hand now only contained a ring finger and the lower half of her thumb from which a small shard of brilliant white bone poked through.

There was a mangled portion of muscle on her upper arm where she had recently begun testing her palette on other areas.

Victor, her grandson, wasted little time with the roast, however. The boy was fourteen and weighed three hundred and twenty pounds. He sliced into the large roast, taking half of it and setting it onto his own plate where he picked it up with his hands and shoved it towards his mouth. He ate like a glutton, barely chewing the meat and swallowing it in chunks that nearly made him gag.

"Slow down," Rosetta muttered to him, rolling her eyes. She did not like resenting one of her grandchildren, but there were times when she found herself very close to hating the boy.

She pulled out her chair to take her place at the table, but the screaming sound came from down the hallway again. Rosetta sighed, smiled reassuringly to the children and got up from the table.

She walked down the hallway slowly, her old knees begging to sit down for a bit. She had been on her feet all day and her seventy-five-year-old frame was getting to the point where even standing for prolonged periods of time was a task.

She heard a light gasping coming from the room at the end of the hall, followed by a retching sound. As she neared the door, another resounding scream filled the house. It was a man's voice, but with this third scream it sounded more like the terrified yelps of a small child.

Rosetta opened the door. A rancid smell hit her right away, but it was one that she was used to. It was sweat, blood, decay and fecal matter. There was another smell, too. This one wasn't as recognizable as the others, but Rosetta assumed that it was simply the smell of death. It was a smell that she was well familiar with and she knew that it had a tendency to fill the air when death was imminent.

The room was lit only by two candles, one on each side of the room. In the candlelight, the screaming man looked as if he were already dead, an angry ghost haunting her house. His condition alone suggested he might be dead: a hole had been etched into his stomach and dried sheets of blood clung to the lower half of his body as well as the floor.

There was a mixture of emotion in his eyes that Rosetta had a hard time reading. She saw hope, despair, agony and a creeping lunacy that would soon take hold.

Seeing Rosetta, the man tried to back away but his naked body was already pinned against the wall. When he moved, the bloody gash in his stomach opened like a mouth and the folds of intestines that spilled out moved in an odd manner, like a worm that could not decide which way was forward and which way was backwards.

The strand of innards hung outward like an umbilical cord. Three feet of them had been uncoiled and straightened out like rope; the end of this loop had been crudely nailed to the wall.

When the man tried to shrink away, his exposed intestine tightened and then relaxed like a rubber band.

"Why…" was all he said.

"You mustn't keep screaming like that," Rosetta said calmly. "My family is trying to eat."

"Why…?" he croaked again.

"If I have to come back in here again, I'll take out your tongue."

She pictured Gabrielle with the man's tongue on her plate, next to the roast, and wondered if it would appease her. She then wondered how long it would be before the girl discovered that the muscle in her own mouth was very much capable of being bitten into. She also wondered if the girl would feast on this agonized man if given the chance. She supposed so. But despite her cravings, Gabrielle would not get to sink her teeth into this man. He was not here to satisfy their personal pleasures. He was to serve a greater purpose.

Rosetta stepped away, headed back for the door and saw a flickering sadness in the man's eyes. Even though she was his captor, he did not want to be alone. To be alone in his state was an invitation to madness; Rosetta could clearly see that he was about two tugs of the intestine away from falling into it.

She closed the door and rejoined the children at the dinner table.

Victor, the greedy little pig, had already started on the remaining portion of the roast.

Gabrielle's plate was still empty but she was eyeing the ring finger of her left hand with much interest.

***

Later, when the children were in bed, Rosetta walked out onto the back porch. She sat on the porch swing and stared out into the night. Her house sat alone in a small clearing in the forests of southern Virginia. Her nearest neighbor was six miles to the east in a similar clearing. Both houses were blocked off by the thickness of the woods to all sides.

Rosetta stared out to the tree line which stood against the dark sky like abstract mountains. The moon was nearly full, casting a sickly glow onto the yard. Somewhere in the distance, she heard a bobcat sounding out, its cry mingling with the constant chorus of whippoorwills, crickets and tree frogs.

Beside her sat an old scarred rocking chair. As she sat there listening to the night, the rocking chair began to rock by itself. It creaked on its ancient rockers and sounded slightly like the joints in her knees early in the morning.

She watched the chair rock back and forth, swaying gently. She studied the space around it, waiting for the form of a man to appear.

His face came first, his eyes as bright and distant as the stars. Then there was his mouth, always wide and smiling. By the time his torso was revealed, covered in simple black cloth, Rosetta could smell him. It was the clichéd smell of Hell—burning things, charcoal, smoke.

"Rosetta, my dear," he said. "How are you tonight?" As always, he was charming. His smile, his eyes, even the tone of his voice…it was all as well-designed as his legends proclaimed.

"As well as can be expected," she said. "My knees are aching. My back is getting weaker."

"Age is catching up to you, no doubt," the man in the rocker said.

"I suppose."

"And the children? How are they?"

Rosetta grunted and shrugged. “Gabrielle’s problem is getting worse. Soon I don’t think she’ll have a left hand remaining. She won’t eat proper food. I’ll catch her in the woods sometimes, eating rabbits, dead birds and squirrels. Victor…well, he’s doing just fine, I guess. But he keeps getting fat and he’s getting sloppy with the work.”

“Yes, I saw how he bound the man in your back room. Quite creative, but messy and unnecessary. We must work on that.”

Rosetta and her visitor sat in silence for a while, looking out to the forest. Rosetta cast a quick glance at him, amazed at how calm he made her feel. She knew what she was supposed to do later tonight and her body demanded that she refuse the work. There was no way that her body could go through it again. But by just looking at the man, she felt thirty years younger and her knees didn’t buckle at the thought of the night’s excursion. Even though she knew that he wasn’t *really* a man and most would fear him, she remained calm in his presence.

“Rosetta,” the man said. “Do you trust me? Surely after all of this time, you know that I am not *quite* the deceiver I am said to be.”

“I know that,” she said. “And yes, I trust you.”

“I will take care of your ailments,” he said. “And as far as your grandchildren, I will see to it that they are taken care of. Gabrielle in particular shows great promise. I will not let any harm come to her.”

Rosetta nodded, assured and disgusted all at once. Hadn’t he made similar promises when he suggested that the children’s parents be sacrificed? Her memories of their father—her own son—nailed to that large oak tree in the back yard were as clear as if it had occurred yesterday. She could still see him bleeding and screaming in the moonlight as the forest below seemed to reach out for him.

"Tonight's task," the man said, "will be hard on you, no doubt. But you must do it, Rosetta. And after it is done, I will heal you."

"Yes sir." She wanted desperately to ask him: *If you're so damned powerful, why must you rely on an old woman to do your work?*

But of course she kept this thought to herself. And even if she had have found the courage to voice it, the rocking chair was empty once again as soon as the thought crossed her mind.

It rocked briefly for two more seconds and was still again.

Rosetta remained outside for another half an hour. When she got up from the swing, there was a brief moment where she was confident that her knees felt stronger, that the aches and pains that had assaulted them for the last year or so had retreated in the presence of her visitor.

But by the time she was back inside, the aches were there again and she felt the true nature of her age upon her.

She sat in her bedroom alone, reading a book. On one occasion, she heard the man screaming from the other end of the house. She thought about going to him and fulfilling her earlier threat of removing his tongue.

But she didn't let it bother her. It would be over for him soon enough. Until then, she would do the proper thing and allow him his last few moments to reflect on the life he'd be leaving and, like all other men that had ever lived, had surely took for granted.

And then she would take him for a walk down Lunatic Mile.

***

When the time came, Rosetta returned to the room at the end of the hall. As she approached the door, she could hear the man muttering something inside. From what Rosetta could tell, he believed that he was talking to a woman named Monica, asking her why she had let the dog in the house.

When she entered the room, the man stared at her with incomprehension. He wasn't sure where he was, nor what had happened to him. He had been somewhere else, within some other memory that his poor brain had summoned up to take him away from the reality of what had happened to him.

Keeping her eyes on him, Rosetta walked to the far end of the room where a small cabinet clung loosely to the wall. She opened it and reached inside, bringing out a small tin. She opened the tin and the latches groaned. Inside were several brown pills.

Rosetta took one of the pills out of the tin and carried it to the man. She reached out, grabbed his earlobe between her fingernails and pinched hard. When he didn't scream, she pinched even harder. When she felt his blood on her fingers, she pulled down violently. There was a quick tearing sound as she tore his earlobe off.

Finally, he screamed. When he opened his mouth, Rosetta shoved the pill in. She kept his mouth covered with her left hand and coaxed his throat muscles with her right. She did this until she was confident that he had swallowed the pill.

"Who are you?" the man asked.
"What…happened…Where am…I?"

Rosetta only waved a hand at him. She went back to the cabinet and withdrew an old knife, its blade stained and slightly crooked. She approached him slowly, amused at the expression on his face. He clearly realized that she meant him harm, yet that dazed state still possessed him and he studied her with befuddled interest.

With a single motion, Rosetta sliced through the crude internal rope that had kept the man attached to the wall. A dull unpleasant smell escaped the severed gut as it collapsed back against its owner.

He opened his mouth to gasp but his jaw simply hung open, as if awaiting food. He narrowed his eyes at her and began to sob.

Testing him, she beckoned him forward. "Come," she said.

He nodded slowly and stepped forward, clumsily collecting his spilled insides as he approached. He obeyed her without question; the pill had already started working.

She led him through the house and onto the back porch. As she made her way down the stairs and into the yard, the man fell to his knees on the porch and collapsed face first down the stairs. He let out a groan and tried to get to his feet.

"Move it," Rosetta said.

He managed to get to one knee. There was grass on his face and his bottom lip was busted open. He looked around the yard and then to the gash in his stomach where he continued to spill out. He looked to Rosetta, frowned, and then fell again.

"Why must this be so difficult?" she asked the night, envisioning the man that had occupied her rocking chair as she spoke. "Once upon a time, this used to be easy, you know?"

She approached the man's body and gave him a swift kick in the ribs, letting out some of her frustration. Sneering at him, she walked to the far edge of the yard where a small shed sat hidden in the shadows. Victor spent a lot of his spare time in that shed, studying tools, blades and experimenting with animals. Such experiments had taught him anatomy and, Rosetta assumed, had inspired him to bind their current captor in such a unique way. The little fool probably thought he was being clever.

In the shed, she looked past Victor's mess and located the wheelbarrow in the far corner. She pulled it out of the shed and wheeled it across the yard to where the man was once again trying to get to his feet.

"Don't bother," she said angrily.

She bent down and lifted him up by his underarms. When she heaved him forward so that he could fall partially into the wheelbarrow, she felt something in her back give. She cried out in pain and once again struck the man to relieve her anger.

With much grunting and cursing, she eventually had him in the wheelbarrow. His left leg hung out and his head bobbed lifelessly over the back of it, between the handles.

Rosetta lifted the handles and aimed the wheelbarrow for the forest. A thin footpath sat at the furthest edge of the yard, winding its way into the darkness of the woods. She followed this path as she had done countless times before and instantly felt the evil of the place caress her.

***

Long ago, when men had been wise enough to revere evil, the stretch of land that the path wound through had been called Lunatic Mile.

Hunters would accidentally venture onto the grounds and return home with emptiness in their eyes and violence in their hearts. Unfortunate hikers that found the land would forever be plagued with nightmares beyond their darkest imaginings. Even animals were affected by it. Birds that flew by fell dead to the ground. Rabbits and squirrels that passed by it would get a taste for blood and turn to their own kind for food.

Even by coming near Lunatic Mile, one could feel some *wrongness* in the air.

Rosetta knew this well and she felt it creeping over her right away. She knew that the Mile did not start at the very beginning of the trail in her back yard. The true start of Lunatic Mile came in the form of two black stones sitting to either side of the trail.

She saw these now, glinting darkly in the moonlight. As she passed by them, she closed her eyes and could feel the world in which she lived begin to slip away.

Even the man in the wheelbarrow groaned. He tried to lift his head but was far too weak. He had lost too much blood and his trauma had been too great. He would open his mouth on occasion and mumble something about Monica.

After passing the stones and stepping onto Lunatic Mile, the chants of crickets and whippoorwills thinned out. The noises that remained of those creatures now sounded wavering and fragmented, nothing more than fearful sighs in the night.

Rosetta had to stop several times along the way. Once, a bump in the trail had jostled the man she carried and his freed intestines went spilling over the side in a heap. She tossed them back into the wheelbarrow in a messy tangle of knots.

Mainly though, her stopping was due to the pains of her body. Her calves felt as if they were on fire and the muscles in her upper arm were as stiff as boards from carrying the wheelbarrow upright.

But she knew that soon it would all go away. Because even though her frequent visitor—whom always smelled of smoke and fancied her rocking chair—was a shameless bastard, he *did* keep his promises. He would mend her pains, would make sure that her family was safe. He would do all of those things so long as she kept the power flowing through this place.

As she went on, she saw several dark shapes crossing the path in front of her. These were usually creatures no larger than a cat, but every now and then she would hear something much larger romping through the woods close to the edge of the trail. She knew that she was being watched. She could feel hundreds of evil eyes on her, their stares like spears of hate.

She did her best to keep track of how far along the Mile she had walked. This was hard to do because along Lunatic Mile, time seemed to become its own creature. Time and space held no relevance here. The Mile was just a physical manifestation of evil that had seeped from Hell onto the earth.

Her dark visitor had never given her any real reason for the powers of this place. He had once indicated that there are spots within the makeup of things where a world's boundaries are worn thin. In such places, two worlds can overlap. It just so happened that Lunatic Mile was a straight stretch of Hell with worldly features to support it.

Or so he said. She often wondered if he told her such foolishness to make her feel as if she were important to him. He was, after all, the most famous liar in the history of the world. Her Baptist upbringing had taught her that. But she had found later in life that once you got to know him, the Devil wasn't so bad.

Her thoughts were broken by sudden movement to her right. Beside her, a figure appeared out of nowhere. It seemed as if the shape had simply materialized out of nothing. Rosetta jumped and nearly shrieked when she saw the figure and then, realizing what she was seeing, rolled her eyes and kept walking.

The figure beside her was the ghost of her former self. It was like looking in a mirror that showed reflections from fifty years ago.

"Remember when we looked like this?" her younger self said.

"Hardly."

"Don't you miss these breasts? Don't you miss the feel of a man's hands on your body?"

At this, the man in the wheelbarrow groaned.

"Fuck off," Rosetta said sternly.

As if on command, the younger reflection did just that. Instead of just winking out though, the form decayed rapidly. Her skin fell away, the tissue beneath rotting too fast to be studied. The skeleton beneath it all seemed contorted somehow; the collarbones were too large and the ribs were exaggerated puzzle pieces. The skeletal shape screamed at her and was then sucked backwards into the darkness of the Mile.

From somewhere further off, another scream filled the night. This one was from the throat of something large and bestial. She could imagine it coming from the throat of the world, an agonizing scream as if it had just discovered the impurity of Lunatic Mile upon its otherwise unblemished face.

To her right, something that sounded almost like a little girl chuckled. Further ahead, something large passed by and temporarily blocked out the light of the moon. Its footsteps filled her aging frame like thunder.

She continued on, knowing that nothing here would harm her. Her visitor would keep her safe as long as she was doing his work.

After another five minutes, she came to her destination. The trail came to an abrupt end and fell into a chasm that was about ten feet wide. Although she had been here more times than she cared to remember and had peered into that chasm each time, she had no idea how deep it was.

"Up you go," she said to her cargo as she positioned the wheelbarrow at the edge of the pit.

"Yeah, Monica never did like that car," he said. "It smelled like mildew ever since that night you left the windows down during that storm."

Rosetta paid no attention to this. She hefted the wheelbarrow upwards and sent him flailing forward. She felt her knees try to give out on her and there was a loud pop in her shoulder. She whimpered in pain and gave one final shove.

As the man fell out, his knee hit the ground first and he had a fleeting second to peer into what awaited him.

"Dark," he said. "Cold…stupid car…Monicaaaaaaa…."

She watched him fall away into the dark, his entrails flowing out behind him in glistening rivulets. He did not scream or complain. He just fell and fell. She watched him, listening for the sound of impact, but she never heard it. She watched the darkness swallow him and sighed wearily.

She then turned around and headed back home, pushing the wheelbarrow along with her.

She heard ungodly cries in the darkness but ignored them. She kept her eyes ahead on the path, on what she knew was real.

At one point something cold and slimy slithered over her forehead like a living spider web. But she looked beyond this and thought of the relief that she had been promised. But, God did her legs hurt. And her right shoulder felt as if glass shards had been inserted into her joints.

But when she passed the two black stones, her knees felt like new and her shoulder felt as loose and flexible as ever.

She carried the wheelbarrow back up into the yard with a slight bounce in her step.

***

She returned the wheelbarrow to the shed and walked up the porch steps with a vigor that she had not experienced in nearly ten years. Behind her, the night crept slowly away from the approaching dawn.

She entered the house and walked into the kitchen to put on a cup of coffee. As she entered the room, what she saw froze her in place. She let out a mangled squeak of disgust and fell to her newly revitalized knees.

Victor lay naked in the floor, surrounded by an expanding pool of blood. Sitting atop him, straddling the immense bulk of his stomach, was Gabrielle. Her hands and face were streaked in blood. In her right hand she held an unidentifiable bloody chunk of meat.

At Victor's feet, Rosetta saw the small tin from the back room. It had been opened and a few of the brown pills were scattered on the floor.

Rosetta's eyes were glued to this horror but she was still very much aware of the third person in the room. He sat at the table, watching Gabrielle's work with amusement. He looked horribly out of place within her house rather than on the porch, in the rocking chair. When he smiled at her, she smelled smoke.

"What…is…this?" Rosetta asked. She didn't know if she was asking her visitor or Gabrielle.

"This," the visitor said, getting to his feet, "is your reward."

She could not look away from the children. There were bite marks all over Victor's body. Whole sections of his enormous stomach looked as if they had been flayed and torn into. Every toe on his left foot had been stripped down to the bone.

"This is no reward," she said.

"Do you not see Gabrielle's left hand?" he asked.

Rosetta looked to the girl and saw that her left hand was somehow whole again.

Not only that, but Rosetta realized that there was something else new about Gabrielle. She looked absolutely beautiful…past the blood and the emphasized chewing motions, she looked gorgeous. Rosetta saw the woman that the child would become and it pained her to know that she would forever be entwined with the visitor, his work and Lunatic Mile.

"I told you that I would take care of your family," he went on. "While it may hurt you to admit it, we both know that Victor was a disappointment."

"But…" She could say nothing else. She was aware that he knew her every thought, so it was useless to refute this point.

"This way we can focus our attention on Gabrielle," he went on. "And while I know your human nature is to grieve your grandson, at least he will meet his end by helping with our work. You and Gabrielle are to take him down Lunatic Mile."

"But why Victor?" she asked. "Why not some random person like we've always done?"

"It takes sacrifice," he said. "You needed to give a sign that you are willing to cooperate with the great work that is yet to come."

"What work?" There was scorn and doubt in her voice and for a moment, she feared that her tone would anger him.

But he only grinned to her. "Why settle on just that small path?" he asked. "Why just that one mile? Why not the whole forest? Why not this entire county?"

She knew that she had no choice. She looked away from the children, taking a seat at the table with the man that had owned her for most of her life.

Rosetta said nothing. The kitchen was quiet except for the wet tearing sounds of Gabrielle tearing into Victor's neck.

"Gabrielle, dear," she said softly.

The girl looked up from her meal, glancing towards her grandmother. "Yes?" she said, blood trickling down her chin.

"Would you go get the wheelbarrow, please?"

Rache

Kendra Lisum

When Tommy was six years old, his parents put the family dog to sleep. Tommy's father explained that Jiffy was old and that he was no longer happy, which Tommy didn't understand because Jiffy had always seemed happy, especially when the family returned after being away.

Two days after Jiffy was gone, Tommy was in bed. His parents had already gone to sleep, and the sound machine next to his sister's bed was cricketing softly.

"Tommy," a voice said in the darkness.

Tommy sat up and looked around. Jiffy was standing next to his bed. The old dog looked the same as Tommy remembered: cloudy eyes, gray wiry fur, and withered back legs that could no longer support the dog's weight.

"I thought you were gone," Tommy said.

Jiffy said, "How can I be gone when I am standing right here?"

Tommy considered. Then, "Are you having trouble sleeping? Do you want to borrow Lisa's sound machine?"

The dog shook its head.

"Where's your collar?"

"It's on the counter where your mom put it."

"Oh. Are you gonna eat me?"

"No. I'm gonna take your eyes."

"My eyes?"

"Yes."

"But, how will I see?"

The sound machine clicked and waves splashed against an absent shore.

Jiffy looked at him through cataract eyes. "You can have them back when you find me."

"Where are you going?"

"Away."

"Heaven?"

Jiffy shook his head.

"Mom said the vet buried you. Will you give me back my eyes if I go to the place he put you?"

"That's not where I'll be."

"Then where?"

"If I told you," Jiffy said, "You would not get your eyes back."

"What if I don't give them to you?"

"Then I will take them."

Tommy glanced at his sister across the room. She was curled up against the wall, her pillow bunched beneath her head. Ghostly birds called over the roar of the waves.

"Are you gonna take Lisa's eyes too?" he asked.

"I only need one pair of eyes."

"So if I give you mine, you won't hurt Lisa?"

Jiffy shook his head.

Tommy chewed his bottom lip. He looked at his sister, then at his old, dead dog.

"Okay," he said.

The next morning, Tommy's mother screamed when she saw Tommy's eyes—gouged and blackened and dripping red. The ambulance came and took Tommy to the emergency room. Tommy tried to explain to his mom and the doctor that Jiffy had his eyes and that he would get them back when he found Jiffy. But no one listened. Instead, they said things like "How could he do that to himself?" or "He keeps talking about his dead dog," as if Tommy wasn't even in the room. Tommy heard his mother crying and his father, who Tommy knew was there because of his smell, said nothing.

Tommy was in the hospital for a long time, learning to do things without his eyes, which meant Lisa had to sleep in their room by herself. It scared her, not to have Tommy there, but her father assured her that she was safe, kissed her forehead, and clicked on the sound machine to a babbling brook.

It had cycled through its recordings once before Lisa startled awake to someone calling her name. She squinted into the darkness.

"Who's there?" she whispered.

"It's me," said the voice. "Jiffy."

Lisa looked over the side of her bed to where Jiffy stood, looking at her through Tommy's eyes.

"You have Tommy's eyes," she said.

"Yes, and I need your legs."

Lisa curled her legs to her chest. "Why?"

Jiffy didn't say anything. The babbling brook chuckled merrily.

"You made mom cry when she saw Tommy didn't have eyes anymore," Lisa said.

"Tommy can have his eyes back when he finds me."

"When will that be?"

Jiffy licked her nose. His breath smelled like the ground beef her mother had forgotten in the car last summer.

"Can I have my legs back when he finds you?"

"No," Jiffy said. "You'll have to find me for yourself."

"I don't want you to have my legs," she said. "I need them."

Jiffy looked at her. Tommy's eyes didn't quite fit, they bulged and never blinked.

"Okay," he said, almost a sigh, and lunged.

***

No one knew what happened to the little Dietrich girl. She vanished one night not long after her brother was found blind and bloodied. The police cordoned off the home and a search was conducted but nothing was ever found.

Upon returning home after his hospital stay, the boy Deitrich, when he did not have hands upon him or was otherwise unbound, would escape through the neighborhood, hands outstretched before him, calling wildly for his dead dog. One night he was taken in a rental car to St Mary's Asylum, and the next week his parents moved away, and soon after everyone forgot about the Dietrichs.

If they had not forgotten, however, they might have understood why, on occasion, the image of a dog with protruding eyes and a small girl, no older than five, would appear in the shadows, the girl watching wistfully in the distance always trying to catch the dog who danced about on human legs.

The Intersection

Brendan P. Myers

Foley opened one eye and saw it was just after one thirty in the morning. He heard sirens in the distance. Reaching out, he turned on his bedside lamp before placing his hand on the phone, lifting it after the first ring.

"There's been another one," Jaworski said.

Foley looked down. He'd fallen asleep in his clothes.

"Be there in five," he answered.

Getting out of bed, he threw on his jacket and drove to Upham's Corner. He arrived upon a familiar scene.

Flashing lights from emergency vehicles lit the intersection a jaundiced yellow and rose red. In the middle of the intersection, a compact car was jammed beneath an eighteen-wheeler. Firefighters bent low beneath the truck preparing the Jaws of Life while EMTs hovered nearby with gurneys.

When Jaworski approached, the two men nodded grimly to each other before the sergeant began to speak.

"Driver's dead," he began. "Young girl. Twenty or so. Two male occupants in bad shape but look to be alive." He paused before adding, "We hear groans anyway."

"What's the truck driver say?" Foley asked.

The sergeant glanced down at his notebook. "The usual. Claims he had the green. Car blew through the light."

"Any evidence of alcohol?" Foley asked.

"Nothing obvious," Jaworski replied. "Truck driver blew clean. Even volunteered to have his blood taken."

Their conversation was interrupted by the chainsaw sound of the Jaws of Life, followed by sounds of breaking glass and crunching steel. When the machine stopped, a brief stillness overtook the scene, until the moans from inside the car began to fill the air. Foley nodded to his sergeant and let him get back to work.

Foley had done his own share of scraping people off this asphalt. He had watched this scene enacted dozens of times before. This night, he only stuck around long enough to watch the injured be removed from the vehicle before heading home to a fitful sleep.

* * *

The next morning, Foley pulled into a parking lot across from the intersection to sip his coffee and watch traffic pass. Mourners had already placed flowers on the stone wall abutting the intersection and a framed photo of a young girl.

The intersection of Bynum and Chambers was the most dangerous in town, often listed as the most dangerous in the state. Over the years, highway engineers had been called in. The road was widened and regraded. Vegetation cut back. Blind spots removed. But the accidents continued.

Only after a horrific crash seven years ago killed a mother and her infant son were lights finally installed. And still the accidents continued. If anything, Foley thought, they'd gotten worse. And from where he sat, sipping his coffee and watching the cars go by, none of it made any sense.

Of the two streets, Bynum was the more major thoroughfare, though it was mostly residential and not heavily traveled. Chambers was residential too, but often used as a cut through from the state highway just down the road. Maybe that had something to do with it, he thought.

A long abandoned rail bed ran parallel to Chambers, visible now only as a low depression by the side of the road. Normal looking houses occupied three corners of the intersection. A non-denominational church the fourth. The sign out front today read: *"God Asks: Have you hugged your child today?"*

Foley glanced at the framed photo of the young girl and thought that was damned good advice. He poured the last of his coffee out the window before starting up his car.

At his desk, Foley saw lights blinking on his phone and decided to ignore them for now. Accidents at Upham's Corner were always followed by residents calling to ask what more could be done. Twenty years on the force and three years as chief had brought no good answer to that question.

On his desk was the manila folder he knew would be waiting for him. The preliminary report from last night's accident. Opening it, he began reading the dry facts of the case.

The girl's name was Marcia Wallace. She was twenty-one, a sophomore at the local college who had been driving friends home from a party. There was no evidence she'd been drinking. Her driving record was clean. Though further tests would be taken, the stoplight was in working order.

The truck was making its weekly overnight run to the supermarket. The driver had been making the run for more than ten years without incident. He too had a squeaky clean record. Results of blood tests were pending. The injured passengers were expected to survive.

Moments after closing the folder, his phone rang. "Foley," he answered gruffly, hoping to forestall a long conversation with whoever it might be.

"Chief Foley? Is that you?"

Foley didn't recognize the voice. "Speaking," he said.

"Marvelous! Chief, you don't know me, but my name is McPhee. Dale McPhee. Perhaps you've heard of me?"

Foley drew a blank. "I'm sorry," he answered.

"That's alright," the man replied cheerily. "Not everyone has. Anyway, I live here in town, over in Brookdale, and I've written a number of books about the town and its history."

The man paused as if that might jog Foley's memory. When it didn't seem to, he went on. "The reason I'm calling is . . . well . . . I understand there was another accident last night."

Foley's eyes narrowed. "Mr. McPhee . . ." he began, not

sure where the conversation was headed.

"Please, hear me out. Believe me, I wouldn't bother you unless I felt it absolutely necessary. Do you have a few minutes to meet with me today? Say, two o'clock at the diner? I have some information you are sure to find fascinating."

Foley took a deep breath. "Mr. McPhee, as you can imagine, I have lots of . . ."

"Chief," the man interrupted. "Trust me on this. You need to hear what I have to say. I'll see you today at two." The man hung up.

Foley held the phone to his ear another moment before putting it in its cradle and leaning back in his chair. He looked at the manila folder, curiosity piqued. He reached for his keyboard and typed in a search for Dr. Dale McPhee.

It didn't take long to figure out that his dozen or so books were geared mostly to the tinfoil hat crowd, investigations into UFO sightings, strange hauntings, prehistoric beasts, and the like. A few sites had photos of the bow-tied and grey-bearded author smiling into the camera. Sighing, Foley closed his browser and went back to work.

***

After finishing hours of the usual paperwork, he leaned back in his chair and took a long stretch before glancing at the clock. It was ten minutes to two. His stomach rumbled.

What the hell, he thought, *couldn't hurt.*

* * *

Sitting alone in a corner booth, the bow-tied man was easy to find. When Foley approached and introduced himself, McPhee smiled widely, revealing bone white dentures contrasting starkly with his healthy, ruddy complexion.

His brown suit was adorned with wisps of dandruff. He wore his longish gray hair pulled back behind his ears. And despite his initial hesitation, Foley found lunch with the author surprisingly pleasant.

Mentioning he'd looked him up on the web, Foley said that McPhee's work looked "interesting." McPhee just smiled.

"Now, Chief. You of all people know we have to keep an open mind on things. Examine all possibilities before arriving at some version of the truth. Isn't that what police work is all about?" Foley couldn't argue with the statement.

While they ate, McPhee told stories about sonic booms in Maine and ghostly apparitions at the Mount Washington Hotel. He had investigated sightings of a pterodactyl-like creature in the western part of the state and found nothing. But the jury was still out on a Bigfoot-like creature rumored to roam the woods of this very town.

As he spoke, Foley noticed a stack of paperwork sitting on the booth beside the author but said nothing, figuring they'd be brought up in time. But by the time they finished their pie and ice cream, he was wondering if the man had any information at all. He pushed away his plate to signal he was preparing to leave, but before he could make a clean getaway, McPhee asked him a question.

"You ever hear of the Pequot Wars, Chief?"

Foley shook his head, knowing only that the Pequot were a local Indian tribe who had long ago vanished.

"Fascinating bit of history," McPhee said. "In fact, this town encompasses one of the Pequot's largest known settlements. Alas, it was destroyed in 1637 by an alliance of Puritans and Mohegans. Together, they burned the village to the ground. And of the two hundred Indians in the village at the time, mostly women and children, by the way, only seven managed to escape."

Foley sat back, waiting to see where this went.

McPhee pushed his now empty pie plate to the side, then reached for the stack of paperwork beside him and lifted it onto the table.

"Now, Chief, you may think what you are about to hear are just the ravings of an old man." He glanced over at Foley and winked. "And maybe they are."

Foley smiled and looked down. He'd been thinking exactly that.

"But before you jump to hasty conclusions," McPhee continued, "I ask only that you hear me out, and try to keep an open mind." Reaching into a folder, he brought out a series of black and white photos and placed them lengthwise on the table. "Now, let's start with these."

Looking down, Foley saw that the first photo was of a railroad station. The word "Chambers" was carved on an elegant wooden plaque above the door. McPhee waited for Foley to take that in before uncovering the next. It was of the same station, taken later and from a further distance, at a place where two roads crossed. In this photo, two gargantuan locomotives belched steam in front of the station, while well-dressed ladies in long skirts and fashionable hats disembarked the train. Only then did Foley comprehend what he was looking at.

It had shifted a little, changed over the years. The tiny saplings in the photo were mammoth trees now. But there was no doubt about it. It was the intersection.

It became clear then too that the railroad station once stood on the same corner where the church stands now, where he'd sat only this morning drinking coffee and watching traffic pass by. Satisfied that Foley understood, McPhee set the photo aside.

The next and last photos were taken from a similar angle, showing a group of grim faced, tired looking men in overalls posed in front of what looked like two stories of wrecked metal and twisted steel. The station was gone. Most of it anyway. You could still see a floorboard here and there. Scorched sections of a rear wall. But the rest had been reduced to cinders.

"The Wreck of the Old Colony," McPhee said sadly. "It ran between Providence and Boston three times a day. The bottom there is what was left of the passenger train. A freight came through moving too fast and derailed. Leaped from its tracks and landed on the passenger train."

McPhee paused before going on.

"July 14th, 1912. Ninety-eight people died that day, forty of them schoolchildren on their way to a summer outing."

He let that photo rest awhile before gathering them all up and putting them back in their folder. He then reached into another and brought out a stack of yellowed newspaper clippings. "Have a look at these, Chief," he said.

The first clipping was dated February 8, 1955. It related the story of a home explosion at 212 Chambers that killed a woman and her two children.

The next was dated March 14, 1952. A school bus crash that killed twelve. Faulty brakes were suspected.

The next was dated August 23, 1959. A late-night altercation that left three men dead.

The next was dated June 29, 1966. The disappearance of a toddler from his backyard. The mother said she turned her back for only a second. The boy was found the next morning in a nearby creek.

There were dozens more. Foley simply flipped through the rest before setting them aside. "So what the hell is this about?" he said, having seen enough.

Foley watched as McPhee seemed to weigh something in his mind. He removed a large, folded piece of paper from the stack and began unfolding it. Looking down, Foley saw it was a topographical map of some sort, showing woods and ponds and brooks and fields. Red lines and black spots as well as various numbers ran across its surface.

"Chief, this isn't easy for me. I told you on the phone I wouldn't have bothered you if I didn't believe it was important. Recall I also shared with you my belief there are some things that can be proven and some that can't. I shared those stories with you for a reason. Do you understand?"

It took a moment, but Foley nodded.

"Good. Because contrary to what my wife might have you believe, I'm not a total nutcase." McPhee smiled. Foley smiled back.

Then McPhee turned serious. "Do you want to go on with this? We can stop right now, if you like. Go our separate ways. No harm, no foul. You can chalk it up to the lunatic ravings of an old man." He stopped to catch Foley's eye. "Do you want to go on with this, Chief?" he asked again.

Foley looked away, unable to hold the old man's gaze. The truth was, he very much wanted to leave. But a small part of him felt there might be something here.

It couldn't all be a coincidence, he thought, then nodded.

"Okay, then. Now, Chief, here is where we are now," he began, pointing to a spot on the map to the north. "Main Street runs east-to-west this way. And here's the right turn onto Bynum. You with me so far?"

Foley nodded.

"Now, let's continue down Bynum," McPhee went on, dragging his pen across the map. "Here's Andy's Food Mart . . . and here's the elementary school . . ."

He moved his pen deeper into the wooded area, tracing the path of the modern-day Bynum Road, moving closer to the areas marked by black spots and intersecting red lines. Foley knew they were nearing the intersection, but something was wrong.

Something that shouldn't be there.

"Wait . . . that's not right," he said.

McPhee looked up and smiled. "They moved it, Chief. Moved the whole bloody river sometime after the Civil War. Dammed it thirty miles upstream."

Looking down at the map again, he slowly moved his pen down Bynum Road, toward the cluster of black marks, stopping at the U-shaped bank of a river that was no longer there.

"And here, right where you'd expect it to be, on the banks of a rushing river, was the Indian village itself." He paused a moment to let Foley digest this before going on. "Few accounts of the attack survive, of course, but what we can piece together is that the Puritans and their allies approached the village from the south and surrounded it, here."

He pointed to a semicircle of red dashes against the river itself, then moved his pen across the river to another semicircle outlined in red on the far bank.

"And here is where their Mohegan allies lay in wait for anyone attempting to escape across the river. Dozens were cut down as they tried to cross."

He waited another moment before taking his pen to the map and completing the circle. Foley watched as it encompassed and fully encircled the cluster of black marks, realizing only then what they were. Places where trains derailed. Where buses lost their brakes and toddlers disappeared and trucks crushed cars.
Taking his pen, he drew a line from one end of the circle to the other, then drew another line across it making an "X". He put his pen down in the center of the circle, at the place where the two lines crossed. "And this, Chief, is our intersection."

Foley just stared.

After a few moments more, McPhee withdrew his pen and folded the map, placing it neatly back in its folder. With that done, he stacked all his folders neatly on the table and waited.

"What do we do?" Foley asked.

He could no longer deny that there was something to what the old man said. And while he sat there waiting for his answer, he realized that all along he knew it was true. It was why he'd left orders to be alerted any time there was an incident at the intersection. It was why reports from those incidents were to be on his desk first thing in the morning.

It was why he always made his way back to the intersection, if only to spend a few minutes wondering just what the hell was wrong with the place.

He glanced over at McPhee, who now appeared to be

having trouble putting thoughts into words. "I don't know what to tell you, Chief. Maybe you think because of my background, or what I do, that I have some answers." He looked up and smiled without mirth. "I'm going to let you in on a secret. Ninety-nine percent of what I do is crap. Pure crap. But I do have a talent with words. I can make the mundane sound mysterious, the pedestrian, supernatural, and the everyday, well... just plain weird. And you know what? People eat it up. There's an insatiable appetite for the stuff. Who knows why? Maybe it allows them an escape from their own boring lives. Or maybe it allows them to forget the real horrors. The everyday horrors..."

He looked over to catch Foley's eye before continuing.

"Like car crashes. And plane crashes. And missing children. That's why I'll never write about this. Never attempt to make money on it or otherwise seek personal gain. Because this is real! Those people are real! And I tell you, it has taken many years to put together what I've shown you today and I don't know what to make of it either. Who can tell? Maybe the Indians are taking their revenge, reaching out across time to wreak the same havoc that was so unmercifully wrought upon them. Or maybe there's a kind of magnetic force at work, something cosmic or quantum that we don't yet understand. Maybe it's a portal to another world or another dimension, something akin to a black hole. But you know what I think, Chief? What I truly think? What sixty-seven years on this Earth has taught me?" He paused a moment to again catch Foley's eye. "Some places are bad, Chief. Just plain bad. They are to be avoided at all costs."

He sat there a moment more, before grabbing hold of his papers and bum-shuffling his way out of the booth. He stood for only a moment to look down at Foley before nodding once.

"Thanks for lunch, Chief. We'll see you again."

Foley shouted as he walked away, "What do we do?" A few of the late afternoon diners stopped and turned their heads, looking at him with embarrassment before turning back to their meals. McPhee stopped halfway to the door and turned around. When he did, he looked to Foley nothing like the kindly professor who smiled back at him from the websites earlier that morning. He looked now like just another stooped old man, who for some reason carried a heavy burden of paperwork that made stand lopsided.

But he also looked like a man who had seen too much of the world, one who knew that at sixty-seven years of age, it wouldn't be long before the answers to these and all other mysteries of this world and the next would be revealed. He paused only another moment before shouting back his answer.

"Move the road, Chief. It's the only way." And then, he was gone.

* * *

For Foley, what followed was a week of fitful sleep and waking nightmares. He hardly ate and barely slept. In his waking hours, he found himself more and more drawn to the intersection, spending most of his free time there, sipping coffee and waiting for…something.

He knew intellectually there was nothing he could do about it. For him to even discuss what he'd learned from the old man, let alone tell anyone who might believe it, was a ticket out of office, or worse.

Still, he found himself cringing watching school buses pass by, almost getting out of his car when neighborhood kids crossed the street, especially when one traveled alone. He was once jarred out of a much needed slumber by a squeal of brakes, not daring to open his eyes until he was certain it wouldn't be followed by the sounds of crunching steel, and later, desperate moans. And on a subconscious level while at the intersection, he found himself delving into the supernatural, trying to invoke the cosmic or karmic or whatever the hell forces were at work or play here that caused so much pain and loss throughout the history of his town, and for all he knew, even further back than that.

He dared them to make an appearance, even dared them to take him. But his gibberish incantations and sacrilegious prayer and appeals to forces both holy and unholy went for nothing. No matter how hard he tried, it felt just like any other place.

A week after his meeting with McPhee, he again found himself at the intersection. It was a gray and cloudy day, with spittle of greasy rain landing every now and then on his windshield. He watched the wind blow the criss-crossing street signs hanging above the intersection like flags whipping in the wind. The sign reading "Upham's Corner" flapped in the breeze, while the sign in front of the church this day read: *"God Says: Your going to heaven or hell. Your choice!"*

Foley smiled to himself, not just at the typo, but also recalling his recent profane attempts to summon the forces of darkness. As he sat there alone in his car, he realized how silly it all was. There were no forces of darkness. Or light. And there were no bad places either. Only bad people. In fact, the further removed he became from his meeting with McPhee, the more he realized how ridiculous the whole thing was.

As if to affirm his thoughts, he looked up and saw the gray skies begin to part. Rays of late afternoon sunshine now peeked their way through the clouds. The temperature too had risen in the time he'd been sitting there. The uptick in humidity caused a foglike mist to spring up above the ground. It would be a beautiful evening, he knew.

He thought back to all the time he'd wasted sitting in this lot waiting for something to happen. And not just this past week either. *What a fool I've been*, he thought. *Boy, did that old man take me for a ride.*

But Foley couldn't blame the old man. He was the one who bought in, hook, line, and sinker. He smiled cynically, realizing McPhee had been right about one thing. He did indeed have a way with words.

Foley shook his head before reaching down to start his car.

It was time to put all this behind him and get back to work. Putting his car in gear, he noticed the mist had thickened. The sunlight that did manage to break through created a strange, prism-like effect, causing the vapor in the air to explode in swirling purples, greens, and reds. The mist itself was no more than five or six feet off the ground. Above it was now bright sunshine. Foley smiled to think there would be a lovely rainbow somewhere once the fog cleared.

He drove to the entrance of the lot. Before turning left toward the intersection, he lowered his visor against the brilliant sunlight. Turning, he looked up and watched the light turn from yellow to red and stopped at the stopline.

The fog was swirling now, glowing all colors of the rainbow. He squinted against the bright sunshine coming through his windshield, and was rubbing his eyes when his car began slowly moving into the intersection. It had already gone three or four feet before he realized it.

He stepped more firmly on his brake as misty colors danced and pulsed but there was no mistaking it. His car was being pulled into the intersection. His panic rising, he glanced into his rearview thinking there might be something pushing, but saw nothing but swirling colors reflected in the mist. His gorge rising, he jammed both feet on his brake and half-stood. The car was almost in the middle of the intersection.

An unholy sound escaped his throat. He reached for the door handle. It flapped this way and that. The door didn't open. The glowing mist enveloped him now, but the sun shone through, creating shadows of darkness and light. He stared helplessly out his windshield, through the holes in the mist, toward the criss-crossing signs marking Bynum Street and Chambers Road. Below them was the sign reading Upham's Corner. Across from that was the church sign. But the shadows and swirling mist made the signs only partly visible, and from left to right, Foley saw what was now being revealed to him and began to giggle.

God Say's: Your

By**NUM** Cham**BERS**

UPham's Corner

He had asked for it. Even prayed for it. And his prayers had been answered. He was in the intersection now. Paroxysms of laughter overcame him when he thought this was the longest light known to man. Tears streamed down his cheeks as he turned his head and saw lights approaching, lights that were curiously far above the ground. Seconds later, words appeared out of the mist, huge black words on a yellow background. He saw them for only an instant.

WIDE LOAD.

And then, all his questions were answered.

What's in a Man's Nose is His Own Business

Brian Barnett

I learned to mind my own business one day last year. I learned it the hard way. Now, I'll never be quite the same. I am just now able to tell the story without feeling physically sick.

I was sitting in traffic at rush hour, just after work. It was a very average day. I was tired and I just wanted to get home. But unfortunately there was a wreck in the intersection, so I had to sit and wait for some time in idle traffic.

Of course, while my mind wandered, so did my eyes. I thought that it was rather humorous how my fellow drivers had felt isolated enough to pick at and groom themselves.

A lady applied a fresh layer of lipstick to my left. Just in front of me, another lady straightened a few strays of her hair while she made playful pouting lips in the rearview mirror. Just to her right, a man unconsciously scratched at his hair. I don't know if it was a nervous habit, or if he had scabies, but he continued to scratch for a solid minute at the very least.

Then, to my right, was the individual who is the subject of my story. There sat a particularly normal looking gentleman. He sat in a particularly normal looking vehicle. And he did a particularly normal looking thing.

He picked his nose.

Of course at first I had to chuckle. For anyone to make such a disgusting act so blatantly obvious was humorous to me. I self-consciously turned away for a moment, afraid that at any time, he could turn and see my gawking face staring at him during his primal desire to grind away at the inside of his nostril.

However, curiosity had gripped me. I looked again, more covertly. He was still digging away. Then something struck me.

The way that he was going about it wasn't normal. It wasn't the desire to unconsciously groom himself that compelled him. He was trying to pull something out—something large.

As you can imagine, I was simultaneously disgusted and intrigued. I slowly turned my head so that I could see the man with both of my eyes. I wanted to see if my mind was playing tricks on me.

My heart fluttered queasily when I saw that he had a stream of blood trickling from his nose. Yet he continued to not only grip something that dangled from his nose with his thumb and forefinger, but tug at it. Perhaps, something, had become lodged in the poor man's nose somehow and he was desperately trying to pull it out.

To this day, I have no idea why he didn't wait until he got home, but I suppose that he was horrified to find something foreign in his nose and wanted it out immediately.

I saw the desperation on his face. His eyes were filled with fear. His chest heaved rapidly, I'd say it was due to pain. I can only imagine what he must have felt.

Again I turned away. I didn't want to make eye contact with him. Who knows what sort of mental state he was in. He might have become angry at me, or worse, he may have asked me to help him.

Just like before, my curiosity got the better of me. My eyes slowly trailed over to him again. The object was nearly out of his nose completely. He had a long wire by both hands that he had pulled from his nostril. It appeared as if a large, ball-shaped object was still lodged in his nostril. His nose was nearly the size of a golf ball. Blood poured steadily.

My stomach churned. I felt hot all of a sudden. I rolled down my window and a cold sweat broke out on my forehead. The stink of diesel fumes stung my nose and made me feel worse.

I tried to ignore the man, but I suppose that I was a glutton for punishment. Once again, I found myself looking over to him. He had nearly completely pulled it from his nose.

His nostril had stretched to its limit. His arms were shaking violently and he cried out a window-muffled scream as he pulled down on the wire. Finally his nostril split and the bloody, metallic orb fell into his lap.

He picked it up with his trembling hands and examined it with a stupefied expression on his face. I could see from my car that the orb had a green light that flashed. It flashed slowly at first, but I could see that it gradually quickened.

Within seconds, the light flashed so rapidly that it appeared as if it had just remained lit. The man seemed panic-stricken. He turned to me and I could see in his torn nostril that he had a light inside his head that corresponded with the light on the orb that he had removed.

Then without warning, his window was sprayed with red.

I tried to wrap my mind around what I had just seen. The man's windshield and driver's side window was covered with blood and small bits of skull and brain matter.

I felt my body get weak and shaky. Then, as if someone had placed a veil over my face, I drifted into darkness.

After a period of time, I'm still not sure just how long, paramedics woke me with their smelling sauce. My car had rear-ended the woman's car that was in front of mine. I wearily looked to the car that was next to mine. A gurney with a bloody sheet-covered body was being strolled to yet another ambulance.

That day was the last day that I ever curiously watched people in their vehicles. Whatever they do, is their own business. I never want to witness anything like that ever again.

Lookers

Brick Marlin

Sherman woke up and felt...different. Something wasn't quite right and he just could not put a finger on it. As if the world around him had changed somehow.

No. Couldn't be, he thought. *Could have just been a bad dream.*

The sun's rays came through the window, an orange glow lay across his face, and he felt its warmth.

The clock on the table read: 8:00 a.m. Time to get up. Time for work. Sherman rose up out of bed, swung his feet around and planted them on the floor. He rubbed a hand through his hair, got up, and stretched.

Sherman went directly into the bathroom, flipped up the toilet lid, and relieved himself. Standing there, he could hear a mower running next door. Probably Carl, his next door neighbor, out bright and early.

After dressing, he walked downstairs and went into the kitchen to make coffee. He looked out of the window that viewed the backyard. The day looked very pleasant with a clear blue sky above. Birds chirped, hidden behind the leaves, and sat on the branches of two oak trees. A few squirrels ran up and down its bark.

Sherman's eyes fell on Chris's swing set. Unused and rusting away.

Poor Chris and Michelle.

Tears filled his eyes and he pushed the sad thoughts away before they could manifest.

Turning on the TV brought a long faced man with glasses speaking about the war overseas, the price of gas going up, and stocks going down. The only bright side was that the weather was going to be very nice, high in the upper eighties and low humidity.

Sherman looked at the clock and knew he had to jet. He drank down his coffee, went through the door into the attached garage, and didn't notice the long faced man following his every move through the TV screen.

After hitting the button to raise the garage door, the smell of freshly cut grass hit him in the face. He started up his car and backed out.

There was Carl tending to his lawn. He always kept the lawn nice and neat. Sherman wondered if he would do the same when he became a retiree.

Rolling down his passenger window, Sherman waved at Carl. At first Carl didn't look up; but when the old man did, he froze in place. He just stood and stared without any emotion on his face while the engine idled.

Not sure if Carl had seen him or not, Sherman waved again. Same pose. Same frozen stare. Sherman looked over his shoulder. No one there, but an empty street.

Sherman shook his head, gave another wave, and pulled out of his driveway and took off. In his rearview mirror, he caught Carl turning his head in his direction. His eyes followed him down the street.

That was weird, he thought. *Something must be wrong with the man.*

Sherman hit the button on the radio and found the eighties station. He loved that era and could remember back when he had hung out with his friends late at night, drinking himself silly, only to wake up the next day and find out that he was still drunk.

He missed his friends, but didn't miss the booze.

Hardly any traffic was out on the main road. A few cars passed him and it almost seemed dead for a Monday morning. Sherman thought it was very odd. Usually, it was bumper to bumper traffic on the main drag.

Rolling up to a stoplight, he pulled up beside a car. While waiting for the light to change, he had an odd feeling that he was being watched. And it was so. A small face peered through the passenger side window of another car, staring, blank faced, with no emotion. The little girl had blond hair and blue eyes.

Sherman smiled at her, but she did not return it back.

What the hell is up with people this morning? he thought.

When the light turned green the car beside him moved forward first and the little face was now pressed against the glass, looking back, trying to see Sherman. Sherman let off the gas a bit, allowing the vehicle to pass and move further on.

Jesus! People this morning are weird!

Cars passed on both sides of him and, for some odd reason, more faces were planted in each of the passenger side windows, staring at him as well. Some young, some old. Each head was turned in his direction. Even the drivers were looking at him.

Sherman figured that it might be a wise thing for them to keep their eyes on the road, and not on him. And why would they be looking directly at him? Why not someone else? Why would any of them take the time to do it?

Sherman began to wonder if something was wrong with his car. Did somebody spray paint something on the side of it while he slept? Some brat? There were a few in the neighborhood, but not any that would stoop that low. At least, he didn't think they would.

Curious, he pulled off into a gas station, got out, and walked around the car. It was fine. No marks. No spray paint.

Okay. That's strange.

And what was worse was that when he slid back behind the wheel, the people that were filling up their vehicles were staring at him. Some even had gas shooting back out of the tank from overfilling, soaking their pants and shoes.

Sherman wondered if everyone in town had gone nuts. Or was he still dreaming? Maybe that was it. He was still in bed asleep, hearing Carl mowing his lawn; the sound possibly blending in with his dream world.

Well, he thought, *I'll just allow the dream to progress and see where it ends.*

Eventually he left the gas station and drove down to where the ramp turned off onto the highway. There, a semi didn't switch lanes so he could merge into the first lane.

Damn those trucks! He hated to be around them. They stank and were dangerous.

And because of this semi, Sherman had to brake so he wouldn't run off into the gravel. He merged over and got behind it. Hampshire's finest chewing tobacco was written across both doors of the trailer and a large face of an old man, scruffy, wearing a straw hat, looked at the world with big blue eyes. The side of his stubbly cheek bulged out.

Sherman looked into his mirror, took a quick look over his shoulder, and switched lanes. He was going to pass the insensitive trucker.

When he did, a car passed him and yet another face appeared in the passenger window. Sherman began to wonder if there was something wrong with *his* face. He looked in the rear view mirror. Nope. Nothing wrong. Same old face with dark hair and hazel colored eyes.

Highway signs read that he should take the next exit. Work wasn't far now. And he really didn't want to go in, but he had to make enough to pay the medical bills. The hospital was kind enough to let him pay only so much a month without interest. And God knows he was already behind on a few other bills. He wondered if Vicki's check would cover the house payment for next month, and the second mortgage...

No. It wouldn't. Because she wasn't working anymore. She wasn't doing anything anymore because she was dead. His son was dead.

Jesus! he thought as tears drained down his cheeks. *Am I ever going to get over this*? Sometimes he asked himself if there was more to live for or not. *Damn that guy for causing their deaths*!

Sherman was on the way home that day and he arrived to an empty house. The last he had heard from Vicki was earlier, when she was going out shopping with Chris. And it had been hours since.

At least he did tell her that he loved her and Christopher before hanging up his cell phone. At least he did get to hear their voices for the very last time, their very last words.

Wiping the tears away, he took his exit and stopped at a light. A car pulled up beside him and the person in the driver's seat bent down and looked at him. A lit cigarette was held between two fingers that gripped the steering wheel.

Sherman looked back. "Got a problem or something?"

The driver said nothing.

"What are you looking at? Ever seen a man in pain?" he sniffled. "Crying his eyes out?"

The driver stayed quiet.

"What? *What* are you looking at? What is up with y-"

A horn blew behind him. The light had turned green.

"Damn!" he spat and took off, hanging a left. Every morning he stopped by a small coffee shop with a drive-thru to add more to his caffeine addiction and to get a bagel. It was just ahead.

Pulling up to the speaker, he waited for someone to ask for his order. A few minutes went by, and no one spoke. Sherman saw that the lot was full of cars, so he was sure that it was open.

"Hello?" he said. "Any one there?"

At first there was silence. Then he heard a crackle and whispers. It was hard to make out what they were saying, it was very low, but he thought that he heard his name.

"Hello?"

Whispering.

Sherman wondered if this was some kind of joke. Were they toying with him? He pulled forward and stopped at the window.

Inside a young lady stood there, wearing a green apron over a white blouse. Staring. Gazing at Sherman. Her long hair was tied back in a pony tail, glasses rested across her nose, spots of acne were on her face, and she held her hands together at her waist.

"Hello?" Can I get a large latte?"

She didn't respond.

"What is up? Talk to me! *Please*!"

The girl kept quiet. Merely a statue with a blue-eyed gaze.

"Hell with it!" Sherman shouted and punched the accelerator. When he left the parking lot, people were out in front of the coffee shop at tables holding paper cups full of brew. They all turned their heads in his direction.

If he was riding out a dream, it was more of a nightmare than anything else.

Sherman drove to work minus his latte and bagel, parked his car, and got out. Walking toward the doors he remembered when the police had called and said that there had been an accident and he needed to get to the hospital quick. Sherman had dropped the phone and rushed to see his beloved and his child.

By the time he got there, the doctors could not bring either one back to this life.

Before their bodies were taken downstairs to the morgue, he confirmed to the cops that, yes, they were his family. He walked out of the room and into the hallway and dropped down into a plastic chair. There, holding his face in his hands, he broke down and cried. And at that point all he wanted to do is to find and kill the person who did this to his family.

Blocking out the rising sun stood a tall building. Sherman's office was on the tenth floor. He entered inside an empty room with no one at the front desk.

Odd. They always had a guy or girl there that said, "Good morning."

He took the elevator up to his floor and got out. Cubicles with desks and chairs ran north, south, east, and west. The place was full of people pecking away on their keyboards. His desk wasn't but a few feet away.

Passing by some of the cubicles, most had their backs to him. Slowly, they began to turn around in his direction, their eyes following his every move.

Usually, Sherman would talk to Sam before he started working. They'd converse about sports or the news. Maybe Sam would let him know that he wasn't going crazy.

"Sam. Something's going on outside. Everyone keeps staring at me and no one speaks."

Sam didn't turn around, just pecked on the keys.

"Sam. Didn't you hear me? Things are really strange. First, I thought I was dreaming; now, I'm beginning to think that I'm *not.*"

Sam faced forward.

"Um, Sam. Hey, man. Can't you hear me?" Sherman reached out and touched the tall man's shoulder.

Sam turned.

First, Sherman noticed the screen. He could plainly see the words: DO YOU DREAM OF US? DO YOU LOVE? written in big letters. Second, his buddy Sam gave him a cold stare through two hollow pits for eyes. His skin was sunken in, pressed against the bone of the skull, showing off high cheeks, and a boney chin.

His mouth opened and revealed the teeth, two missing from the lower jaw, and whispers of many voices, spoken in long drawls. Some young, some old, calling out his name.

Sherman...

He backed away as Sam began to stand. This was no dream. Reality clawed into his gut.

Sherman ran toward the elevator and all of the people at their cubicles were standing up, reaching for him. Fingers brushed both of his arms, touching, feeling—but he didn't stop. And his eyes found more writing on other computer screens.

DO YOU DREAM OF ME? DO YOU LOVE?

Pressing the button frantically so the elevator's doors would open, he saw that they were all walking toward him with hollow eyes and skin sunken back against the skull and their arms down by their sides. Slowly drawing near to him, like zombies.

Finally the doors opened, Sherman slipped inside. As they slid closed, Sherman saw Sam in the lead reaching out a clawed, arthritic hand for him. His heart beat fast. He was out of breath. He knew this was no dream or nightmare. What was going on? Was he really going crazy?

The light above lit up the letter L with a *ding* and the doors opened. He flew out and was in his car in a matter of seconds. The ignition sparked and the tires peeled away.

He hit the road and wondered what was going on. He had no idea. First everyone gazed at him like a freak; now they were after him? Nothing made sense.

He crested a hill, rolled down it. He took a corner too fast, the back end fishtailed, and he had to slam on his brakes. The car slid sideways and came to a stop.

Two people stood in the road. One woman and one child, holding hands. Both looking at Sherman. A huge tree stood tall over on the left and a wooden fence was under it, running along the shoulder. The wind blew, dead leaves fluttered across the pavement.

Sherman opened the car door and got out. He walked to them and couldn't believe what he saw. Definitely not a dream anymore.

Vicki was drenched in blood, as was Chris. Both of their bodies looked mangled, deformed, and hardly human from all of the dents in their flesh from the car's tires that had rolled over them. A torn open hole in Vicki's cheek revealed her back teeth as she gave Sherman a smile. Dark hair, draped past her shoulders, hung off of her scalp and both of her eyes were hollow pits.

As if she never had eyes at all.

Chris was smiling with no lips. A couple of front teeth were missing and wet blood covered the front of his favorite Ultra Man shirt. No eyes sat in his sockets; hollow like his mother.

Sherman felt sadness behind his eyes and they drained more tears.

Vicki and Chris reached out their hands to him and when he grasped them, he could feel the wet blood. And it was warm.

***

Days later Carl, Sherman's neighbor, called the police and said that he hadn't been able to get Sherman to answer the door for days. An odd smell hung around the front door to his house when he knocked. He knew that the poor man had lost his family by some nut that mowed them down in a car in front of the department store down on Market Street.

The police arrived, broke down the door, and found Sherman at peace in the bloody water of his bathtub. Oddly, he had cut both of his eyes out, leaving two hollow pits.

Gravity Hill

Jenna M. Pitman

Her fingers were in my brain. She dipped and twisted them, twining them through the delicate rubbery mazes and folds of my mind. I could feel her moving and stroking, prodding and yanking. I could feel her tongue, wet and rough and unnerving; running over its ridges and chasms. I shuddered in response, an involuntary spasm that racked my body. I felt torn between ecstasy and terror.

Her icy breath tickled the back of my neck, spreading a sickening chill down my spine and making my stomach clench. Her corporeal arms dropped to drape my shoulders and she pressed herself firmly against the back of the driver's seat; I felt her every shift echo through my body.

Amelia.

She had been my friend once. My sister. My lover. Now she was my curse. I had thought she loved me at one time. And at one time I had loved her back.

I tightened my grip on the steering wheel and accelerated a little more. My eyes flicked briefly to the sleeping form of Abby, a friend from years ago, slumped beside me, her body wedged horizontally between the passenger door and the armrest. A bottle of Jack Daniels, mostly drained, had overturned in her lap seeping slowly into a puddle on her pants. Everything inside of me wanted to snatch it up and guzzle down the remaining quarter, numbing the conflicting emotions.

I pulled myself away from those urges and tried to ignore the dead girl who tugged on my senses from behind. It amazed me when I succeeded.

"Ana."

The word flooded the cab, filling me with dread and anticipation. In spite of the warm summer night the temperature inside the car plummeted, I could see my breath emerging in puffs. Frost crept up the sides of the windows, slowly expanding, just like the amber stain that slipped down Abby's legs.

"Ana," her voice was quicker now. Louder, more insistent. I wasn't sure if it was inside my head or ringing in my ears. Maybe it was both.

We were nearing her hill, the place that had haunted me for ten years. Gravity Hill it was called. To me it was Amelia's Hill.

Some people said that it was the location of an ancient Indian burial ground. Others said a white settler had been raped there and left to die. Most claimed a teenage girl had been eaten by her mother and father in the midst of a terrible winter. Either way, all the stories ended the same, with the dead victim pushing a car up the hill, defying gravity, lending the nickname to the popular rise of road.

Bits of those stories were true of course. There had been a mother, crazed with rejection, who had slaughtered her children in the dead of some blinding snowstorm, devouring them in part and whole to hide her projected shame. Her oldest, a sixteen-year-old daughter, chose to fling herself from the top of their barn rather than succumb to that horrid end. The corpse had never been recovered. Even in death, the daughter was too frightened of her mother to let her body be found. Would-be rescuers later said it was as though she'd flown away rather than plunging to her demise but it wasn't that at all. She, this dead sixteen-year-old girl, pushed the wagons away, pushed the cars. She shoved away anyone who might discover her body, away from her resting place.

To the majority of town it was a game. Gravity Hill was just some place they could go on a weekend night to scare that special girl or boy. But once a generation Amelia chose a handful of girls and lured them into friendship before offering them as placation to her mother.

No one knew about *that* but Amelia's special friends.

Ten years ago I had been one of those girls. So had Abby. For months the two of us and three others had been overawed with the new girl who had arrived at school, withdrawn but sweetly soft-spoken. She wasn't like the other kids; she made us feel extraordinary and made us feel cherished. All five of us believed that we were the most important thing in Amelia's world, that we were as meaningful to her as she was to us. It never crossed our minds to question why we were never invited to her house and why she was always dressed so strangely.

She took us to that hill nearly once a week, sometimes more. The last day, that final trip, hadn't seemed strange or out of the ordinary. It wasn't until the Explorer started speeding, until the world got *different* and we could feel that seething malevolence that we understood just how much danger we were in. And when the car had been ripped apart like a piece of dried newsprint, when Shelly, Megan, and Carla had been eviscerated before our eyes…

I don't know how Abby and I got away. Somehow we'd managed to make it out of the carnage alive. We'd never been the same after. There have been times since when I have wondered if it wouldn't have been better if we had just died out there.

"Ana, come now. We're almost there.. Listen to me." Her voice cut through me like a frozen knife, it rattled my brain. I thought I was going to be sick.

I'd tried to stop listening to her long ago. Abby had too, I had seen it reflected in her eyes when I bumped into her at the bar earlier. She'd tried to drown that voice in alcohol like I had. Drown it in drugs and boys and girls and blood. We'd run and run and blunted the edges until we couldn't feel her anymore. But she had always been there, hovering in the periphery of our awareness, waiting for us to make a slip, to look to the side just once.

We both knew she was there, knew she waited for us. Despite our best efforts we could hear her, we could see her. We simply tried to ignore it. We were on borrowed time, we already belonged to her and we knew it. We didn't like to dwell on it and tried to hide from that knowledge.

"Don't you want to be strong, Ana? Don't you want to be special? It doesn't take much, Ana."

"Shut up," I mumbled. I'd been drinking too. "Shut up, Amelia. I'm here. We're here. It's what you've wanted. I'm giving you what you wanted, you persistent bitch. That should be enough, right? Don't push it."

She knew what I was thinking, knew I was nowhere near as sure as I hoped I sounded. Amelia knew everything about me. I couldn't fool her, I could only try to fool myself.

"I don't think I want Mother to have you, Ana," she crooned, suddenly switching tactics. "She's had everyone else I ever brought her, Ana. Mother always took them and took what she wanted. But you? I want to keep you, Ana. You're already special and I can make you more so. *We* can be special, Ana. We can help each other, Ana! You and me. Together. Isn't that what you've always wanted?"

Yes! But I didn't tell her that. She knew anyway.

Instead I said, "No. No, I've never wanted that, Amelia. Don't be stupid."

She laughed, the sound of it vibrating against me. It sounded hollow and distant, like it ricocheted off the ethereal bones and cavities of her ectoplasm body before reaching my ears.

"What can you do for me anyway? It's because of you that I'm in this mess."

She turned away from me then, slightly amused, as though the answer was so obvious I shouldn't even have had to ask. Abby moaned and flinched, her face distorting as it screwed up in pain. I didn't know if it was physical or mental torment that affected her but I knew Amelia was with her now. I should have been concerned for Abby's sake but I was just relieved that she wasn't toying with me at the moment.

The landscape flashed by, the barren steppe dotted with sagebrush and a patchwork of carefully hemmed in crops. Empty and lonely, dark and unending.

I had tried to escape this place. I fled to the lush greenery across the mountains, to the rain that meant life and foliage. I tried to leave behind the tones of sepia and jaundice and dead, dried grass but this land had imprinted itself upon my soul. Just like Amelia had. Or maybe it had imposed itself on me because of her. This open space, marred by its hills and crevices, a land that needed man-made engineering to support life, had seared itself into my head. I had become this place, empty and barren. No matter where I went it would follow, withering anything I touched.

I wanted it to end. More than anything I wanted something resembling peace and security. I longed to let my guard down and rest a while, without thinking about the past that was or the future that would be. It had been so long I wasn't sure I was even capable of living a life without the stress anymore. Maybe the terminal embrace of death wasn't such an unthinkable option.

In the distance her hill grew closer. I could make out the silky ribbon of antiquated highway winding up and around its sides. There was an old farmhouse up there, at the top, grey and weathered. A barn would be sitting by its side, sad and dilapidated next to the creaky, old weathervane. The details came from memory; we weren't close enough to make those out. They would become apparent soon and when they did we'd be closer to Amelia's goal. Which meant we'd be closer to her mother.

I eased my foot off the gas pedal at the thought. A decade's worth of shock and terror came flooding back. I wanted just a little longer to forget the worry and forget her, to pretend that it wasn't destiny.

Amelia was behind me immediately.

"Don't get scared now, Ana. We're almost there and then it will be over. I know you're tired, Ana-dear. I'm tired too. But soon we can rest. So let's just get there, ok?"

Her fingers ran lightly up my arm then down again, tracing a line of ice along my skin. She brushed them into my lap and spun them across my thigh. She started to massage my leg, caressing and pushing. Gently at first, then harder, more purposefully. I gave up my prerequisite resistance and watched the speedometer creep higher. Resigned now, I gave her what she wanted, giving into her pleas and her desires. She was all I had ever really wanted anyway, why not make her happy? I should have known by now that Amelia would always get what she wanted and that what she wanted was hardly any different than what I wanted.

"That's it, Ana," she encouraged, "That's it! Just a little faster. Let's make Mother happy."

Then Abby awoke, screaming.

The bottle of whiskey tumbled from her lap to the floor of my Sentra, the smoky smell of it bursting into the air. Her screams turned to shrieks when she saw where we were headed.

"Oh god, Ana, no!" she choked out between sobs. "Ana, we can't go back there!"

I set my jaw, allowing my agitation to overpower my fear and confusion, letting it cycle into anger. I gripped onto it like a drowning man clings to the first thing against which his fingers brush. Then I unleashed it on Abby.

"I'm tired of running. She's had us this whole time. We're dead anyway, there's nothing left inside. You know it. I know it. What's the use? We're hers." I didn't know if I meant Amelia or her mother but it was true about either of them, each in their own way.

"Please!" her voice snapped and she started to sink into her seat, drawing away from that looming hill. Tears were streaking her face, her already smudged make-up trailed down her cheeks and landed in black speckled pools on her fists and chest. "We got away! We got away, Ana! Why would you want to go back?"

I pushed away her protests. This was more important than anything else, I decided. I was disappointed that she didn't understand but not really surprised.

With Abby quivering beside me I approached the foot of the incline, slowly braking until I'd drawn to a complete stop. Amelia wasn't with us, I couldn't feel her frigid presence hovering or leaning over the backs of our chairs, couldn't feel her dry hair against my skin. She'd gone outside. I couldn't see her but I knew that's where she was. Gravity Hill, Amelia's Hill, never worked when she was in the cab.

I felt the telltale tingle of electricity and the ever-present chill grow even colder. A foreboding presence, full of anger and seething with hatred, suspended above us, not near enough to touch but close enough to feel. Amelia's mother waited for us from her vantage point at the peak of this cursed hill. Every step Amelia took drew us nearer to that roiling cloud of emotion.

I turned the car off. I moved to switch it into neutral but Abby's hand shot out to grab my wrist.

"Don't do this," she pleaded. Her eyes and face were red and puffy, her voice thin and watery. "We can still turn around. Head to town. Forget this happened. Forget *that* happened!"

"If it were as easy as all that then why haven't we?" I demanded, turning on her with vehemence.

"You're crazy," she whispered, shrinking away from me, fumbling for the latch on the door.

I hit the power locks and snatched up her hand. My nails bit into the flesh of her palm. She shrieked again but I felt her go limp, giving up and giving in. Resigned. Just like me but without the power of furor behind it. She'd never had much of a backbone.

"I'm ending this! Right here, with the both of us. I can't take any-God-damned-more."

She sniffed and nodded. Weak. Abby had always been the weakest of us all. How she'd managed to make it out with me all those years ago I would never understand.

Amelia was growing impatient. Her displeasure struck against me, sliding into my mind and pounding against its walls. So I slipped the shifter up a notch, letting the wheels choose where it was they wanted to roll. This time all that came from the seat beside me was a terrified whimper.

We rolled up, tires crunching on the worn out blacktop, the sound deafening in the void left by the engine. Slow at first. One mile per hour. Two then three. Faster it came. Ten, fifteen, twenty. We raced upwards, barreling toward the house and barn, the air darkening with that uncontained enmity with every inch. We'd never gone this fast before and we were still gaining speed. Thirty, forty, fifty, sixty.

The world began to shift as we drew closer to the peak. The layers of time sighed and expanded, falling away and clinging closer all at once. The structures in the distance, that house and barn, they seemed newer now than they had at first, taller and looming, a foreboding facsimile of the buildings I was used to. We were in that scattered and chaotic realm, the one that drifts and teeters between both the land of the living and the land of the dead. A realm of ghosts and spirits; home to Amelia and to her mother.

In the rearview mirror I could see her, that pale, girl in a yellowed-white dress with lank, brittle-black hair. She pushed us up, her hands braced on the trunk, her back hunched as she thundered forward, up the curling road.

I knew she wouldn't keep me safe. There was no love between us any longer, only the hard realization that she was using me.

No, that wasn't entirely right.

I had always loved her; even as she sent us to our deaths I loved her. It was only that she had never loved me. The words she had said, the promises she had made, the feelings she had made me feel? She had played with me. Played with my hormones, my insecurities, my lusts, and my desires. She'd been inside and she knew me. She'd known just what to say. Just as she had always known what to say to all the others. It had all been a part of her plan.

Take off your seat belt, Ana. The words rang in my head just before we reached the crest. I didn't have time to obey.

The Sentra slammed to a halt, tossing me forward and striking my chest against the steering column. I heard the weathervane creak.

And then Amelia's mother moved, that dark presence enveloped us.

She invaded the cab like a gust of wind, popping the locks and blowing the seals of my doors. They bowed out at the center; red-tinged moonlight came streaking through those jagged open holes. She hung inside, dank and oppressive, leaning into us, smelling and testing. I felt Her pressing the air out of my lungs.

But I couldn't see Her.

"No!" Abby moaned, closing her eyes tightly. "Not again!"

She shimmered. She no longer had a shape, the fury and madness had long ago taken over, rendering Her a specter. But She could flash and flicker in translucent shapes of iridescent yellow, purple and green. In the right light you could see Her snaking through the air in a serpentine spiral.

This was Amelia's mother. The source of all of Amelia's fear, her driving motivation. She was as terrifying as any monster ever to haunt the subconscious of the human race. She was malicious, vicious, invisible, and indestructible. She could enter your mind like Amelia but thought nothing of tearing it apart as She did. Amelia made you feel treasured as she manipulated, cajoled and bent you into doing her will. Her mother left you a husk of your former self, wrapped in painful insanity.

Abby remembered Her too. She made a sound like a wounded animal.

Amelia's mother stiffened, focusing Her attention on Abby. Then She exploded.

The car bucked and buckled, straining. Abby's cries suddenly dominated my ears despite the whoosh of energy that accompanied the attack. Abby was being pulled against the nylon seatbelt that restrained her; her body went rigid. Amelia's mother tugged at her, trying to pull the straps *through* her. Abby's eyes bulged, protruding from her skull unnaturally. She was warping and fraying. Blood began to seep from her skin where the seatbelt dug into her. The liquid oozed and bubbled, thicker than it should be, redder even. It seemed to boil, pouring out of her as she was slowly picked apart, fiber by fiber, strand by strand.

I looked away, I couldn't keep watching. This was to be my fate too. After she was done with Abby, Amelia's mother was coming for me.

Take off your seatbelt, Ana! Amelia's voice rang inside of me, frantic now. I felt something different about her, almost as though she was reaching inside and blending her voice with mine. I didn't have time to comprehend that though.

Instead I scrabbled to comply with her request, hands shaking. They felt sticky. Was that blood? Was it Abby's? She was still screaming so it had to be hers.

I freed myself just as another burst of power hit the car. Abby's voice grew louder, a devastating, heartfelt wail of pure agony. I didn't know a human could sound like that. The force shattered the windows. I felt someone grabbing my arms, lifting me from the wreckage of my car. It pushed me away, tossing me down the hill, away from the carnage and the unearthly cries of a girl I'd once called a friend.

Amelia's mother focused on me, as my bruised form started to slip back down her sacred hill. I felt invisible tendrils reaching for me, sucking me back.

That other being, the one that had pushed me, grew stronger, throwing me away, desperate to avoid detection and scrutiny.

It didn't disappear as we descended the hill, instead weaving itself into me as we spiraled away from the land of spirit.

Amelia.

I finally understood, as my body tumbled down, hitting rocks and sagebrush and clumps of mud, catching on the crumbling asphalt and tearing. She did love me; she loved me as much as I loved her! She'd meant it when she said she needed me. More importantly, however, she'd meant it when she had said we'd be together.

The ruthless and relentless anger was fading as I fell. Skidding away from the last vestiges of the spirit realm. I could still hear the screaming, Abby's inhuman howls, filling the night sky as I finally came to a rest at the bottom of that cursed hill.

Everything had returned to normal, the sky a dark and distinct navy blue, pricked with points of light and interrupted only by flimsy gray clouds that caught the clean, white moonlight.

People had started shouting, scrambling out of that old farmhouse near my car. Rushing to help poor Abby. They wouldn't be able to, of course. Amelia's mother had been given the blood she'd needed. Abby was gone now. Or would be soon enough.

I started laughing hysterically, lying broken in the middle of the steppe.

You would think that by now that family would be used to mysterious disasters outside their home.

I know we were.

***

They'd said that Abby had been charred and mangled beyond recognition. I never doubted them.

The state charged me with driving under the influence and involuntary manslaughter. The lawyers sent me to a mental ward instead.

Once it would have shattered me, losing Abby out there just as I had lost the others ten years before. But now?

Now I understood. With Amelia I was ok. She loved me, she was me. Abby's blood had been necessary to bring us together. All of those deaths, the girls I had known and the generations before us, all of that had been necessary. We were safe from her mother here, with each other. And she loved me!

To think that I had run from her for so long.

The Language of Colors

Deena Lyvang

I know why you're here. You think I'm crazy. Well, let me tell you something. I'm not. They just stuck me in this hospital 'cause they think I hear voices inside my head. Well, I don't hear voices. And I know I'm not Abe Lincoln or Napoleon like some of the other crazies living here. No sir, I ain't crazy. I have a gift, that's all. I hear the Colors. Mama always said I was special. She said there was a reason for me being able to hear the Colors.

Do you still think I'm crazy? Well, you might just wanna check out that Learning Channel on the TV. There are other people just like me. Doctor's call it synaesthesia or something. Some people can even taste the Colors, but I wouldn't want that.

So you wanna know what the Colors say? Well, Colors don't talk like you or me. Colors talk by giving off feelings. Like take this blue shirt for instance. They always make me wear blue here. What do you feel when you go down by the water or look up at a clear blue sky? You feel calm and peaceful, don't ya. That's what the color blue says. That's why blue's my favorite color. I like yellow too, but they don't like me wearing it here. They say I get too happy. I like that color. It's the color of the sun. I can't help but feel the happy thoughts yellow gives off. Purple's a curious color. I always think it's a color meant to study. It's pretty and it's dark at the same time. It's not bad, no sir it's not. It's curious, that's all.

What about green? I'll get to that horrible color in a moment. You see every color speaks to me, but brown. I don't hear brown at all. Maybe 'cause it's all the Colors mixed together, or maybe 'cause it's so neutral. So, I don't mind brown. When I can't feel anything, I can't say I hate it.

You want me to talk about that ugly color, don't you? Why? I hate green. I hate what it says. Mama says I got this gift, but I hate it 'cause I have to hear green talking. You should consider yourself lucky you can't hear it.

Do you know what it gives off? It gives me the feeling of being sick, like some kinda virus, or somethin'. It spreads and spreads in this world. There's too much green, it's almost overpowering. That's why I hate summer so much. There's green everywhere and it drowns out the other Color's words. I can barely hear the blue singing its lullaby or the yellow saying all those happy jokes. No sir, that green is bad. Drowns out everything. I like the autumn though. Green dies. The red takes over and turns it to brown. Red does that. Red says love. That's why all those hearts on Valentine's Day cards are red. Red says love. Red's a helpful sort. It really is. Orange can be pretty helpful too, but not like red.

I know what else you're thinking. You want to know why I did it. Well, I ain't ashamed to admit it. I started that fire. I don't feel guilty at all. You see, the green was spreading, coughing over everythin'. That whole forest was green. I had to stop it. It was like a weed. It kept growing and growing and spreading and spreading. So I called on red and orange to help me. I heard yellow in those flames as well. Yellow sure was happy to kill off that sick Color. That fire sure did wonders, didn't it? It turned all that green to brown. It finally shut up. I don't hate the trees though. It's not their fault that they have the green. I was just doin' them a favor by making the green stop its yammering.

They told me that's not why I'm here though. They said it's 'cause of that girl. Oh, that poor, poor girl. She had no idea. I remember when I first saw her. She wore that green dress. I had to put my hands over my ears to block out the green's hollering, but I could still hear it. It was so loud. And her eyes. They were green too. Not that she could help that.

I had to help her, I had to quiet the screaming. I wanted to burn the green like they did to those witches in Salem, like I did to that forest, but I couldn't. I couldn't get the fire to start for some reason. I think it was 'cause it had just finished raining and everything was so wet. So I thought and thought about what I could do to stop that ugly yelling. Then I remembered how loving red was. So I got out my pocket knife and I cut her. I kept poking her with the knife and what joys! That red really sung out loud. Oh sir, it's simply the most beautiful sound you could ever hear. That red covered up that green just so. I thought that would have been the end, but I could still hear the green howling it's horrible, sickening screech. I didn't know where it was coming from until I looked at that girl's eyes.

There was nothing I could do to save her you see. I told her she had to lose those eyes. Too bad she didn't have blue eyes. I like blue eyes. They make me feel so good inside, so peaceful, so calm. Brown eyes I don't hear anything. But this girl had the green eyes. And those green eyes hurt my ears so bad. I told that girl I had no choice but to get rid of that green. Felt sorry for her, really I did. But I had to do it, don't you see? I had to take out those green eyes. And I did too. I'm sure you've heard the story.

I took that knife and cut into that green. The girl started screaming, but it wasn't as loud as the green. Once I got rid of all that Color, things were good again. Things were quiet. Too bad she had to die. I didn't mean for her to go, but I had to make things quiet. Oh, that horrible, horrible green. You understand that now, right?

Now these doctors here, they think I'm crazy. They know there are others like me, hearing the Colors and all, but they say my hatred to green isn't normal. It's making me sick or somethin'. I told them that green says sickening things all the time, so of course it's making me sick. I shake my head at those quacks. I ain't crazy. Green doesn't make me crazy. I'm just on a mission to get rid of it all.

That one doctor, the one with the short brown hair? I don't like him. He thinks I'm crazy and stupid. He wears that green shirt under his sweater. He thinks I can't hear it 'cause it's all covered up. Oh, but I can hear it. I can hear its yelling quite clear. I ain't stupid either. I know he's playing me, wearing that sick Color around me like he does.

So, do you know what I did? I took his pen. See this here? See this red pen? Oh, it's singing to me right now. It's singing me a beautiful song and it wants me to use it on the doctor, the one with the green shirt. I don't plan on coloring the green with the red. No sir, but the tip of this here pen will do. It's sharp. I can't wait to shut that green up and this pen will help me do the job just fine.

Somewhere Anywhere

Kevin Brown

5:45 a.m.

Skylar Mosely gunned the throttle on his old man's fishing boat and the nose lifted high off the dark water, the current splitting white around the aluminum body. Squinting, he snaked around the bends of the river, watching the dark treetops lined ahead. His earlobes were red and stinging. His eyes watered in the cold air.

An hour ago, he snuck out dressed in layers of hunting clothes and hitched the boat to the pick-up. It was his dad's truck and boat, and Skylar wasn't allowed to take them out alone. But he'd decided to after his dad came home tanked and smelling not like his mom's perfume. They'd yelled and cried and slammed things until he passed out and she went to the Motor Inn Motel. This had been happening more and more and Skylar figured that if they could have their places to go, so could he.

Skylar watched the snow-splotched banks slide by. Felt the foamy spray of water on the backs of his hands like ice needles. He bit down hard, and his jaw squared off and popped. He was sick of the liquor and women, the fighting and cruelty. Lately, he wondered what was going on in his old man's mind when he slammed tools in the garage. When he stabbed food on his plate as if it were alive, shoveling it in his mouth faster than he could chew and swallow. Always looking down or to the side, answering questions in grunts or nods. He wondered where that anger had come from and how far it was going to go.

Skylar eased off the throttle and angled the boat toward a fallen cedar near the bank. His dad had never taken him upriver this far and the land felt foreign and undiscovered. He heard game ran wild in this area because few people hunted it—if you were lucky enough to bag a good sized deer, getting it back would be a chore and most folks didn't bother. But he figured he'd cross that bridge when and if he came to it.

He'd also heard stories of these woods being haunted. It was where that family, the Otis', had supposedly lived. Where, if you believed the tales, they were murdered—burned alive, one at a time. Son and daughter first. And according to the older folks in town, where the house stands to this day, there are four charred spots still burned into the floorboards.

Skylar stepped onto the muddy bank bottom and tied the boat off. Shouldered his .30-06 and looked around, his breath ghosting out white. Currents rolled and flecked in the river, but everything else was a numb silence. He climbed the bank by the jutting tree roots and stepped into the woods, sinking calf-high in the snow. He felt oddly comfortable, as if the land was closing its arms around him. Pulling him in a hug to its breast.

6:40 a.m.

Nature began to form and take shape with the light. The world resembled one large Polaroid being shaken until it developed. The brush came alive, rattling. Twigs snapped. Parts of dead trees cracked off and popped the snow. It seemed the lighter it got, the louder. And colder.

Skylar sat on a dark tree root crooked out of the snow like a burned elbow. The wind seemed to come from all directions, chipping away at his face and neck. A few feathering snowflakes had turned into a sideways flurry and it was hard to see more than thirty yards out. The snow's surface was smooth as white cake icing.

He flipped his collar up and slid his hands under his armpits, balancing the rifle in his lap. He imagined his mom shifting and tossing under worn motel sheets. Her face clenched in the middle, eyes red and raw. And his dad, still sprawled sideways on the bed, half-dressed and snoring. He couldn't understand why his father continued to stray off the straight, simple road he and Skylar's mom had been on for twenty-one years. Why he took highways and side roads headed in every direction but home.

He thought about their vacation a year ago. It was the last great time he could remember them having together. They'd gone to Clearwater, Florida, and everyday they ate at a different seafood restaurant. He and his dad played Frisbee on the beach. Tossed hunks of bread in the air for the screeching seagulls to dive and catch, and watched the sun deflate into the horizon, where it watered off and on to somewhere, anywhere. In beach chairs behind him, his mom and dad sipped margaritas and laughed and kissed, while Skylar sat in the surf, curling his toes in the warm wet sand. The water foaming in and over and around him, then sliding metallic back into the sea.

He shifted on the root, looked out ahead, and thought about that old house. If it was really out here somewhere, all decayed and folding in on itself. Animal tracks and wads of shit everywhere. He wondered what direction it was supposed to be in. If he was close.

The way he'd heard it, the Otis' lived back here in the thirties. People called them river rats because they lived on what they took from the river. Some claimed to have seen them occasionally, running trotlines and barrel nets for fish and turtles. They were supposed to be inbred and ravaged by syphilis. Disfigured by chancres and patchy hair, pegged and notched screwdriver teeth. Brain disorders.

Story goes, they took in a couple of guys lost in the woods one night. What they didn't know was these guys had robbed and killed a goods store owner twenty miles north and took to the woods. They fed them, gave them a change of clothes, and a bed for the night.

And sometime the next morning…

Skylar looked around, scanning the thickets and bottoms. He wondered if years ago, killers had actually come through this exact area, maybe rested on this same elbow root. If they saw chimney smoke mouse-tailing above the trees. Faint candlelight in the windows like eyes. He wondered if all those years ago, you could smell burnt flesh in the air. Blood and charred hair in the leaves. He figured not, because he'd also heard the Otis' weren't actually fried like witches, that they'd just moved on, farther upriver where the fish were more abundant. Lived and died the way most people lived and died. Uneventfully.

Some swear they never even existed at all.

To his left, there was a loud crack in the underbrush and he jerked around. Leaned forward and raised his rifle. Another snap and he saw it—a Jackrabbit working its nose in the air, ears twitching. It spun and sputtered into the tangle, and Skylar eased his gun back across his lap. Wiped his nose with the back of his hand. He glanced to his right and nearly fell backward, off the root.

Standing there, forty yards out and staring at him, was a large, wide-racked buck.

It never made a sound. Just appeared out of nowhere like a ghost.

6:45 a.m.

Skylar whipped his gun up as the buck turned to bolt. He squinted, threaded the bead on its shoulder, and fired.

6:46 a.m.

Blood was everywhere. Standing where the deer had been, breathing heavy, he could still hear it bouncing through the thicket ahead. He wasn't sure where he hit him, but it was deep enough. Thick ropes of blood trailed off from where he stood, toward the sounds the deer was making.

Skylar ate a handful of snow, pinched his collar, and fanned his shirt. He looked back in the direction he'd come from, toward the river. Large foot divots in the snow like candle holes in cake frosting.

He turned back toward the unseen world snapping and popping and dying ahead. He started after it.

8:15 a.m.

Skylar leaned over, hands on his knees, trying to catch his breath. His lungs felt scrubbed raw inside and he coughed and spat. He'd come a ways, the deep snow hampering his movements. Several times he thought he'd lost the trail and was about to turn back, when a slash of red on a tree or a glob in the snow pulled him along. He'd been through a rotten cane patch woven with vines of briers, and farther, until looking back, the black oaks and cedar trees looked like walls. Like jaws closing out the open world forever.

Still coughing, Skylar yelled, "Better be one big fucking deer!" and his voice sounded small.

He kept going—up the incline of a ridge, along its spine. Down the slope, the snow sliding around him, and—

Before he heard it, he almost ran right into it. He dropped to his knees, slipped his coat off, and clutched a tree trunk. Leaning forward, he drank handfuls of icy stream water that swirled by, dark as the trees, then disappeared around the bend.

8:23 a.m.

Skylar wiped his mouth on his shirtsleeve and looked around. The trail picked up on the other side of the stream, and unless there was a narrower spot to cross, that was it. Curtain call. He was done.

He leaned back down for another drink, and the small bank loosened and caved. He whimpered and slipped face forward toward the water. Never breaking grip with the tree, his body spun and his legs went in instead.

He sunk gut deep, his feet hitting the bottom.

As quickly as he went in, he grabbed the tree with his other hand and pulled himself out. The water had taken his breath, and his clothes were slick and shiny and clinging to his body as if they were melting.

An Hour Later.

Skylar's hands fluttered. His jaw quivered. He started back, following his own ghost of a trail, as the older tracks were disappearing, erased by the storm. He slid his coat on and jammed his hands under his armpits, carrying the rifle in his folded arms. But the shaking had intensified. His toes seemed to have disappeared a while back and his pants were stiffening and freezing to his legs. He fell several times and each fall he seemed to leave a little more of his energy, of himself, in the snow.

He reached the cane patch and made his way in. He scanned the ground, the tracks barely imprints on the surface. He went left, lost the trail. Turned back and followed the tracks he'd just made. The briers bit into his clothes, tore at his cheeks and ears. Cane sprung at his face, popping him in the forehead. He stumbled and regained balance. Turned and went in any direction, clawing, trying to find some landmark that looked familiar.

"Please," he said, and saw an opening ahead. He went toward it in a rush, the thorns ripping into him, and finally made it out of the tangle. He stopped. Dropped to his knees.

There was the stream, the bank caved in by the tree.

He looked around. Every thicket and stunted cedar, log and bush looked the same. Black and white Xeroxed copies in all directions. He tried to stand and dropped his rifle. Tripped and sunk. He slammed his fist into the ice and screamed, but it muffled in the flurry. The wind moaned around him. For some reason, he pictured his mom on the nights she waited up for his dad, her eyes rimmed in tears. Imagined the *tack, tack, tacking* of her wedding ring on the tabletop.

And for the first time, he began to think he might die. Started to wonder if his death would somehow reunite his parents. Maybe make them see what real unhappiness is. Through his tragedy, their marriage would live on. A sacrifice of him for the better them.

He smiled and began to cry.

Later.

Skylar nestled between two oak logs, draped his coat over his legs, and closed his eyes. His hands trembled in a violent blur and his lips had gone the color of the veins under his skin. His eyelids bruise-purple and as translucent as a baby bird's. He tried to listen for a passing boat. Some sign that would show him the direction the river was in. Back to where his dad's boat was roped off and waiting to take him somewhere warm. To his family. His home. He was about to nod off when he heard a child's voice giggle and say, "You dead?"

He opened his eyes.

In front of him, a little girl was wrapped in a dirty brown coat, wearing yellow socks as mittens.

He started to cry again.

"You *ain't* dead!" she said. Tears slid off his cheeks and he shook his head "no."

She reached out and wrapped both hands around one of his, grunted, and tugged. He winced, snakes of pain coiling through his legs. She tugged harder and said, "Come *on*, silly." He shifted and the cold around his joints seemed to crack and release. He staggered to his feet, a lapful of snow dusting down.

She turned to go, still holding one of his hands, but he didn't move. "Well?" she said. "You coming or ain't ya?"

He took a step and fell. She helped him up and he took another, then another, his movements jerky and stilted. He stared at the back of her head, her dirty blonde curls floating in the wind. In a breathless fragment, he said, "Where...we going?"

Not looking back, she giggled.

"Hey…" he said, "do you…know?"

"Course I do, *silly*," she said, and giggled again. She

stopped and pointed down the hill at a small, earthy looking house. "Home."

She yanked his hand and he fell again. They staggered down the hill.

The house looked like it had been twisted in opposite directions from the center like a half-turned Rubik's Cube. A maple had grown through the back porch and bent over the roof. Smoke spiraled from the chimney, which was crumbling and leaning in the opposite direction of the house. The windows were glazed in a caul of ice and a shutter creaked back and forth on its hinges like an oscillating fan.

They went in.

The front door was crooked and the house shifted and bowed under his footsteps. The walls were decayed and peeling like skin. In the beams of light filtered through the tattered curtains, he saw rats crisscross on the countertops. Something dark slipped across his boot and disappeared in the shadows with liquid grace.

The little girl began to hum "This Little Light of Mine." She skipped ahead, into the living room, and said, "In here, reindeer."

"Where's your…mom and dad?" Skylar asked. He jerked forward.

Backlit by the fire in the hearth, she giggled and sang: *"Let it shine, let it shine,* le-*et it shine!"*

The wind gripped the house and shook it. The shutter slammed against the sill. He jumped and looked around.

"You can sit down," she said, and he heard her moving around in the dark. He eased into a dusty chair that wobbled under his weight. She poured something and appeared out of the shadows with a coffee mug. He watched her face—her dirt-smudged cheeks and runny nose. A missing front tooth.

She handed him the mug. "Cocoa," she said, and winked. Still humming, she slipped a moldy gray blanket around his shoulders. She stepped back into the dark.

"Your...parents?" he said again, his words cutting out. He cupped the mug in both hands. Felt the heat in his palms. He took a drink and his chest warmed.

"You ought not wander around out there by yourself," she said. "There's bears, ya know?"

He took a drink, never taking his eyes off her. The house shook again and popped. The shutter slammed. He pulled the blanket tight and held it under his chin. "What's your name?" he said, his voice stronger.

And she said, "Wanna hear a story?" She stoked the logs in the fire and it lit up the room.

And there it was.

Four charred spots in the floor, burned straight through the boards to the ground.

His throat went dry. Skin needled and detached from everything it held inside.

"One a ponce of the time," she said, giggling, "there was a beautiful princess—"

"This is the Otis house, ain't it?" he said, unable to take his eyes from the floor. "It's really real."

"—and one day the princess was captured by a mean ol' dragon and locked in a fiery dungeon—"

"How…?" he said, and his voice was weak again.

She stepped out of the shadows, still smiling, and said, "—one day, a handsome prince arrived at the dragon's den to rescue the princess…" and a fleshy bubble pulsed and formed under her right eye, and wormed down her face. It dropped in a hot pucker mark on the floor. Her hair singed at the ends of her curls, hissed, and began to blacken in spirals to her scalp. More bubbles rose, shiny in the light, and slid off and onto the floor.

He tried to move but was frozen.

Her lips peeled back in a gap-toothed grimace. Steam wavered around her.

"...and he told the dragon: 'Release the princess, dragon, or face the blade of my sword!"

He swallowed, starting to shiver. "You're...dead," he said, barely a whisper.

She stopped talking. Then, her voice dragging slower and slower like a damaged audiotape, said, "I'm not dead, *silly*," and disappeared.

His breath caught. He looked down and his hands were cupped, holding nothing. He looked back up and there was no house. No darkened living room or fire in the hearth. No charred floor. Only snow and thickets and trees that all looked the same.

Sitting on the ground, half-covered from the blizzard, there was not even a moldy blanket draped around him.

Sometime. Anytime.

Skylar huddled against a large oak between its flanges that opened out into thick roots. Eyes closed. Face pale and puffy. From somewhere far away he heard the faint growl of a boat motor on the river, but he didn't open his eyes. He'd just sit awhile and wait. Stay here and rest a little longer, because he knew sometimes boats weren't boats at all. Sometimes, you heard boats like you saw old houses and little girls humming in the woods. He'd just stay here and relax, listen to the seagulls screech in the warmth of the sun. Smile at his mom and dad sitting in beach chairs behind him, laughing and sipping margaritas. Together and happy. Maybe he and his dad would toss the Frisbee along the beach. So what if that was a boat, there'd be more. There was always more. There were boats and boats, and he could sail away anytime. Toward the sun deflating into the horizon, where it watered off to somewhere, anywhere. But now, he just wanted to sit in the surf and curl his toes in the warm wet sand. Listen to the waves hiss and burst. Let the salty water foam in and over and around him, then slip silver back into the sea.

Really, it could wait.

He was warm now.

Even the shivering had stopped.

The Bitter Taste of Rapture

Monique Bos

I'll come to you one last time tonight.

You're wondering now as you walk through the halls of your high school whether I'll grace your dreams. You slouch in your trenchcoat and hide your pimply forehead behind greasy hair and think of me. I have kept myself from you for nearly a month, and you've stopped eating, stopped washing, driven to despair by futile desire. Still, you gloat. *If only they knew*, you tell yourself, looking with contempt at your classmates – loathsome specimens of a contemptible race, you think, and I concur. If they knew of my nighttime visits, of the way you who have never had a mortal lover (and never will) carry me to ecstasy on your almighty cock, they'd look at you with respect.

Or so you believe.

Ah, that cock, so insignificant and forgettable. Truly, they all are. A thousand generations of proud manhood merge and blend and fade. And yet they do serve me well. Without them, it's quite possible I would cease to exist.

You move toward your locker, covered inside with posters of Korn and Cradle of Filth and beautiful, vampiric women who remind you of me. As you spin the combination lock, one of the football players passes and jostles you, deliberately rough.

"Hey, loser," he says. "Watch out."

You're unusually feisty today. You turn to respond, but I reach out to soothe you. You sense me as a light, cool breeze across your cheeks, a vague scent of clove and musk, the echo of a whisper in your ear. He's baiting you and I don't want to see you humiliated on your last day, humiliated by anyone except me. For me you will be abject, you will crawl, you will grovel, as you always do.

He shrugs and walks away. I watch his swagger, his letter jacket, the girl on his arm. Enjoy him now, I think to her, because soon he too will be mine.

She shivers and looks over her shoulder. My green eyes glow. For an instant she seems to see me and I wink.

Yes, I'll take him, too, this football player; I'll take him just for you, my toy, so he can know what you've known, at least the anguish of it. Him I'll enjoy quickly and destroy because he deserves no better.

You don't either, of course. You weren't a challenge or a conquest. It's holy men I enjoy the most: monks, saints, lamas. Men whose passions rage through their intellects or their faith, men who believe they have overcome the temptations of the body or who have never experienced lust until the vision of me descends to torment them. Their surrender is sweetest, their agony and betrayal profoundly erotic. Ah, the men I've broken, the magnificent and proud, the wise and brilliant. I prefer to leave them alive, bereft, sorrowful, ruined: shells who will spend the rest of their days in warped longing for me and abhorrence of their own frailty. Yes, they are my favorites. The sumptuous desserts of my feasts of men, but they have grown ever more rare.

And so I sustain myself on boys like you, lonely and awkward misfits, and on pompous ministers and hardened prisoners and whomever else I please. And I do a service, I think, to the race I despise, because left alone you might bask in your rejection and rage. Your desire for vengeance might fester; you might take too seriously the lyrics you hear; you might begin to sketch lists, stockpile guns, study ways to create bombs in the womb of your bedroom. You might take life if I did not visit you and take, instead, your hunger and your longing and your soul, all diffused into the pearl droplets of your cum.

***

I found you when you were a child, when you were

encountering for the first time the bewildering fury of lust and its disquieting physical manifestations. I came to you then in dreams; I touched and taunted and teased you. Before you ever saw a *Playboy* your eyes had devoured my sumptuous curves, my breasts and thighs, my belly and cunt. My tongue stroked your pubescent cock; my lips embraced the shaft; I drank your first nighttime emissions while your peers, ashamed, wondered at the stains on their sheets in the mornings. I trailed my long red hair across your concave chest. I brushed my fingertips across the thin treasure trail running south from your navel. I whispered and caressed; I exhaled ancient spices. I sculpted erections from lethargy. I swept you to the verge of orgasm and then pinned you to the edge until your endurance nearly failed. And then I straddled you, I impaled you inside me, I swallowed you. I rode with the abandon of a whore and the urgency of a virgin desperate to redeem lost time.

When I finished, I flowed from you like a river, sucking away your seed. I slid from your bed like a satin garment off white shoulders and slipped into the night. I left you drained and exhilarated, emptied and fulfilled.

You are mine. You always have been mine, from the first time I slipped into the dark purity of your sleep.

***

Only once did my hold on you waver, and then only slightly. She was never a threat; you would have forgotten her soon enough, I would have made you forget; but I am Lilith and I tolerate no rivals.

You were fourteen that summer and she a year older, a bright and golden creature who moved in a swirl of blond hair and giggles. You wanted, I think, to escape from me, or at least to diminish my power over you. Other boys went on dates or played video games or traded Magic cards, and you had begun to envy them. Never an athlete, you had grown scrawny, sun-starved. You craved sleep like an addiction. You compulsively desired and dreaded my visits. My presence sapped you, but my absence deprived you of a fix more compelling and commanding than heroin. You loved me and you loathed me.

You had not yet learned how wholly and completely you belonged to me.

She noticed you, this girl, and encouraged you, perhaps only to bolster her own tenuous confidence, perhaps because something in your pathetic attempts appealed to her. Your approaches were gauche, laughable: unfunny jokes, blurted compliments, stammered conversations full of long pauses. She flipped her bangs and batted her eyelashes, shifted, scraped her foot across the ground. Said she'd see you later, or told you where she and her friends would be the next day so you could show up and pretend coincidence.

I decided to end your paltry effort at flirtation one June afternoon at the old rock quarry that has served as a swimming hole to more than a generation of teenagers. You had fantasized about her the night before. When I came to you, you superimposed her hair on mine, her eyes and the shape of her face onto my features. You imagined adolescent breasts and slender hips. I spat in your face and struck your cheek. I dug my fingernails into the tender skin of your shoulder and pulled, tore, clawed my marks onto you. You cursed me, forgetting that I myself am the curse.

You, isolated and despised, had never been out to the old quarry until that afternoon. How absurd you looked: hunched on a flat stone, a black t-shirt over your concave chest, a shy grin creasing your face as the girl skipped past you. A giggle, a ribbon of blond hair, a squeal as her tanned foot slid off the edge of a rock and then she plunged into the pool. She looked back at you, splashed playfully, told you to come in. You laughed and ducked your head. You were flattered, happy.

She stroked out toward the middle of the swimming hole. An older boy, college age, catapulted off the cliffs opposite you and exploded into the water, splattering her face and hair. She shook her head and sunlight caught the water on her eyelashes.

You wanted to reach out across the space that separated you and brush those glistening droplets from her dewy skin. You disgusted me.

I swam from beneath and saw her silhouetted against the sky. I looked up through layers of blue and turquoise to the darkness of her arms and legs, her torso and head, shadowed by an invisible sun. I surged upward from the indigo depths and grasped one of her slim ankles and plummeted downward again.

You didn't see her vanish. Another boy was leaping off the cliffs and you watched him enviously, wondering how you could work up the courage to try that yourself, wondering how the girl would react. Your eyes followed him as he ran to the edge and jumped, as he fell flailing past the graffiti-scarred rock walls and crashed through the surface.

At last you looked for the girl and she was gone.

At first you thought she had just ducked under. Then you thought the diver must have hit her, and you were on your feet on the slippery rock, hollering at him across the water. But he hadn't seen her and he didn't appreciate the hysterical note of accusation in your voice. Still, he and his friends dove down into the freezing water over and over as deeply as they could go, looking in vain for any sign of her, because the girl's friends were screaming now too and sobbing.

Far beneath the commotion I laughed. My fingers were steel around her fragile bones. Her hair floated like kelp. She fought so little, as if life held little appeal to her in the end. Her lips and her skin chilled, taking on a blue tinge. I wish you could have seen her then, as lovely as she would ever be, locked eternally in her youth and glory, her vanity and idiocy.

I left her there on the bottom, after the last breath had seeped from her lungs. I pinned her feet and hands beneath heavy boulders that no buoyancy could move, and then I amused myself watching the increasingly desperate search for her body: the college boys, then rescue workers with cadaver dogs, later her distraught father. And you huddled miserably under a towel the whole time, unable to join in the search because you couldn't swim, loathing yourself for your helplessness and because you knew, even before I brought you the certainty that night, that your meager adolescent affections had cost the golden child her life. That steep-sided quarry, plunging forty or fifty feet below the water's surface, filled by melted mountain snow and reachable only after a half-mile hike up a narrow valley, made a perfect setting for disaster. Two or three drownings every summer, and who but you to suspect that the girl wasn't just another casualty of an ill-timed muscle cramp?

I have never let you forget. And you have never again been tempted to stray.

***

On your last lunch break, you score some Oxycontin from a geek who claims to mail-order his stash from a pharmacy in India. You don't care where it comes from as long as it works. You're such a cliché; I've driven far better men than you to abuse any potion you can name—opium, absinthe, peyote, mead, cocaine, whiskey, wine, even blood. Anything they can find to dull the craving for me, to blunt the minutes and hours and days between my visits.

And some, those who are wise enough to recognize what they've lost and strong enough to act on their self-loathing, turn to more lethal substances to author their own endings. I've held men in the throes of death by cyanide, arsenic, heroin, hemlock, nightshade, bleach. I've brought them to the final delicious orgasm at the moment their souls leave their bodies. I've stroked them and whispered in their ears, taunted and soothed their broken souls. That I'll do for you too, although you won't die by your own hand; you don't have the resolve or the nerve. Still, it's the least and last gift I can provide, I who after all am your ruiner, both demon and tormenting goddess.

You take two pills before afternoon classes begin and save

the rest for later. You endure geometry and chemistry and political science in a pleasant daze, conscious but transported to another part of your mind than what your teachers try in vain to reach. Amid your jottings about compounds and cosines, the electoral college and the Bill of Rights, you try to write poems and songs to express your adoration for me, the terrible and sweet longing, but your talent isn't worthy of such a muse. Eventually you surrender to your inevitable failure and instead of original lyrics you borrow the words of others who express the exquisite beauty and agony that, despite my best ravages, you'll never be capable of fully experiencing. You doodle in the margin of your notebook: my gamine eyes; my round breasts. My warm, wet, welcoming cunt.

***

You walk home from school through the woods, along a small creek. Your boots, designed for urban streets and sidewalks, slide on the mossy rocks, and pebbles splash into the water. You peel a twig, tossing the discarded pieces away. Dead leaves swirl in the current. You see the tawny hide of a deer between tree trunks but are too preoccupied to register the staccato fury of a squirrel in the branches above or the pair of raccoons that waddle crossly from your path.

In the house you grab a bottle of Maker's Mark from your parents' alcohol cabinet. You don't realize how weak you have become, how badly the whiskey and the Oxycontin are straining your liver and kidneys and heart. Ensconced in the sacred principality of your bedroom, you wash down two more pills with the booze and gaze on walls papered with more posters of women who remind you of me. They look at you with eyes seductive, sly, challenging, imperious. They bare fangs and wield whips, strain against chains and ropes, rest phallic guns against leather-clad thighs. But none of them is me, and none excite you in the way I do.

You close your eyes and think of me. A lazy hand drifts toward your crotch. You beg me to appear, though I've never come to you in daylight. You talk to me, tell me how badly you want me, need me. Fingers unzip your jeans and move to your cock.

"Please," you breathe. In my invisible silence I gloat. Your hand moves quickly up and down the shaft of your penis and your eyes flutter. You don't need much time or stimulation to come and when I see the precious seed spurting out over your thighs and stomach and the sheets, I want to stick out my long tongue and lap it up.

But there will be time enough for that later.

Afterward, you settle into a restless doze. A vague sense of loss, the absence of something vital and irreplaceable, follows you into dreams. You churn in the bed. I lean over you and breathe onto your fluttering eyelids and you gasp in the texture of my scent. When I draw back, you whimper and struggle and fling out a searching hand. Your fist closes and opens.

I leave you then, locked in ungentle sleep, mad with lust for your own destruction.

***

Time has edged past midnight when I return. The moon stipples your room with pale light, mutes the sexism and rage in your posters. Your face looks older in sleep, gaunt, troubled. Whiskers sprout unevenly along your jaw and chin and upper lip. Your breath smells of sour whiskey and rot.

I exhale onto your forehead: desert fire, ancient musk. Your lashes flicker. "Awaken," I whisper. My voice, my vision, my voluptuousness have inspired anguished works of art and tortured symphonies, immortal poems and lifelong quests into arcane powers. But you're a cowering child of a cynical century, I am wasted on you.

Your eyes open. "You're here," you murmur, aroused already. I slide onto you, into you. My nipples rub your lips. My auburn hair brushes feather-light across your cheeks. You reach out to hold me, to run your hands over my smooth cool skin, but I grip your wrists and hold your arms against the pillow above your head.

"Hush now," I say.

I begin to move rapidly. You pant. I am furious, demanding. I draw you so far inside me you are annihilated. I pull your body into myself, I possess your soul. Just before the end, you look into my green eyes and know. You are mine: mine for eternity, and no hell you could imagine will touch the torture that awaits you.

I feel your weak heart strain and falter. Your seed bursts into me as your eyes roll back. And the last sensation you experience in that final, fatal orgasm, sweeping across your tongue like the barren wind across the desert sands, is the bitter taste of rapture.

Amy-Lou's Ice-Cream Parlor

Harper Hull

The tiny sliver of chalk crumbled against the blackboard and Gwen Meadows simply sighed and walked back behind the counter to find another piece, brushing pink dust from her hands. This was her favorite part of the work day, writing up the daily flavors of ice-cream on the board. There was always chocolate, strawberry and of course peach, this being a peach-growing region and all, but that fourth flavor, that could be anything under the sun and was rarely the same thing twice. Gwen always made the ice-cream herself the night before, five nights a week, and had been doing so for two years. That was when she opened her little business, *Amy-Lou's*, part ice-cream parlor and part knick-knack and craft store. She had named it after her only daughter, the love of her life, her precious gift from God. Amy-Lou's daddy had left town before Amy-Lou could walk, but Gwen had managed just fine as a single mom, for sixteen years now. Fit as a fiddle too. A little overweight maybe—cuddly at worst—but generally in good shape.

Well, apart from the voice thing.

She had been hearing the same strange voice in her head for a while now and it scared her, a lot, but it didn't diminish her abilities as a great Mom. She reckoned it was a side effect of the awful migraines she got quite frequently. Hopefully nothing more serious than that. A weird chemical kick from her prescription sleeping pills, perhaps, or a spark in the brain caused by codeine overuse, something simple and everyday like that. She bet a lot of people suffered from similar afflictions and just didn't talk about it.

'WRITES NOT TALKS'

Gwen heard the familiar voice again and shook it out of her head. It always came echoing from what felt like the depths of her mind, like a trapped miner shouting for help from down in the coal-pits to the clear air far above.

She found a box of yellow chalk on a shelf beneath the cash register and slid a piece out, cool and smooth to the touch. She smiled as she stepped back over to the blackboard on the wall. Today's special flavor was honey and cream, because that's what Amy-Lou had decided upon the night before. Amy-Lou decided the special flavor every night; it was a ritual that Gwen enjoyed more than *anything*. They'd sit at the big, oak kitchen table beneath the cooling ceiling fan and Amy-Lou would come up with some wonderful idea, and if Gwen didn't have all the ingredients in her oversized pantry she'd make a quick trip to the all-night supermarket just outside the neighboring town of Winter Creek. She'd spend a couple of hours making batches of the ice-cream in her *Electrolux* machine, making sure it was packed into scoop buckets and put away in her chest freezer ready for the store the next day.

Gwen stepped back from the board, making sure everything was in proportion and looked pretty. It was perfect, as always, neat and simple just like Gwen liked it. She did a quick trot around the store, humming to herself, eyeing everything quickly to make sure it was all neat and tidy. The merchandise was arranged in perfect formation on the shelves, from the local peach salsa and jam to the hand-decorated bird feeders and the beautiful paintings Gwen sold on behalf of local artists. Truth be told, there weren't that many local artists, this was still a redneck town at heart and always would be. It made her week whenever someone did come in wanting to sell their work.

The little cluster of brass bells above the front door jingled and a tall, gaunt man in dark blue overalls and a tan cap walked into the store, with a rusting, battered, once-red tool-box in his hands. He nodded at Gwen and strode over to the far wall where a rare blank space glared emptily from between the rustic coat hooks and home-made civil war dolls. He set his overflowing tool-box down and headed back past Gwen and out the front door.

"Gotta get the shelves from my truck," he muttered without looking at her, "be right back."

Gwen sighed. Walter Hertz was a puzzle to her. She had him come in to do odd jobs and handyman work around the store when she could afford it. Unemployment was horribly high and Gwen felt like she was doing a little something by paying the man an odd twenty dollars here and there for a new shelf or a painted wall. He used to work in the cornfields but business was bad and a lot of the agricultural laborers had been laid off in the last few years.

Gwen had actually invited Walter to dinner at her house one time; a few years back, and had even entertained the thought of romance. She secretly desired a new man in her life, mostly for the little things like a hand to hold during scary movies or someone to take the trash out, and she knew that Walter's wife had left him a long time ago.

The meal had been a disaster though. The man barely spoke and when he did it was usually one or two words at a time. Gwen never invited him back and kept things on a purely professional level from that point on. The one thing he had shown interest in that evening was Amy-Lou, asking about her grades and how she was doing without her daddy around. Gwen got the impression he regretted not having any kids of his own, and although that made her like him a tiny bit more, it was obvious there was no attraction between them and she filed the idea of Walter away in the shuttered side of her brain.

'WET AND FAT'

She rubbed her temple hearing the voice again and went back to the counter to make sure there were toppings and sauces ready for the sweet-toothed schoolchildren and hot, tired local workers who would be stopping by later. It was a scorcher today and business would doubtlessly be good.

She took a small, folded piece of paper from her pocket and dropped it into a wooden box decorated with blue flowers on the counter-top. Amy-Lou had made the box at school when she was twelve—it was rough, over-varnished and the lid didn't quite sit right, but Gwen loved it. Every morning she dropped a piece of paper inside the box, each one had the flavor of choice from the previous night written on it. It had become a tiny ritual.

Gwen brushed down her apron, checked herself in the mirror she kept on the back wall, and went across to the door and flipped the sign over to *Open*. The customers would come streaming in today; *Amy-Lou's* being one of the few actual air conditioned sanctuaries from the shimmering heat on this street. Most places around here still used floor fans and propped open doors for air conditioning.

Not one of the customers stopping by today would even get an inkling that Gwen Meadow's mind was completely snapped in two.

***

That evening, back home, Gwen sat at the kitchen table waiting for her daughter, drinking an iced tea and browsing the new Cracker Barrel catalogue. It was almost six o'clock; Amy-Lou was due home any minute. Teenagers, though, usually rolled in on their own sweet time. As long as she came home, that was all that really mattered. Gwen finally heard a familiar step coming down the hall, and smiled to herself.

"Baby, come in here sweet-girl. I want to tell you how well the honey and cream went over," Gwen called.

The spirit of Amy-Lou Meadows, who had been abducted, tortured, raped and murdered two years ago, at the age of fourteen, lurched into the kitchen on cracking bones and awkwardly fell into a chair at the kitchen table opposite her mother. Amy-Lou's slit throat gaped like an angry red mouth, her snapped fingers and broken arms hung at horribly wrong angles past her broken legs, and her eyes were hollow black slits in a mass of red, puffy flesh. She was naked, her distended body a ghoulish tapestry of bruises, cuts and burns, the canvas of an especially twisted psychopath who had sent her screaming and begging to a way too early grave. Her body had never been found—it had been thrown into a backwoods creek outside of town where it was hidden from view, bloating then rotting away as the critters took turns devouring it. The killer remained uncaught and still had Amy-Lou's little tongue and bloody panties inside a freezer bag in his sock drawer.

'DEAD AND GONE'

Gwen Meadows rubbed her eyes before she looked across at her beautiful daughter with her pretty smile, pretty eyes, and perfect hair wearing her best dress and smiled proudly. The pad and charcoal pencil was set in front of Amy-Lou just like they were every night.

"What's tomorrow's flavor, darlin'?"

Amy-Lou grasped the charcoal pencil from the table and somehow held it between her back-bent fingers. She scrawled some letters with the pencil, whining, and then pushed the notebook across the wooden surface with the back of her hand. She groaned, gestured at the pad with her head and then stumbled to her feet and shambled away down the hall, disappearing back to the awful place she had come from.

Gwen reached for the pad and read the words beautifully printed on it in her daughter's curly and feminine penmanship. "Caramel pecan, ooh that sounds good!" said Gwen, standing up and stepping over to her large pantry. "Good idea as usual, baby!" she called down the empty hallway.

The caramel pecan ice-cream was a hit the next day. The store was busier than usual, welcoming in familiar faces from town as well as some curious first-timers. Walter Hertz was back too, touching up the new shelves so they would be ready for Gwen to stock over the weekend.

Around three o'clock a gaggle of schoolchildren exploded into the store with a solitary, weary parent in tow. Gwen watched them anxiously as they zoomed around her shop, touching things and generally making her nervous. The lone mother finally corralled the group over to the counter and ordered ice-cream cones for the lot of them. The kids cheered and waved their arms around. One of the boys swung his hands a little too wildly and sent the wooden box that Amy-Lou had made tumbling to the floor. The wonky lid went flying and a shower of small, white pieces of paper fell across the floor.

"Oh! I'm so sorry—Sam, you start picking those up right now!" the mother apologized, skipping over to the spill to start picking up alongside her red-faced charge.

Gwen went looking for the lid that had slid beneath an old dresser she used to hold serving implements. "It's alright. Kids will be kids!" she crooned, reaching a chubby hand beneath the large piece of furniture. "There it is!"

The mother was crouched down gathering up the pieces of paper and suddenly stopped, holding one up in front of her face. She grabbed another, then another, and each one had the same phrase written on it in barely legible scrawled black letters.

'IT HURTZ'

Furrowing her brow the mother quickly pushed all the paper back into the box and gathered her children. Behind her loomed Walter Hertz, looking down on the scene with cold eyes. One slip of paper had escaped retrieval and lay on the floor almost beneath the corner of the counter. Walter Hertz stared at the words written on it and glowered. He looked at Gwen, who was putting the lid back on the resituated wooden box, then turned sharply, gathered his tools and left the store.

A few minutes later he was in his truck driving towards Gwen's home, toolbox beside him in the passenger seat.

The Elephant in the Marble

Desmond Warzel

I met Ryan on a website—if you were gay, you'd probably be familiar with it. I've got a lot of friends on there. I might have more, but I don't come up in guys' searches—no tags on my profile to categorize me.

This is Dean, we've been exchanging emails for years, but he chickens out when I call him. This is Jerome, he lives here in the city. We saw each other a few times, but it just didn't happen. He's sweet, though. A lot of these guys are like that.

And this is Ryan. Ryan and I have been talking on the phone for months. I almost can't fall asleep without his voice in my ear. He's exactly my—well, I don't really have a type, but now I know I never needed one. I think Ryan is everything I want and there's no one else like him.

He's rich, too. But I don't care.

He's coming all the way from Seattle just to see me.

***

We have dinner downtown near the theater district, with lots of champagne. I know I won't remember eating—my eyes remain focused on his, barely sparing a glance for the filet mignon. Our knowing waiter deftly serves each course and removes our empty dishes and refills our champagne, remaining expertly outside our awareness.

"I never expected to meet such an interesting guy on a dating site," he remarks. "Someone who doesn't fit into any of the categories."

"You mean like twinks, bears, chubs, leather, drag?" I laugh. "Give me a break. I'm a person, not a fetish."

"And TV isn't helping," he said. "Everyone's either an

impeccably-dressed corporate suit or a mincing ninny in a gay minstrel show."

"Oh, you mean being some underfed neurotic woman's best friend isn't your lifelong ambition?"

Ryan laughs so hard he nearly chokes on his champagne. "You *do* understand." At some point during the discussion, his hand began touching mine.

"I'd just like to think that someone could love me as a person, without cross-indexing me."

"You want someone who loves you for who you are," he says.

"Yes."

"And what you can become." Ryan smiles.

"Yes."

We leave the restaurant and loiter on the sidewalk, the chilly evening air yanking us out of our self-absorbed reverie. I summon more courage than I've pulled together in years and ask him which hotel he's staying at. He says he didn't make a reservation, thought he'd "play it by ear." Imagine James Bond by way of Cary Grant—that's how self-assured he is.

When the sun streams through my venetian blinds and rouses me, Ryan is already awake. He asks me to move to Seattle and be with him. "But my work," I say, immediately wincing at my pretentiousness. I don't spend my days splitting atoms—I herd a bunch of teenage baristas at Starbucks, and surely I can do that anywhere, as Ryan points out.

I suggest we drive my car back to Seattle and get to know each other along the way. He squeezes my hand and says that'll be just fine.

***

Ryan's house is enormous. My first night there, I literally get lost making my way back to his bed—our bed—from the bathroom.

Over breakfast, I ask Ryan what he sees in me. I don't

usually get that girly about things, but I really want to know. "You're indefinable," he says. "I can make you my own." He doesn't ask me what I see in him. I love his self-confidence.

I really should look for work, but being with Ryan has shown me how little I really got out of my old job and my narrow, tenuous circle of friends. Ryan discourages it, anyway. He has more than enough money to support us and he says no job would provide me with enough satisfaction to make up for the time we would have to spend apart. I know he's right.

***

Along with all his other qualities, he's also an expert cook. After a month of living with him, I've gained almost twenty pounds. When did he have a chance to hone his skills so finely? He eats like a bird.

I should join a gym, or at least start jogging again. Ryan pooh-poohs my concerns. Did I give up everything to be with him, he asks, only to be worried about what other people think? "My opinion is the only one that matters and I'll love you no matter what," he says.

***

I stare at myself in the hall mirror. I think I must be fifty pounds heavier than when I arrived. Most of my clothes just plain don't fit anymore, but I rarely wear clothes around the house anyway. Ryan likes to look at me without them and I oblige him.

He comes up from behind and encircles me in his arms. "Admiring yourself?" he whispers in my ear. "Not really," I begin. "I—" He kisses the back of my neck. "Wanna go to bed?" he asks, and he can see in the mirror that I do.

Afterward, I stare at the textured ceiling, driven to distraction by its formless patterns. "You seem agitated," says Ryan. "I'm not surprised. Your whole life has changed, and we've just brushed that under the rug instead of dealing with it. I'm sorry. I've got something that'll help." He leaves and comes back a few minutes later with a glass of water and a pill. "This'll calm your nerves," he says gently. "My nerves are fine, it's just—" He won't have it, though. "Let me take care of you," he says. I take the pill and drink the water. "That's a good man," he says. "You'll thank me." He reaches down and takes me in his hand. "You think you could go one more time?" I raise a playful eyebrow. "At least." Ryan laughs. "I'll settle for once more. I don't think you'll be awake after that."

***

I've lost track of the days and months, but I don't care. Calendars and clocks are for miserable people, people who have to subdivide their lives into work and play. For me, there are no schedules. There's only Ryan, all day and all night. He cooks my meals, he gives me my pills, he gives himself to me. We're never apart.

I've never been so content for so long a time. It's not perfect, but what relationship ever is? Sometimes I get a little bitchy and try to make Ryan take me out somewhere, but he's always so understanding and I always apologize. Usually he'll give me two pills instead of one, to show me he forgives me.

One day I notice just how fat I'm getting. I bring it up, but Ryan reassures me that he loves all of me. "You know," I joke, "if you're into big guys, you're going to an awful lot of bother. There're plenty of chubby fish in the sea." He laughs, then gets up and leaves. He returns with three pills. "Someone like me," he says, "doesn't buy off the rack."

***

I have no idea what time it is. Why would I care? All time can do is bring an end to things. What Ryan and I have is forever. I can barely move now, but why would I want to? Time and motion are for outside. I am inside.

We are inside, Ryan and me and the bed, and there is nothing else. It's always dark, so I'm never sure how long I've slept, but that doesn't matter because Ryan is with me whenever I'm able to open my eyes. He looks at me with such longing.

On one occasion, I awake feeling numb and tingly all over. I can still feel the sheets, but I can't move my arms and legs. Ryan is at the foot of the bed. He says he has a surprise for me, but he needed to give me something to deaden the pain. He's holding something that looks like a shiny pen in the dim light. He says he's going to make me beautiful—that it'll last forever, like true art should. He can tell I'm nervous. He leans forward and takes me into his mouth. Right after I finish, I drift off again, lulled by the buzzing of the needle.

I awaken hours or days later. My chest and stomach are sore. My face, too. It's too dark to see what Ryan has drawn on me. He assures me it looks fantastic, and when it heals he'll take me out to the hall mirror so I can see. I ask if I can give him a tattoo someday. We should match. I'm asleep again before he can answer.

***

I am awake. I can't make much out anymore except for my own tattooed stomach, but on the floor next to the bed are a basin of water, some towels, and some other things I can't really see. Ryan is lying next to me. He notices that my eyes are open.

He retrieves a pill and some water from the stand. He places the pill on my tongue and holds the glass to my lips. As I swallow it down, he asks me, "Do you know what Michelangelo said when someone asked how to carve an elephant?" I giggle, spraying droplets of water. "Michelangelo never carved an elephant, silly. I think you're mixing up your riddles." He gently dabs at my lips with the blanket. "He said you just take a piece of marble and chip away everything that doesn't look like an elephant." We laugh. He kisses me gently.

This is a good pill. I feel light as air. I'm almost asleep already.

When he draws the blade of the saw across my leg, it is as sensual as one of his caresses. "I love you," I whisper.

Only Three Dead Presidents

Robert Essig

Mervin was like a kid in a candy store. His girlfriend, Tanya, like a cheerleader in a slaughterhouse.

"Oh God, Merv. This place is filthy."

"Filthy?" His eyes were glowing at the sheer intensity of something even his wildest dreams couldn't fathom. "This place is brilliant. Two please," he said to the decaying man at the ticket box. Leathery fingers handed over two tickets.

They walked through the turnstile and into the summertime amusement. A carnival, but not exactly what Tanya remembered from when she was a little girl. No, this carnival was of a different caliber and Mervin loved every bit of it.

"Wow, look at this!" Mervin's eyes were all but popping out of their sockets.

Tanya said nothing.

Once again Mervin was thinking only of himself. What she hoped would be a romantic night alone ended up in a third rate carnival. At times she wondered what it was that attracted her to Mervin—surely not his fascination with all things weird.

"Check this place out!" Mervin exclaimed.

She regarded him as if he were a weathered cigarette butt. *How could he like this place*?

The carnival was oddly constructed within the foliage of a forest. Trees stood tall, lined with trouble-lights and wrapped with white Christmas lights creating a dimness that could hide anything in the shadows. There were booths with carnies who looked like throwbacks from the beatnik era of the sixties on acid. Their eyes were bloodshot and floating in a sea of baggy flesh, and many of them were sporting frizzled moustaches and goatees, all hailing and chiding to gather a mark up to their table.

"Let's play a game," said Mervin.

"Yeah, whatever." Tanya had no interest in the midnight carnival.

"Hey you!" came a boisterous voice from a deep black booth, his face hardly visible. "Your girl looks unhappy. What the hell have you done to her?"

"Who, me?" said Mervin, looking around as if there was someone else the carnie was referring to. There really wasn't many people there at all.

"Yeah, you! Come over here and I'll guarantee you can win her something great!"

Mervin chuckled and proceeded to walk on by. He didn't want to stop at the first heckling carnie.

"Hey! Where you goin'? Have you even seen what I got here? What you can win for your little lady there?"

Mervin turned to look over his shoulder and stopped in his tracks. Tanya stopped, irritated, and had a look for herself. As much as she hated this place, her mouth fell open in awe for the booth was now illuminated and instead of the normal cheap prizes there were glimmering gold necklaces, rings and bracelets.

The sheer luminescence of the booth shone on the carnie leaving him an indistinguishable silhouette, his eyes seeming to glimmer as wildly as the jewelry behind him.

"No stuffed bears here! No hokey pictures of talentless pop singers. This is what she really wants buddy, and the game's as easy as they come, I swear you. E-A-S-Y, easy. You can't lose."

Mervin looked to Tanya. "Should we?"

She was ever the skeptic, but the array of glimmering jewelry was tempting. "Sure. Why not?"

As they walked up to the booth, the carnie chuckled like a lifetime smoker, "I knew you'd turn around. Come on over here and win her something she really wants, only three clams a pop and easy as pie. Step up, buddy."

"So what's the game?" asked Mervin, trying to sound confident and secure.

"Name's Goby," said the carnie, striking his hand out, the fingernails painted black, tattoos above his knuckles that spelled out: D-E-A-D.

Mervin shook his hand and said, "Mervin."

"All right, watch closely. I'm only gonna show you this once. All you have to do is throw this ring," Goby held up a grimy looking ring that may have once been red, "around the hook of whatever piece of jewelry you think would look best on your girlfriend here. Got it?"

It seemed easy enough, but that's the way carnival games always were. Each piece of jewelry was on a hook, and though Mervin knew he couldn't possibly choose a certain piece of jewelry, he asked Tanya which one she liked best.

Tanya pondered at the glimmering gold, noticing that there appeared to be diamonds embedded in some of the rings. *Probably fakes*, she thought. *It's all probably fake, has to be.*

She lost her interest and pointed to a necklace, any necklace just to be through with the charade. Goby was a strange one; his eyes dancing in the darkness his top hat provided them, wild and sleepless. *Probably high on meth*, thought Tanya.

Mervin handed over three wrinkled dollars. "All right, buddy, take a stab at it." Goby handed over the dirty ring.

"Kiss it for good luck?" Mervin asked sarcastically.

Tanya grimaced.

"Here goes nothing."

Mervin focused and made the toss. It missed the piece Tanya selected, but did catch on another hook, the weight of the ring pulling the hook down, dropping the necklace onto the ground.

"We got a winner!" yelled Goby.

Goby kneeled down to retrieve the prize, but what he came up with puzzled both Mervin and Tanya.

"What?" said Goby slapping the tarnished waist of necklace on the table with his other hand, tattooed with F-U-C-K above the knuckles. "Don't like?"

On the wall behind Goby all the pieces of jewelry were immaculate and shinning, but the piece he pulled from the ground was old and beat. The chain had knots and kinks in it; the medallion—a circular piece of rusted junk with an intricate pattern on it—chipped and dinged. It was an insult.

"Take it. You won it." Goby handed the insult to Mervin, then redirected his attention to no one in particular, beginning his pitch again. "Step right up and win a talisman! Yes sir, you heard me—a real life authentic talisman!"

"What is he talking about?" asked Tanya as they walked off. "Throw that away. It's ugly."

Mervin regarded the necklace. "A talisman? He didn't say anything about that when we walked up, did he?"

"I don't know. We should just go, Merv."

"Go? Why? We just got here."

"This place..." she looked around. " It's not right. I don't like it. And where are all the people? Aren't carnivals usually packed with people?"

"It's a midnight carnival. Maybe it hasn't caught on yet. Let's get something to eat." Mervin pointed to a lunch truck. "There's a roach coach, we'll get a bite there."

"Gross."

They sat on paint-chipped benches eating chewy burgers followed by fries drowned in grease, all washed down with Coke (which was the best part of the meal) when Mervin further regarded the necklace.

"I'm not putting that thing around my neck," she said.

"I'll wear it then."

"This place is dead. Do you think they're closing for the night or something?"

"Naw, the carnival's open until daybreak."

"Where did you hear about this place?"

"Got a flyer somewhere."

Mervin put the necklace around his neck.

"Where are all the people?" she asked. "I feel like I'm in the *Twilight Zone*."

As the necklace hung around Mervin's neck things came into focus. "What are you talking about? There's actually a lot of people here."

"You're kidding me, right? I see, like, four people walking around. It's creepy."

"What? This place is packed. They all must have come at one time."

Tanya sighed. It was becoming more and more difficult to humor Merv. He loved carnivals and circuses, was nearly obsessed, but this was taking it too far. The place was a miserable dump and here he was trying to make it out to be on par with Barnum and Bailey.

But Tanya couldn't see what Mervin could see, what the necklace opened his eyes to; couldn't hear what the necklace opened his ears to.

"Oh wow! A haunted house!" Mervin grabbed Tanya's hand. "Let's go."

She screamed as the herds of people appeared suddenly with his grasp on her hand, the necklace causing her to be transformed into the bustling carnival Mervin's eyes had been opened to.

"What's wrong?" he asked.

"All these people... Where did they come from?"

When Mervin put on the necklace, the sudden abundance of people didn't surprise him. The sudden large crowds seemed normal, expected.

"Like I said, they must have all come at once."

She pulled her hand from his to wipe away the sweat that formed there from her nerves, and that's when things changed back to the dismal carnival. The lights seemed dimmer, the trees large and foreboding. And the people were reduced to only a few wanderers like lost souls.

"They're gone!"

"Who's gone?"

"All the people, they're gone."

"What are you *talking* about, Tanya?"

She looked back, toward Goby's booth, and he was staring at her, his eyes like diamonds embedded in his filthy face. His teeth seemed to gleam as well, red and blue like rubies and sapphires, but she knew it was just a façade to cover the rot therein, the old decrepit carnie.

"Let me see your hand," she said.

Mervin held out his hand for her, and when she took it, she wasn't quite as surprised to witness a miracle. The carnival was suddenly bustling and noisy with laughter and excitement, people as far as her eyes could see.

"Don't let go of my hand, okay?" she said.

"Yeah, sure, whatever."

She could see that he didn't get it, didn't see what was at play here.

"Let's get out of this crowd for a moment," said Tanya. "I want to talk to you about something."

There was brightness in the distance, perhaps a large light source. "Over there," she said. "Let's go over there."

They worked their way through the crowd, hands separating but for a lonely moment that stole away the crowd and replaced it with a dismal ruin, a parallel carnival that grew more disturbing every time Tanya saw it. She grabbed his hand ferociously to take the grim carnival away.

As they neared the intense brightness that seemed to come from between two large trees, what they saw could only be a projection or some kind of illusion.

"Take a look at that!" said Mervin. His smile showed Tanya that he really had no idea what was going on, that the necklace was indeed some sort of magical talisman creating this whole thriving carnival that she knew wasn't really there.

They stood before the immaculate screen, for it had to be a screen of some sort. The picture was of a lush, green pasture, the light blindingly bright; the image so clear it seemed they could walk right into it.

"Only three dead presidents, kids, if you want to bask in the sunlight on that grassy knoll," came a voice from behind them.

They turned to get a look at the guy.

"Hello, folks!" he said, his voice ragged and torn, the odor of booze permeating his body. "It's like nothin' you've ever seen, I'll guarantee you that. Nighttime on this side, daytime over there. Why not take a look-see?"

There was no trust in his grubby five o' clock shadowed face, his smile revealing black teeth that had probably been rotten since his mother dipped his pacifier in whiskey to shut him up when he was a baby.

But the wall of daylight was so intriguing, even Tanya wondered.

It's a trick. This whole place is a trick.

She wanted to tell Mervin about the necklace, try and get him to take it off so he could see what was really going on, but the bizarre screen of daylight stretched between two trees was so real that she was completely taken aback.

"It's only three—" the carnie took notice of Mervin's necklace. "—free to you, sir, and your lovely girl. I see you've won one of Goby's gold necklaces. That, my friend, is a ticket to ride. Walk on through to the other side and bask in real sunlight at two in the morning. You'll never experience anything like this again, I assure you."

"Free?" asked Mervin. "We can just walk through?"

"With that there gold necklace you can."

Mervin grabbed the necklace with his free hand, Tanya's grip on his right hand like a vice.

"It's gold again," said Mervin.

Tanya gasped. Indeed the necklace was as gold and shiny as it had been hanging on the hook in Goby's game booth.

Tanya looked back to see if Goby was still watching them, but he was too far off, concealed by distance and midnight carnival goers.

"Let's go!" said Mervin as if the fact that his necklace changing appearance was nothing to be shocked about.

"Go, have fun," said the greasy carnie, his breath hitting the both of them in a cloud like the air of a busy tavern.

"C'mon." Mervin pulled Tanya toward the screen of bright day that led to a picturesque vision of a vibrant field. She tried to protest, but before she could stop him he was already walking into the picture, his body suddenly taking on a glow as he entered, as if the sunlight was suddenly shinning over him.

She tried not to enter, afraid of what lay therein, but she was more afraid of what she would see were she to let go of his hand.

As she walked through what she thought was a projection screen, she could feel the warmth wash over her. As her head came through, the brightness caused her eyes to close tight like a sea anemone.

"This is amazing!" said Mervin. "I've never seen anything like this."

Mervin tried to squirm his hand from her grasp to look at his watch, but her grip was intense. "Want to loosen up your paw there, Tanya. You're cutting off my circulation. I want to see what time it is."

"I can't let go of your hand."

"What are you talking about? What's wrong with you tonight?" He looked around at the blue sky and green pasture. "Or today, or whatever."

He pulled his hand free and looked at his watch. "It's two thirty at ni—"

Tanya screamed in horror at what she saw around her. She grabbed Mervin's hand to bring her back to sanity.

"What's your problem?"

"You need to see what I see, Merv. Take that necklace off."

"Oh, now that it's gold again you want to wear it."

"That's not it at all. You don't understand. You need to take it off and see what I see when I let go of your hand."

"Here," he began taking the necklace off. "You can wear it."

As he lifted the necklace over his head, the day turned into night like someone placing a drape over the birdcage called Earth. The necklace was suddenly transformed back into a rusted piece of junk.

The wide-eyed look on Mervin's face relieved Tanya, but the darkness around them filled her with dread, and worse, the lush prairie was replaced with a weed-riddled graveyard.

"What the..." said Mervin. He quickly replaced the necklace and winced as brightness filled his eyes.

"Grab my hand!" said Tanya, feeling as if she were estranged from him, knowing he was in a better place.

He grabbed her hand. She cringed as the light hit her, driving a nail of brightness into her eyes.

"What the hell is going on?" asked Mervin, finally recognizing what Tanya had been trying to tell him.

"We need to leave, Merv. This carnival is bad, it's wrong. We have to get out of here."

The grassy plains were inviting, but not with the certain knowledge that there was a graveyard out there, hidden beneath a veneer created by the necklace, the talisman.

From between the same two trees, they could see the darkness of the carnival, the bustling of imaginary people stuffing their faces with cotton candy and peanuts, hotdogs and fried foods, laughing and jolly.

"Let's go back through," said Mervin suddenly fearful of the paranoid consequences that filled his mind. The grim possibility that the movie screen sized swatch between the trees that now showed them the midnight carnival would shrivel up extinguishing their doorway back to reality.

"Run! Quick!" he said.

They ran together, their grip precariously sweaty from shared nerves, and just before they made it through the portal and back into the Midnight Carnival Tanya's foot caught a rock, pulling her down, the sweaty grip they held ripped apart as Mervin went through the portal, unable to stop inertia as his body disappeared into the darkness of the carnival.

Tanya was in darkness as well, her mind wrecked as the portal swallowed itself leaving her in a graveyard all alone.

"Mervin!" she screamed. "Mervin! Where are you?"

But there was no answer. There was no portal where she could see the gluttonous carnival goers stuffing their faces, or the grim-faced carnies hollering and chiding for people to waste their money on games and cheap prizes.

And Mervin had the necklace.

"Help! Mervin! Help me! Where are you?"

Again, there was no answer, but there was a noise in the still night, a sort of rustling from behind her. She turned, and that's when her worst fears, the very irrational fears that kept many people out of graveyards after dark, became a reality.

They were coming out of the graves, corpses filthy with soil and crawling with nocturnal insects, all eyes and empty sockets on her.

Then she recognized one of them. It was Goby. They all had a look in their eyes like she was a mark, that greedy passion as if everyone who enters the carnival is a piggy bank that just needed to be shaken a little to get the money out.

They were carnies, all of them. Some were freaks, their forms strange and more menacing than the rest, pinheads and rubber-band men, clowns and people with horrible deformities.

And they were all walking toward her.

"Mervin, help me!" she screamed into the forest, but the portal remained closed, the forest devoid of the carnival that was the real world.

They inched closer, without a word, some smiling, others so decomposed they were skeletons with mere morsels of dried tissue remaining on their bones.

Tanya screamed.

They were only an arm's length away.

A hand shot out of nowhere disembodied and floating in the air. For a split second she feared the arm, but realized it was Mervin's. She grabbed it, and in that split second before he pulled her back to the midnight carnival, there was a flash of brightness that seemed to shock her retinas like staring into the sun. She couldn't see, but knew the undead carnies and freaks had been banished in that brightness.

"Oh God, I thought I lost you," said Mervin.

Tanya's face was saturated with tears, not only of fear, but relief too.

"Let's get out of here," he said.

"Wait!"

"What is it?"

"The necklace. Take it off. This is not reality." She let go of his hand. "This is."

Mervin nodded then took the necklace off and dropped it. It tarnished immediately, before it hit the ground. "What the...?" he said.

Tanya followed his eyes and saw the sign, arched above what the necklace showed them as a portal to a sunny, green field. The sign said: Vagabond Cemetery.

Instead of a warm summer day, now they could see the truth—the cemetery that lay beyond the gates, only now the graves were still.

"You wanna visit the final restin' place for our deceased brethren?" said a drowsy looking soul in a little ticket booth they hadn't noticed. "Only three dead presidents."

The Good Father

E.R. Delafield

When Adrian came home after work, his thirteen-year-old daughter was in the living room, dancing on her toes. He was exhausted and the place was a mess, but he was glad to see a smile on her face for the first time in weeks.

"Hey, sunshine."

"Gretchen and I got an A on our project."

Jenny followed Adrian as he picked up the scattered newspapers around the room. She chatted about science: the teacher was impossible to please, but she and Gretchen had worked really hard for weeks on their photosynthesis project.

Adrian was just glad that the project was finally over, the whole thing had been nerve-wracking for him. Jenny had demonstrated a natural talent for it and of course her plants had been kept in the house, making it difficult for him to sleep. How many times had he checked on them, wrestling with his fear over the way he caught Jenny humming to them? So much like her mother.

He shoved the newspapers into the recycling basket and gave Jenny a weak smile. "Would you like to invite Gretchen to go to a movie?"

"Gretchen's not into movies," Jenny said.

Adrian watched Jenny; aware at the way she bit her lip and played with the fringe of the rocking chair that she wanted something specific. "A sleepover?"

"Dad," Jenny said and then in a large breathless statement, "Gretchen's parents are taking her to Lyman Lake this weekend. They want me to come. Her dad's going to show us how to fish."

Adrian's stomach turned to ice. He could smell the bleach

in his nostrils, and remembered how the earth had tried to pull him down into her embrace.

"I'll think about it," he said. *Coward*, he thought.

Jenny's face dimmed. "Daddy, I need to tell her tonight."

"I said I'd think about it," Adrian said. He and Emory had barely made it out of the woods alive; the trees had struck out at them. The last thing he wanted was Jenny anywhere near a wooded area.

Jenny's knuckles were white as she clenched the sofa chair. "They go all the time."

"You usually have a lot of homework over the weekend," Adrian said. *It's not safe, don't let her go.*

"I'll do it Sunday night. Please, Daddy."

Adrian's rational mind tried to reason with his gut. It wasn't likely that anything would happen to her in just a weekend. There was no logical reason why not — *remember the project? Remember Mrs. Costello's damn garden last summer? You don't know what could happen. You don't want to know what could happen.*

"Daddy?"

You'll regret it. "No, Jenny. Not this weekend." He faced her crushed expression head-on. "Maybe another time."

Jenny kicked the back of the chair with her shoe. "You're just saying that! It's not fair."

The flash of anger in her eyes gave Adrian a punch to the gut. *Just like her mother.*

"It's not fair," Jenny said. "Just because you hate the outdoors."

"Don't be melodramatic."

Jenny kicked the chair again. "Stop saying that."

"Don't kick the furniture. The way you're behaving—"

"It's not fair."

"Jenny."

Tears were in her eyes. "Please, Dad."

Adrian almost gave into her, but the reasonable part of himself reminded him that such inconsistency would only teach her that she could get what she wanted. Her mother was the same way.

"Some other time," he said.

A final kick to the chair and Jenny plunged up the stairs. Adrian stood in the aftermath, looked at the pile of old newspapers and cursed himself. *Idiot.*

***

Beer washed the plastic taste of the reheated pasta out of Adrian's mouth while he stared at the four or five feet of lawn allotted to his townhouse. He moved to this neighborhood because of the lawns; everything was so safe here. Even the grass was boxed in.

He knew it was right to stick to his guns. He couldn't go back and forth like a cuckoo. Besides Jenny was impossible.

But it's your fault that she's impossible. You should have told her.

Jenny had only been a child when it happened. And how could he have explained it to a child when even he didn't completely understand it himself.

Fifteen years ago, he'd been a half way normal guy. He'd put a down payment on his little cabin. He had a garden, his sanity and a naïve passion for the world. He'd found his little piece of paradise; was going to write a book, study the wildlife, maybe raise a family. How could he explain what had happened instead? How could he even describe it?

"I was living in New York, out in the country, where they were going to bulldoze these beautiful woods. This Indian I palled around with, whose daughter I was seeing, said—look, I know what my people'd do in this situation, I know what they shoulda done when you people first showed up..."

No,—he couldn't tell her that. He couldn't put it into words or expect her to believe him. She didn't remember her mother, didn't remember anything about New York. He was sure of that. He just wanted her to have a normal life.

Which brought him, in a circular way, back to his dilemma. Adrian shifted uneasily, his dress shoes pinching his feet. He stood half the day, dealing with window shoppers, and now he stood for relaxation. He needed his head examined about more things than one.

Jenny has to have a normal life.

He swished beer in his mouth. He glanced up at her window. As his eyes trailed over the back of the townhouse he could see the green veins of a plant, slick against vinyl, nearly at the window.

It's found her.

He dropped his beer, not even registering the noise of the bottle shattering, as he jumped in two leaps across the patio. His fingers snagged the plant and started to yank.

The plant was stubborn. His fingernails cut open the stalk, its sticky innards coated his skin. It snapped in tiny pieces, which he ignored as he tried to get more of it. He snapped up the broken bottle and gouged it into the plant's flesh. The damn thing looked hooked—no, burrowed—in the siding. In his frenzied attack, he sliced it in half.

Where the hell did it come from?

Adrian began ripping it off the bricks. He followed it to the next-door neighbor's patio, and through the narrow black railing that separated Adrian's porch from Mrs. Costello's flowerbed. The plant's tendrils grew thicker as it reached the bed, becoming a heavy stalk as wide as his fist. It was nested carefully among rose bushes; the thorns stabbed his skin.

Damn woman! Her stupid garden!

Adrian tried to pull the vine loose, but its barbs cut his hand. His heart hammered in his ears, but he remembered his lessons. He grabbed a bottle of bleach from the kitchen and poured it onto the bed, barely able to see the clear fluid spilling and swirling into the earth.

Take that you damn thing. Drink up.

"Mr. Kerensky?"

The old woman's tremulous voice came from her porch. She was in a sunflower yellow robe, her hair in pink curlers, and she waddled over.

Adrian tried to hide the bottle, but the toad's round, glassy eyes caught sight of it immediately.

"You can't do that." Her lower lip shook like a child's. "That's against the law."

Shut her up before half the neighborhood notices, Adrian thought wildly. *Shut her up before Jenny notices.*

"Your plants are out of control. Look at my house."

Mrs. Costello wailed and embraced her flowerbed. "My babies, my babies. I'm calling the association. You can't do this to people's plants. It's not right."

Oh, shit, Adrian thought. He backed off, moving towards the sliding glass door and the safety of his kitchen. He could have the homeowner's association on his side, he was sure of that, if he was able to offer evidence of its digging into the side of his house.

In the corner of his eyes, he saw the plant slither across his patio.

***

His fingers shook as he dialed, but he was sure if he stopped to think about it, he wouldn't be able to remember the number.

It rang six times. An unfamiliar voice said: "Hello?"

"I'm calling for Emory Blackfeather. He still there?"

"Just a sec," said the man.

Adrian was jittery, trying to remember the last time he and Emory had talked. He couldn't even remember half the plans they'd discussed, once they were free of those damned trees. Only Emory saying, "I'd get my ass to a city and stay there, if I were you."

Well, I half made it, Emory. I half made it. And it hasn't been bad—only I've got no clue what to do now. And I'm scared. First time in nine years, I'm terrified.

A woman's voice came on the other end. "Hello?"

It was Mattie. *Hell.*

"Hey, it's Adrian." He cleared his throat in the strained silence. "Adrian Kerensky."

"I remember."

Just great. "Look, your dad there?"

"What trouble are you in?"

"It's an emergency. I have to talk to him. Please, Mattie?"

"Oh, you have to talk to him. Old days, isn't it? You had to talk to him the last time, then he comes back looking like death warmed over."

Adrian knew that last day in the woods had taken a lot out of both of them. He'd found gray hairs all through his beard and hair in the motel mirror the next morning. As for Emory, God only knew.

"Just two minutes, Mattie. Two minutes and I swear to God—"

"You can swear all you like, but you won't get it."

Adrian felt the receiver slip a little in his hand. *Why the hell can't she just let it die*? "Mattie..."

"He's dead."

Adrian felt his stomach sink. *What the hell am I going to do now*?

"I didn't know," he managed to say. "I'm sorry."

"The sun doesn't rise and set on your wanting it," Mattie said.

"I'm sorry," Adrian replied. He felt sick to his stomach.

Emory was his best friend and all Adrian could do was think of himself. He was a selfish son of a bitch; Emory had put his life on the line for Jenny. What had Adrian ever done in return? "If I'd known... How'd it happen?"

"It finally up and killed him."

Adrian felt his bladder go cold. "What?

"Those damn woods. I knew nothing good would happen you getting him all worked up—"

Adrian's heart stopped. "Wait," he said, or he tried to say. His tongue was thick and now he could hear hammering in his ear. "Wait."

"—I knew it would kill him, but he wouldn't listen. What did you ever do for him?"

"What about the woods?" He could hear the air around him, and his fingers shook.

"They bulldozed it," Mattie said. "Just like they planned."

***

He told Jenny it was an emergency. Her grandfather was dying and they were going to Texas before it was too late to say good-bye. She argued with him. She pleaded to stay with Gretchen. He shut her down, got her in the car and on the highway.

It was nine years ago all over again. Except that now Ataensic was loose, and God knew where, and Adrian was running cold. He could still hear the cut in Mattie's voice when he asked her: "You think that woman would come see me?"

Adrian's hands were slick on the steering wheel. He glanced in the rearview mirror to catch sight of Jenny's face. Nine years ago, she'd been a toddler in a footed pink sleeper and she hadn't woken up the whole long drive out of New York. In a motel, in Pennsylvania, he had explained her mother was dead and she had cried, but she hadn't argued. She had trusted him.

I was supposed to give her a normal life, he thought in agony. His stomach ached fiercely. Would San Antonio or Dallas be far enough? There was a lot of pollution in those cities, smog, too. But Mexico City—he definitely knew Ataensic couldn't reach them there. It would kill her. He hoped it would kill her.

You think Jenny's just going to sit still while you drive to Mexico City? You think this is some kind of fucking normal life?

It's time to tell her. It's time to sit her down and explain the whole damn thing.

Adrian swallowed the bile in the back of his throat and focused on the highway in front of him. He didn't know where to begin.

Perhaps he could start by saying he loved her? That she was more important to him than all his values, all his beliefs? That he'd walk through hell itself so that she could have the kind of life she deserved to have?

But when Adrian looked at Jenny's face in the mirror, all he could see was this mask of anger and resentment. She was plugged into her iPod, deliberately looking away from him.

You coward, he thought bitterly. At the same time, his heart said: *One more night. Tomorrow morning, explain everything. Beginning to end.*

Adrian gripped the steering wheel tighter.

***

Adrian stopped at one of those hotels along the highway. Its neon light welcomed them off the highway, and although he saw trees behind the sign, they didn't look close enough to harm them. Besides, his eyes were too exhausted to stay open.

The hotel should be safe enough for tonight, he decided

Jenny didn't even speak to him when he got a suite. He asked for one next to the pool, thinking Jenny might swim in the morning. He remembered, only after she threw herself into the bedroom and slammed the door, that of course she wouldn't have packed a suit.

Adrian laid down on the couch, even though he was exhausted he couldn't get to sleep. His mind kept recycling old thoughts and ideas. The humidity seeping under the glass door left him sticky, but the blast of the air conditioning made him sick.

Adrian walked barefoot out into the pool area, which was dead and dark. He sat down on a damp chair near the water and poked his toes about on the wet tiles.

Some normal life.

The chlorine smell burned his nostrils. The water was a milky blue, churning quietly as it waited for the inevitable tide of guests who would come plunging out in the morning. Adrian could imagine the noise of the children.

He remembered, without wanting to remember, the pond outside their tiny cabin in New York. He taught Jenny how to swim that last summer; he saw Ataensic's quiet, contemplative face as she whispered beneath the trees or coaxed wildflowers out of hiding. He had built a bench swing overlooking the pond, and in the evening he would find Ataensic there, cradling Jenny in her arms and whispering.

It was on that bench, his hands sweating, and his clothes sticking to his damp skin, that he had tried to compose himself after he saw what happened to the construction crew. It was on that bench that Adrian served Ataensic the glass of bleach and watched her choke, writhe and cry out. He heard the trees howl in agony with her, his spine quaking.

He had loved her so much; even now he could remember the awe of seeing her, listening to her, teaching her about the modern world while she taught him all the secrets of the woods. It had been a good life; but at that time Adrian and Emory didn't know what had happened to that first developer. If they'd known...

Adrian wiped his cheekbones with the side of his hand. If he could go back, would he take it away? Would he cut Jenny out so neatly? Or would there have been another Jenny? Mattie's Jenny, maybe; some other kid. In that other, more peaceful world, would he be looking into the backyard of the development, wishing to hell he'd done more to stop it?

You made your choice. It was a bad choice. So make good ones from now on.

His hands trembled like they had nine years ago. He wanted to bawl, but he had to hold it together. He had to explain to Jenny, tell her all of it and then... He didn't know. God help him, he didn't know.

Adrian knocked lightly on the bedroom door, and when she didn't answer he pushed it open. The room was empty, lit by the bathroom light. He didn't even see her backpack.

"Jenny?"

He went into the hall and there was no sign of her. He ran to the lobby, where the clerk frowned over Sudoku.

"Have you seen my daughter?"

"Huh?"

Adrian grabbed the clerk by the shirt and yanked him forward. "My daughter," Adrian said. "She's thirteen."

The clerk pointed towards the front door. Adrian bolted. What was Jenny thinking? Was she running away? Was she going to try to take the car?

The asphalt cut his feet. He saw his car exactly where he'd left it. He looked all around, hoping Jenny had walked over to the 24/7. He couldn't see from where he was standing and questioned if it was worth it to dart over and check. He didn't know. He could think clearer if it weren't for all the whispering.

The whispering.

Adrian glanced over the parking lot for signs of trees. It had seemed farther from the highway. He ran, sure he recognized the murmuring of trees, spreading news on the wind.

Please don't take her.

His heart raced as he reached the top of a small embankment at the edge of the parking lot, and saw that a broken creek ran below. A little ways further, standing out in the night, Jenny stood near a pair of deformed trees.

"Jenny!"

He plunged downwards, slipping in the grass. *Don't take her, don't take her, don't take her.* His heart thundered the rhythm out while he screamed Jenny's name again.

The creek was cold and his feet burned with pain. The trees bent their branches towards Jenny, and Adrian wept in his panic.

He reached her, threw his arms around her, and cried into her soft brown hair.

"Jenny," he said.

She pushed him away, scowling.

"Jenny." Adrian put his hands on her shoulders and looked into her dark, angry face. "It's not safe."

Jenny took a step back, towards the trees. Adrian grabbed a hold of her hand and tried to pull her towards him. She wrestled free.

"Jenny, you don't understand. I'll explain, but we have to get away from here."

Jenny was surly in her adolescent anger. "I understand."

"You don't."

Jenny huffed and threw up her hands. "I do!"

"Jenny...."

She grew calm, her frown replaced by a guarded expression. "You'll tell me."

"Anything. But let's go inside."

"You tell me what you did to my mother."

Jenny's words echoed in the open space. Adrian could have sworn the trees had paused to listen.

"Jenny," he said, "I only wanted you to be safe."

"You hurt my mother."

"You were too young to understand. What your mother did to those people—what your mother was—"

"She's my mother."

Adrian wanted to explain. But how can you explain something elemental brought to life? In the end, he suspected not even Emory was aware of what they had awoken.

"Your mother was special," Adrian said, "but she was also dangerous. I'm so sorry, Jenny."

The whispering began, and his legs burned in fierce response. He glanced down to see what the hell he'd done to himself and saw instead gnarled roots and the rough, brown bark of a tree.

"Jenny..."

He looked into his daughter's face and saw her whispering. Her lips moved the way her mother's had once done to coax seedlings and heal a tree damaged by a storm.

The transformation of his lower body left him rooted in the ground, unable to move.

"Jenny, I wanted —I had to protect you—" Adrian gasped for breath. "Don't do this—I'll take you back, I promise—"

"My mother is coming for me," Jenny said. She stared at him and he tried to read compassion on her face. "She's been looking for me. Even the trees have been looking for me."

Adrian tried to rock himself loose. Only his head moved; the tree had now encased his abdomen. He would have cried, but it had become hard to breathe. "Let me go, Jenny."

"I don't want her to hurt you," Jenny said.

"It'll be okay," Adrian said wildly. He felt the air pressure grow in his lungs.

"But I don't want you to hurt her, either."

"Jenny," Adrian said, "no one—we can—we could get away."

"Dad, you don't understand."

"Stop," Adrian said. The part of himself that was no longer human but something vegetable, something alien, had now reached his throat. He wasn't sure how much longer he could speak. "Jenny—" it came out harsh, and when he tried to clear his throat, there was no more speech. The bark crawled over his chin, swept up against his lower lip.

Jenny touched one of his branches. The tree part of him could feel the power coursing through his veins; he could recognize the energy and the life she radiated.

"You'll be safe," Jenny said, and she smiled at him, like a final apology. Adrian wanted to hug her, to try and explain one last time.

She looked away, and his last sight of his daughter was as she stared into the distance, a strand of her hair stuck against her cheekbone.

Then Adrian was buried in the warmth of his cocoon. His veins ebbed and flowed in the rhythm of whispers, to the murmur of power that shivered in his roots.

While Gabriel Slept

Matt Moore

Pray: Deliver Your strength to my loved ones...

—soul spirals away like wisps of smoke shredded to nothing. reclaimed by darkness. like i belong to it. strength, love, feeling. gone. this place takes all i am. only certainty remains: must do something—

Was in kitchen, now in nursery. Don't remember getting here.

Been like that a lot lately.

Pain like a white hot needle twisting under my left temple. My wife—

–can't think of her in any other term–

–just a description–

–the liar doesn't deserve a name–

—looks up, gives a look like: *Why am I doing all the work?* then makes *gootchy gootchy goo* noises, tickling the baby's feet. The baby—

–also undeserving of a name–

—giggles.

Dry, sweet smell of baby powder, formula, wet wipes—overpowering. Stomach clenches and does a slow roll. Should run to bathroom, but can barely move my feet.

"So that's that," is Mom's conclusion to a topic I don't remember. Phone's heavy as a brick. Struggle to keep it to my ear. She asks: "And how's my granddaughter?"

Look at the baby. Needle twists harder. Hope to keep pain from voice. "Fine," I lie. Baby is fine, but don't have the heart to tell Mom she isn't her granddaughter.

"I do hope you and"–my wife's name–"can bring her up and

visit some time soon. I can't wait to meet her."

There is power in what Mom didn't say: bring her up and visit some time soon *while I still have time.*

"Sure, some time soon."

My wife pulls a blanket over the baby, shushing her to sleep. Sings a lullaby.

Needle punctures something. Fury sprays hot like arterial blood.

Should smash her head with the phone. So tiny, so small. Rage-fueled strength to crush, to pound...

To...

Pray: Please God, tell me I don't need to do this...

—not darkness. darkness is the absence of light. no concept of light here. a realm god passed over. heaven and earth, light and life, created elsewhere—

Outside on balcony. Wind has picked up, cold against face and arms. Smells clean. Mom is talking about visiting Dad this afternoon.

Turn, see wife bent over baby, smiling.

Safe.

Needle now an icepick, jabbing inside skull.

Phone bad idea, anyway. Just shattering plastic, a welt, some blood. Then cops. Cuffs. Comments about what kind of a monster could do that. And Mom wondering why the phone cut out.

"Be nice if you could make it out to see your father," Mom hints.

Look down at street, nine stories below. "I know. But it's hard with the baby." Jump would kill me, but my priest said I'd go straight to Hell. No chance to tell God what He will not hear in prayer: that my wife and mother and father need His strength and grace. He may not act, but He must hear.

And I will not escape the pain of my wife's betrayal through death. Not if she's still alive.

But after...

Barely lift feet to step back into living room. Like moving through syrup. Pain quivers with each footfall, wringing the back of my neck.

"Sound good?" Mom wants to know.

No idea what she said. "Yup."

She might hear indifference in my voice. Might ask: "What's wrong, dear?"

How to respond? "Nothing really, Mom," I could say. "I got the results this morning. Amazing what technology can do. Swab my cheek, then the baby's, and mail them off. A week later, some lab tells you your wife got knocked up by some other guy and didn't even tell you."

"That's horrible, dear," she might reply.

"Did I mention she tried to make it out like it was my fault? When I asked her about the credit card charges at lingerie and 'adult toy' stores, she doesn't deny it. Like she wasn't trying to hide it. She tells me I'm boring and shallow and she'd hoped she could change me, but it never happened. So she sought out other men."

And Mom might say: "No, dear, you never mentioned that" but instead says: "You sound tired, sweetie."

Soft footsteps. Small, bare feet on hardwood. I turn. "I am." Truth for once.

"You should—"

Lose the rest. My wife is saying something.

Hear neither of them.

Ice pick scraping inside my skull, scoring jagged grooves.

"Hold on, Mom." Hand over mouthpiece. Look down at my wife. So tiny. Not even five feet tall. I played fullback in college. Making love, I had to be careful. Could have crushed her.

Maybe that is how I could do it. Make it look like an accident.

But thought of my hands on her repulses me, like handling human filth. Only way I would touch her is hands around throat.

"Sorry?"

Wife rolls her eyes, looks back up. "What I said was 'I'm going to take a nap. Make sure the baby doesn't cry'." She motions to the door of the bedroom we made the nursery—

—No, not "we" made--she picked everything, I did the work

—paint, assemble furniture, hang pictures. Barely had the strength for it. My wife's role was to find the flaws, tell me our child deserves the best.

Envy Dad. Unable to remember anything—his name, where he is, who Mom is. "I'll try."

"Do more than try. I did the work for nine months. Least you can do is keep her quiet for an hour." She turns, heads for our bedroom.

Wish phone wasn't cordless. Phone cord looped over her head, pulled tight around throat until she stops moving.

What would Mom hear? Gasping, struggling, cartilage cracking.

My wife shuts bedroom door and for a moment I can believe she's gone for good.

—never here in the first place—

—never met her, fell in love, confronted her about the credit card charges and what she was doing all those business trips and late nights at the office.

She confessed and vowed she was done. Stopped trips, late nights. But resisted counseling.

Six months passed. Started getting home an hour later than normal. Then two. Sometimes not home until midnight. Wondered if cheating again. Prayed she would remain strong and faithful, but felt nothing. Only darkness. Darkness filled me. Headaches clouded thoughts. Unfocused at work. Tired all day, but could not sleep at night. Strength gone. Trouble making love.

Told me she was pregnant. Should have been happy—a baby would bring us together—but suspicions remained. We had not been together often and sometimes I could not finish.

Was baby mine?

Ice pick pries something loose. Thick as my pinky finger, it squirms deep in my skull.

Break into a sweat. "Sorry, Mom. What were you saying?"

"Are you okay, sweetie?"

"Far from it," I could answer. "Do you remember teaching me to pray, Mom? How to clear my mind and open myself? You used to tell me God cannot answer all prayers, but He hears them. So praying brought me peace, Mom, because I knew God heard me. But I don't think God hears me anymore. Everything's dark when I pray."

"That's terrible, sweetie," she might say.

"It's worse than that," I'd continue. "I could kill her. But my priest said God does not hear prayers of sinners unless they repent and ask forgiveness. I do not know what sin I committed so God will not hear me, so how can I ask forgiveness? And I would never be sorry for killing her. But I think I have found a way."

Talked to another priest on other side of city. Lied and said infant son had heart defect. No hope. I asked: Can he hear me and understand when gone? Priest said while alive, infant cannot understand, but can as spirit.

Had found way for God to hear me. Tell baby my prayers—my wife needs God's strength to remain faithful and not stray. And my mother needs strength in the face of the illness that will take her life. And my father needs God's grace while his mind slips away.

"And then if I kill the baby," I might tell Mom, "she goes to heaven as my messenger."

"Sweetie?" Mom asks, waiting for answer.

"Just tired, Mom." Thing in my head wriggles, borrowing deep. Hold back a gasp of slashing pain.

"That lasts another ten years, dear." Trying to be funny.

Look back toward bedroom door. How would it feel to put

hand over her mouth and pinch her nose? Imagine her struggling —surprisingly strong—arching her back and awkwardly kicking and punching, pivoting her head, desperate for breath? Would I have the strength and resolve to hold my hand in place until she stops fighting?

For that, I do. If I have sinned so that God does not hear me, I am lost. What is one more sin? Or two?

Approach the door. Soft, gentle sounds of sleep. "Gotta go, Mom."

"You take care now."

"I will."

"Kiss"–the baby–"for me and tell"–my wife–"I said hello."

Open door. See her sleeping. The serpent in my mind stills, waiting. I don't answer Mom. Instead I drop the phone to the floor.

"Sweetie?" Mom asks. "Sweetie?" More urgent.

Open myself again, searching.

Pray: Show me a sign I am heard...

—cold, boundless nothing. not indifference. indifference would mean something was there. here is the void—

Wind carries sirens through open patio door. Living room is cold, clean-smelling. Phone on floor by bedroom doors, both of them open.

Tires squeal to stop outside.

Mind is free. Twisting, wriggling thing is gone.

Pick up phone. Feels light, like it should. Strength in my hands and arms. I can move. I could run if I wanted. Rapid beeping from earpiece like forgot to hang it up. Voice mail light blinking. Dial in code. Mom's voice: "What was that?! What just happened?! Is everyone OK? It sounded like... sweetie, I'm... I'm calling 911." Message ends.

Pounding on front door. "Police. Can you open the door, please?"

Drop phone and step through patio door. Cool breeze on skin. Inhale. Look down at street. Crowd has gathered around something.

Pray: Forgive me...

About the Writers

Pete Mesling lives in Seattle, Washington, and is an affiliate member of the Horror Writers Association. Horror luminary Mort Castle has said of Pete's work, "Nicely surreal and quite Kafka … This is impressive." Thomas F. Monteleone, on the other hand, has gone only so far as to say, "This is bizarre stuff." Pete has sold fiction to such publications as *Doorways*, *Black Ink Horror*, and two of the *Potter's Field* anthologies. Keep up to date on his fictitious pursuits at www.petemesling.

Deena M. Lyvang lives in a quaint little fishing village along the shoreline of Lake Erie with her husband, daughter and two spoiled cats. She loves writing scary tales almost as much as she enjoys reading them and because of her macabre imagination, her husband sleeps next to her with one eye open, gripping a baseball bat.

Somewhere in southern California lurks a creature by the name of **Robert Essig**. This beast is known to have a macabre fascination with horror and is fortunate to implore an imp of whom whispers dark delicacies to him in the night. Visit Robert's website to find out where his offerings have been published at robertessig.com.

Raised under the perpetually overcast skies of northeast Ohio, **Kendra Lisum** developed a penchant for horror at an early age. She attended the University of Nevada, Reno, where the sunshine and blue skies did nothing to undermine her enjoyment of the macabre. In pursuit of her writing goals, she moved to Missoula, Montana, and has since had works published in the Brushfire literary arts magazine, as well as on Alienskinmag.com. She recently took second place in a short story contest sponsored by LongShortStories.com.

Desmond Warzel has always labored under the assumption that he was a science fiction writer, but the relish with which he has been torturing or bumping off the characters in his recent stories (in such publications as Shroud, Alternative Coordinates, Whispering Spirits, and Return of the Raven) has got him reconsidering. He writes from northwestern Pennsylvania.

By day, **Matt Moore** is an online communication specialist. By night, he is a science fiction and horror writer with work in *On Spec*, *Tesseracts Thirteen*, *Tesseracts Fourteen* and an e-book from Damnation Books. By later at night, he is the marketing director for ChiZine Publications, a small Canadian publisher. Raised in small-town New England, a place rich with legends and ghost stories, he lives in Ottawa, Ontario. He blogs at mattmoorewrites.wordpress.com.

Jessy Marie Roberts lives in a "haunted" house in Western Nebraska with her husband and two dogs. She grew up in Morgan Hill, California.

Lawrence Conquest is a writer from Frome, England. He has had short fiction published in Black Static, Crossed Genres, A Thousand Faces and Fantastic Horror along with the forthcoming anthology Inner Fears (Lame Goat Press). He has also had comic strips published in FutureQuake and Something Wicked, (full bibliography online at www.lawrence-conquest.blogspot.com) Lawrence is also a musician, and has released several albums of experimental electronic noise under the name Hate-Male (www.myspace.com/hatemalenoise) He does not swim, and rarely visits the beach.

Adrian Ludens lives with his family in the Black Hills of South Dakota. He works as a radio personality on a classic rock station. Adrian has contributed stories to several anthologies: Night Terrors, Bonded By Blood 2, Love Kills, 52 Stitches, Glassfire Anthology, The Middle of Nowhere and Don't Tread on Me. His fiction has also appeared in Alfred Hitchcock's Mystery Magazine, Morpheus Tales, Crossed Genres and many others. He invites you to visit him on Facebook or MySpace.

Stories from **Brendan P. Myers** have appeared in the *Northern Haunts* anthology from Shroud Publishing, *Malpractice: An Anthology of Bedside Terror* from Stygian Publications, and *Dead Worlds: Undead Stories* from Living Dead Press. The first novel in his vampire saga *Applewood* is coming in 2011 from By Light Unseen Media.

Monique Bos earned a master's degree in literature from the Pennsylvania State University, where she submitted her thesis on the characters of Morticia Addams and Lily Munster. She has worked as a newspaper and magazine writer and editor, and has taught college writing courses. Currently, she teaches ESL to Korean students and covers the Seattle museum scene for Examiner.com. "The Bitter Taste of Rapture," inspired by the Dimmu Borgir song "A Succubus in Rapture," is her first fiction publication. She has also completed a horror novel. Visit her blog, the Literary Gargoyle, at www.moniquebos.wordpress.com.

As his short tales of terror and his novels have began to surface throughout the years, **Brick Marlin** has been married to a woman who keeps him chained up in a room so he won't try to escape and turn this odd fiction into reality..

Stephanie Kincaid inherited a deep love of horror from her father and a passion for great books from her mother. The result was a deranged insomniac muse, who forces her to stay up nights and write grammatically correct stories that disturb people.

Harper Hull was born and raised in Northern England but now lives in a 19thcentury farmhouse in the American South with his much smarter and prettier Dixie wife. He grew up in a home crammed with classic sci-fi, fantasy and horror books, started writing his own stories in 2009 and has 20 credits so far. If you ever read one of his pieces, he just hopes you enjoy it. Harper can be found at http://harperhull.weebly.com

Joshua Scribner is the author of eight published novels and over 100 short stories. He currently lives in Michigan with his wife and two daughters. Up to date information on his work can be found at joshuascribner.com.

Trying her hand at everything from horror and fiction to poetry and erotica, **Piper Morgan** has been writing for years, but until recently said works never saw the light of day. Two of her previous works were published in Strange, Weird, and Wonderful Magazine. She's bitter, angry, and always pissed off about something so you can catch her bitching and ranting at: http://pipermorgan.blogspot.com or drop her a line at piperdmorgan@gmail.com

Kevin Brown recently won the Permafrost Literary Journal's Midnight Sun Fiction Contest, the Touchstone Fiction Competition, and placed third in the Cadenza Fiction Contest. He was nominated for a Pushcart Prize and a 2007 Journey Award, and has published in GUD, Space & Time, Murky Depths, Twisted Tongue, Morpheus Tales, Horror Express, sub-TERRAIN, Rosebud, and Underground Voices. His first book, *Ink On Wood*, will be published by Virgogray Press this summer. His website is: InvisibleBodies.com

Stephen Hill is a Toronto, Ontario based writer whose short fiction has appeared on numerous eZines such as Thrillers, Killers n' Chillers, MicroHorror, The Oddville Press, and Flashes in the Dark. His work has also been published in 6 Sentences: It's All About Love and The Broken Pencil, and new fiction will be featured in such upcoming anthologies as Don't Tread on Me, 31 Days of Halloween, and Flash Fiction: 365 Days of Flash.

Barry Napier has had fiction and poetry appear in several online and print publications. His collection of short fiction, Debris, is currently available through Library of Horror. He also has a chapbook being released through Strange Publications later in 2010. He lives in Lynchburg, VA with his wife and children.

Craig Saunders is 37 years old (likely to change sometime in the near future) and lives in Norfolk, England, with his wife and three children. Craig started writing on his first computer in 1998, with fantasy, followed by science fiction, then humor. It took eight novels before he figured out he was a horror writer, but Craig hasn't wasted any time since, with thirty horror shorts and three horror novels under his belt. When he's not writing, Craig pretends to listen to his family while making up stories on scraps of paper. Sometimes he even gets a story published.

Brian Barnett lives with his wife, Stephanie, and son, Michael, in Frankfort, Kentucky. To date, he has published over sixty stories since he began publishing in November 2008. He has been accepted by over twenty-five publications, online and in print, including four anthologies. He was co-editor of the *Toe Tags* anthology with William Pauley III. For up-to-date news on Brian: http://merrilyhauntingfrankfort.blogspot.com

Lawrence Salani has always enjoyed living in coastal areas, and now lives around Cronulla, Australia. He completed an Associate Diploma in fine arts, with the feel that painting and writing complement each other. Salani's interest in horror came about by reading the early pulp writers when he was at school; his favorite being H.P. Lovecraft and Clark Ashton Smith. This led to painter/writers such as William Blake and Austin Spare. His only other published work has been in Eclecticism E-Zine, issue # 5, called *A Fragment of Yesterday.*

Michael Hughes is a freelance author, commercial writer and journalist whose short works of horror and adventure have appeared in a number of horror magazines including *Yellow Mama* and *Astonishing Adventures Magazine.* Hughes covers geopolitics for some of the top news sites in America, including The Huffington Post and Examiner.com. He has interviewed world-renowned foreign policy figures such as the assistant Secretary of State, and has appeared as a geopolitical analyst on an international news network to cover the Afghanistan war. He currently spins his tales of iniquity in a dark room somewhere within the bowels of the South Side of Chicago.

G. Winston Hyatt lives in Chicago. His work has appeared in *Necrotic Tissue*, *Thuglit*, *The Harrow*, *Whispers of Wickedness*, and elsewhere. *Malagon Rising*, his dark fantasy novel, will be released in fall 2010 by Leucrota Press.

Growing up in an increasingly suburbanized area, **E.R. Delafield** has long been fascinated with what nature might do if given the power to strike back. Today she writes dark fantasy and steampunk, while in her spare time she teaches history at a local high school.

David Bernstein started taking his writing seriously in 2009, having decided to stop spending hours of his time playing MMO's—writing instead. Since May of 2009, he's had 40 stories published in various anthologies and magazines. He is currently working on a novel—Amongst the Dead—of which the first four chapters can be read at Tales of the Zombie War. He lives in the NYC area. You can visit him at davidbernsteinauthor.blogspot.com and email him at dbern77@hotmail.com.

Born and raised in London, England, **Keith J. Scales** worked as a professional actor and director for over thirty years in the Pacific Northwest, where he received many local awards and several research fellowships. His play *What Mad Pursuit* was a finalist for an Oregon Book Award. As Artistic Director of the Classic Greek Theatre of Oregon he created English versions of sixteen of the ancient texts. He recently moved to Eureka Springs, Arkansas, to concentrate on writing and seeking publication. His stories are published by Roastbooks, UK; Story-Me and now, he is happy to be able to say, Night Terrors.

Jenna M. Pitman is a 20-something-year-old writer from Washington State. Her work has appeared in a variety of local and national locations from The Seattle Sinner to Planet Lovecraft to American Gothique and her comic debut can be found in Strange Aeons issue 2. She is very active in the local horror community and looking to expand her reach. *Gravity Hill* is based on an eastern Washington legend in the town where she spent her teenage years.

Bryan Oftedahl was raised in the Tongass forests of Alaska. Having spun dark stories since a child, greatly appreciated for nights around the fire, it wasn't until well within his second decade he started putting the stories to paper in an amateur manner that has only recently begun to develop into a style of his own

Murphy Edwards most recent works of fiction have appeared in Trail of Indiscretion, Dark Discoveries, Escaping Elsewhere, Samsara; The Magazine of Suffering, Hardboiled Magazine, The Nocturnal Lyric, Barbaric Yawp, Night Chills Magazine and in the anthologies *Dead Bait* (Severed Press), *Assassin's Canon* (Utility Fog Press) and *Abaculus*, Volumes II and III (Leucrota Press).

After earning his bachelor's degree in English at the University of South Florida, **Lee Clark Zumpe** began working with Tampa Bay Newspapers as a proofreader. Lee is now the publisher's chief entertainment columnist. His nights are consumed with the invocation of ancient nightmares, each dutifully bound in works of fiction and poetry. His short stories and poetry have appeared in a variety of publications such as Weird Tales, Space and Time and Dark Wisdom and in the anthologies Horrors Beyond, Corpse Blossoms, High Seas Cthulhu, Arkham Tales, Abominations, Frontier Cthulhu, Withersin's Unkindness and Cthulhu Unbound, Vol. 1. Lee's work has earned several honorable mentions in the annual Year's Best Fantasy and Horror collections.
Visit http://muted-mutterings-of-a-mad-poet.blogspot.com.

www.ingramcontent.com/pod-product-compliance
Lightning Source LLC
LaVergne TN
LVHW091122080826
845145LV00008B/2012

* 9 7 8 0 9 8 4 5 4 0 8 0 8 *